For Chris Gleason and Mike Eigen.

Who listened. And heard.

And sometimes carried.

. . . must we dream our dreams
and have them, too?

—Elizabeth Bishop,
"Questions of Travel"

ACKNOWLEDGMENTS

Thanks to Sheila, George Bick, Jack Driscoll, Dawn Ellenburg, Mike Flynn, Julie Anne McNary, David Robichaud, and Joanna Solfrian.

Three texts were indispensable in writing this novel: *Boston Harbor Islands* by Emily and David Kale; *Gracefully Insane,* Alex Beam's account of McLean Hospital; and Robert Whitaker's *Mad in America,* which documented the use of neuroleptics on schizophrenics in American psychiatric institutions. I remain indebted to all three books for their outstanding reportage.

As ever, as always, thanks to my editor, Claire Wachtel (every writer should be so blessed), and my agent, Ann Rittenberg, who gave me the book by giving me the Sinatra.

PROLOGUE

FROM THE JOURNALS OF DR. LESTER SHEEHAN

MAY 3, 1993

I haven't laid eyes on the island in several years. The last time was from a friend's boat that ventured into the outer harbor, and I could see it off in the distance, past the inner ring, shrouded in the summer haze, a careless smudge of paint against the sky.

I haven't stepped foot on it in more than two decades, but Emily says (sometimes joking, sometimes not) that she's not sure I ever left. She said once that time is nothing to me but a series of bookmarks that I use to jump back and forth through the text of my life, returning again and again to the events that mark me, in the eyes of my more astute colleagues, as bearing all the characteristics of the classic melancholic.

Emily may be right. She is so often right.

Soon I will lose her too. A matter of months, Dr. Axelrod told us Thursday. Take that trip, he advised. The one you're always talking about. To Florence and Rome, Venice in the spring. Because Lester, he added, you're not looking too well yourself.

I suppose I'm not. I misplace things far too often these days, my glasses more than anything. My car keys. I enter stores and forget what I've come for, leave the theater with no recollection of what I've just seen. If time for me really is a series of bookmarks, then I feel as if someone has shaken the book and those yellowed slips of paper, torn matchbook covers and flattened coffee stirrers have fallen to the floor, and the dog-eared flaps have been pressed smooth.

I want to write these things down, then. Not to alter the text so that I fall under a more favorable light. No, no. He would never allow that. In his own peculiar way, he hated lies more than anyone I have ever known. I want only to preserve the text, to transfer it from its current storage facility (which frankly is beginning to moisten and leak) to these pages.

Ashecliffe Hospital sat on the central plain of the island's northwestern side. Sat benignly, I might add. It looked nothing like a hospital for the criminally insane and even less like the military barracks it had been before that. Its appearance reminded most of us, in point of fact, of a boarding school. Just outside the main compound, a mansarded Victorian housed the warden and a dark, beautiful Tudor minicastle, which had once housed the Union commander of the northeastern shoreline, served as the quarters of our chief of staff. Inside the wall were the staff quarters—quaint, clapboard cottages for the clinicians, three low-slung cinder block dormitories for the orderlies, the guards, and the nurses. The main compound was composed of lawns and sculpted hedges, great shady oaks, Scotch pines, and trim maples, apple trees whose fruit dropped to the tops of the wall in late autumn or tumbled onto the grass. And in the center of the compound, twin redbrick colonials on either side of the hospital itself, a structure of large, charcoal stones and handsome granite. Beyond were the bluffs and the tidal marsh and a long valley where a collective farm had sprung up and then failed in the years just after the American Revolution. The trees they planted survived—peach and pear and chokeberry—but no longer bore fruit, and the night winds often came howling into that valley and screeched like cats.

And the fort, of course, which stood long before the first hospital staff arrived, and stands there still, jutting out of the southern cliff face. And the lighthouse beyond, out of service since before the Civil War, rendered obsolete by the beam of Boston Light.

From the sea, it didn't look like much. You have to picture it the way Teddy Daniels saw it on that calm morning in September of 1954. A scrub plain in the middle of the outer harbor. Barely an island, you'd think, so much as the idea of one. What purpose could it have, he may have thought. What purpose.

Rats were the most voluminous of our animal life. They scrabbled in the brush, formed lines along the shore at night, clambered over wet rock. Some were the size of flounder. In the years following those four strange days of late summer 1954, I took to studying the rats from a cut in the hill overlooking the northern shore. I was fascinated to discover that some of the rats would try to swim for Paddock Island, little more than a rock in a cupful of sand that remained submerged twenty-two hours out of every day. When it appeared for that hour or two as the current reached its lowest ebb, sometimes they'd swim for it, these rats, never more than a dozen or so and always driven back by the riptide.

I say always, but no. I saw one make it. Once. The night of the harvest moon in October '56. I saw its black moccasin of a body dart across the sand.

Or so I think. Emily, whom I met on the island, will say, "Lester, you couldn't have. It was too far away."

She's right.

And yet I know what I saw. One fat moccasin darting across the sand, sand that was pearl gray and already beginning to drown again as the current returned to swallow Paddock Island, swallow that rat, I assume, for I never saw it swim back.

But in that moment, as I watched it scurry up the shore (and I did, I saw it, distances be damned), I thought of Teddy. I thought of Teddy and his poor dead wife, Dolores Chanal, and those twin terrors, Rachel Solando and Andrew Laeddis, the havoc they wreaked on us all. I thought that if Teddy were sitting with me, he would have seen that rat too. He would have.

And I'll tell you something else:

Teddy?

He would have clapped.

DAY ONE

Rachel

1

TEDDY DANIELS'S FATHER had been a fisherman. He lost his boat to the bank in '31 when Teddy was eleven, spent the rest of his life hiring onto other boats when they had the work, unloading freight along the docks when they didn't, going long stretches when he was back at the house by ten in the morning, sitting in an armchair, staring at his hands, whispering to himself occasionally, his eyes gone wide and dark.

He'd taken Teddy out to the islands when Teddy was still a small boy, too young to be much help on the boat. All he'd been able to do was untangle the lines and tie off the hooks. He'd cut himself a few times, and the blood dotted his fingertips and smeared his palms.

They'd left in the dark, and when the sun appeared, it was a cold ivory that pushed up from the edge of the sea, and the islands appeared out of the fading dusk, huddled together, as if they'd been caught at something.

Teddy saw small, pastel-colored shacks lining the beach of one, a crumbling limestone estate on another. His father pointed out the prison on Deer Island and the stately fort on Georges. On Thompson, the high trees were filled with birds, and their chatter sounded like squalls of hail and glass.

Out past them all, the one they called Shutter lay like something tossed from a Spanish galleon. Back then, in the spring of '28, it had been left to itself in a riot of its own vegetation, and the fort that stretched along its highest point was strangled in vines and topped with great clouds of moss.

"Why Shutter?" Teddy asked.

His father shrugged. "You with the questions. Always the questions."

"Yeah, but why?"

"Some places just get a name and it sticks. Pirates probably."

"Pirates?" Teddy liked the sound of that. He could see them—big men with eye patches and tall boots, gleaming swords.

His father said, "This is where they hid in the old days." His arm swept the horizon. "These islands. Hid themselves. Hid their gold."

Teddy imagined chests of it, the coins spilling down the sides.

Later he got sick, repeatedly and violently, pitching black ropes of it over the side of his father's boat and into the sea.

His father was surprised because Teddy hadn't begun to vomit until hours into the trip when the ocean was flat and glistening with its own quiet. His father said, "It's okay. It's your first time. Nothing to be ashamed of."

Teddy nodded, wiped his mouth with a cloth his father gave him.

His father said, "Sometimes there's motion, and you can't even feel it until it climbs up inside of you."

Another nod, Teddy unable to tell his father that it wasn't motion that had turned his stomach.

It was all that water. Stretched out around them until it was all that was left of the world. How Teddy believed that it could swallow the sky. Until that moment, he'd never known they were this alone.

He looked up at his father, his eyes leaking and red, and his father said, "You'll be okay," and Teddy tried to smile.

His father went out on a Boston whaler in the summer of '38 and never came back. The next spring, pieces of the boat washed up on Nantasket Beach in the town of Hull, where Teddy grew up. A strip of keel, a hot plate with the captain's name etched in the base, cans of tomato and potato soup, a couple of lobster traps, gap-holed and misshapen.

They held the funeral for the four fishermen in St. Theresa's Church, its back pressed hard against the same sea that had claimed so many of its parishioners, and Teddy stood with his mother and heard testimonials to the captain, his first mate, and the third fisherman, an old salt named Gil Restak, who'd terrorized the bars of Hull since returning from the Great War with a shattered heel and too many ugly pictures in his head. In death, though, one of the bartenders he'd terrorized had said, all was forgiven.

The boat's owner, Nikos Costa, admitted that he'd barely known Teddy's father, that he'd hired on at the last minute when a crew member broke his leg in a fall from a truck. Still, the captain had spoken highly of him, said everyone in town knew that he could do a day's work. And wasn't that the highest praise one could give a man?

Standing in that church, Teddy remembered that day on his father's boat because they'd never gone out again. His father kept saying they would, but Teddy understood that he said this only so his son could hold on to some pride. His father never acknowledged what had happened that day, but a look had passed between them as they headed home, back through the string of islands, Shutter behind them, Thompson still ahead, the city skyline so clear and close you'd think you could lift a building by its spire.

"It's the sea," his father said, a hand lightly rubbing Teddy's back as they leaned against the stern. "Some men take to it. Some men it takes."

And he'd looked at Teddy in such a way that Teddy knew which of those men he'd probably grow up to be.

TO GET THERE in '54, they took the ferry from the city and passed through a collection of other small, forgotten islands—Thompson and Spectacle, Grape and Bumpkin, Rainford and Long—that gripped the scalp of the sea in hard tufts of sand, wiry trees, and rock formations as white as bone. Except for supply runs on Tuesdays and Saturdays, the ferry ran on an irregular schedule and the galley was stripped of everything but the sheet metal that covered the floor and two steel benches that ran under the windows. The benches were bolted to the floor and bolted to thick black posts at both ends, and manacles and their chains hung in spaghetti piles from the posts.

The ferry wasn't transporting patients to the asylum today, however, just Teddy and his new partner, Chuck Aule, a few canvas bags of mail, a few cases of medical supplies.

Teddy started the trip down on his knees in front of the toilet, heaving into the bowl as the ferry's engine chugged and clacked and Teddy's nasal passages filled with the oily smells of gasoline and the late-summer sea. Nothing came out of him but small streams of water, yet his throat kept constricting and his stomach banged up against the base of his esophagus and the air in front of his face spun with motes that blinked like eyes.

The final heave was followed by a globe of trapped oxygen that seemed to carry a piece of his chest with it as it exploded from his mouth, and Teddy sat back on the metal floor and wiped his face with his handkerchief and thought how this wasn't the way you wanted to start a new partnership.

He could just imagine Chuck telling his wife back home—if he had a wife; Teddy didn't even know that much about him yet—about his first encounter with the legendary Teddy Daniels. "Guy liked me so much, honey, he threw up."

Since that trip as a boy, Teddy had never enjoyed being out on the water, took no pleasure from such a lack of land, of visions of land, things you could reach out and touch without your hands dissolving into them. You told yourself it was okay—because that's what you had to do to cross a body of water—but it wasn't. Even in the war, it wasn't the storming of the beaches he feared so much as those last few yards from the boats to the shore, legs slogging through the depths, strange creatures slithering over your boots.

Still, he'd prefer to be out on deck, facing it in the fresh air, rather than back here, sickly warm, lurching.

When he was sure it had passed, his stomach no longer bubbling, his head no longer swimming, he washed his hands and face, checked his appearance in a small mirror mounted over the sink, most of the glass eroded by sea salt, a small cloud in the center where Teddy could just make out his reflection, still a relatively young man with a government-issue crew cut. But his face was lined with evidence of the war and the years since, his penchant for the dual fascinations of pursuit and violence living in eyes Dolores had once called "dog-sad."

I'm too young, Teddy thought, to look this hard.

He adjusted his belt around his waist so the gun and holster rested on his hip. He took his hat from the top of the toilet and put it back on, adjusted the brim until it tilted just slightly to the right. He tightened the knot in his tie. It was one of those loud floral ties that had been going out of style for about a year, but he wore it because she had given it to him, slipped it over his eyes one birthday as he sat in the living room. Pressed her lips to his Adam's apple. A warm hand on the side of his cheek. The smell of an orange on her tongue. Sliding into his lap, removing the tie, Teddy keeping his eyes closed. Just to smell her. To imagine her. To create her in his mind and hold her there.

He could still do it—close his eyes and see her. But lately, white smudges would blur parts of her—an earlobe, her eyelashes, the contours of her hair. It didn't happen enough to fully obscure her yet, but Teddy feared time was taking her from him, grinding away at the picture frames in his head, crushing them.

"I miss you," he said, and went out through the galley to the foredeck.

It was warm and clear out there, but the water was threaded with dark glints of rust and an overall pallor of gray, a suggestion of something growing dark in the depths, massing.

Chuck took a sip from his flask and tilted the neck in Teddy's direction, one eyebrow cocked. Teddy shook his head, and Chuck slipped it back into his suit pocket, pulled the flaps of his overcoat around his hips, and looked out at the sea.

"You okay?" Chuck asked. "You look pale."

Teddy shrugged it off. "I'm fine."

"Sure?"

Teddy nodded. "Just finding my sea legs."

They stood in silence for a bit, the sea undulating all around them, pockets of it as dark and silken as velvet.

"You know it used to be a POW camp?" Teddy said.

Chuck said, "The island?"

Teddy nodded. "Back in the Civil War. They built a fort there, barracks."

"What do they use the fort for now?"

Teddy shrugged. "Couldn't tell you. There's quite a few of them out here on the different islands. Most of them were target practice for artillery shells during the war. Not too many left standing."

"But the institution?"

"From what I could tell, they use the old troop quarters."

Chuck said, "Be like going back to basic, huh?"

"Don't wish that on us." Teddy turned on the rail. "So what's your story there, Chuck?"

Chuck smiled. He was a bit stockier and a bit shorter than Teddy, maybe five ten or so, and he had a head of tight, curly black hair and olive skin and slim, delicate hands that seemed incongruous with the rest of him, as if he'd borrowed them until his real ones came back from the shop. His left cheek bore a small scythe of a scar, and he tapped it with his index finger.

"I always start with the scar," he said. "People usually ask sooner or later."

"Okay."

"Wasn't from the war," Chuck said. "My girlfriend says I should just say it was, be done with it, but . . ." He shrugged. "It was from *playing* war, though. When I was a kid. Me and this other kid shooting slingshots at each other in the woods. My friend's rock just misses me, so I'm okay, right?" He shook his head. "His rock hit a tree, sent a piece of bark into my cheek. Hence the scar."

"From playing war."

"From playing it, yeah."

"You transferred from Oregon?"

"Seattle. Came in last week."

Teddy waited, but Chuck didn't offer any further explanation.

Teddy said, "How long you been with the marshals?"

"Four years."

"So you know how small it is."

"Sure. You want to know how come I transferred." Chuck nodded, as if deciding something for himself. "If I said I was tired of rain?"

Teddy turned his palms up above the rail. "If you said so . . ."

"But it's small, like you said. Everyone knows everyone in the service. So eventually, there'll be—what do they call it?—scuttlebutt."

"That's a word for it."

"You caught Breck, right?"

Teddy nodded.

"How'd you know where he'd go? Fifty guys chasing him, they all went to Cleveland. You went to Maine."

"He'd summered there once with his family when he was a kid. That thing he did with his victims? It's what you do to horses. I talked to an aunt. She told me the only time he was ever happy was at a horse farm near this rental cottage in Maine. So I went up there."

"Shot him five times," Chuck said and looked down the bow at the foam.

"Would have shot him five more," Teddy said. "Five's what it took."

Chuck nodded and spit over the rail. "My girlfriend's Japanese. Well, born here, but you know . . . Grew up in a camp. There's still a lot of tension out there—Portland, Seattle, Tacoma. No one likes me being with her."

"So they transferred you."

Chuck nodded, spit again, watched it fall into the churning foam.

"They say it's going to be big," he said.

Teddy lifted his elbows off the rail and straightened. His face was damp, his lips salty. Somewhat surprising that the sea had managed to find him when he couldn't recall the spray hitting his face.

He patted the pockets of his overcoat, looking for his Chesterfields. "Who's 'they'? What's 'it'?"

"They. The papers," Chuck said. "The storm. Big one, they say. Huge." He waved his arm at the pale sky, as pale as the foam churning against the bow. But there, along its southern edge, a thin line of purple cotton swabs grew like ink blots.

Teddy sniffed the air. "You remember the war, don't you, Chuck?"

Chuck smiled in such a way that Teddy suspected they were already tuning in to each other's rhythms, learning how to fuck with each other.

"A bit," Chuck said. "I seem to remember rubble. Lots of rubble. People denigrate rubble, but I say it has its place. I say it has its own aesthetic beauty. I say it's all in the eye of the beholder."

"You talk like a dime novel. Has anyone else told you that?"

"It's come up." Chuck giving the sea another of his small smiles, leaning over the bow, stretching his back.

Teddy patted his trouser pockets, searched the inside pockets of his suit jacket. "You remember how often the deployments were dependent on weather reports."

Chuck rubbed the stubble on his chin with the heel of his hand. "Oh, I do, yes."

"Do you remember how often those weather reports proved correct?"

Chuck furrowed his brow, wanting Teddy to know he was giving this due and proper consideration. Then he smacked his lips and said, "About thirty percent of the time, I'd venture."

"At best."

Chuck nodded. "At best."

"And so now, back in the world as we are . . ."

"Oh, back we are," Chuck said. "Ensconced, one could even say."

Teddy suppressed a laugh, liking this guy a lot now. Ensconced. Jesus.

"Ensconced," Teddy agreed. "Why would you put any more cre-dence in the weather reports now than you did then?"

"Well," Chuck said as the sagging tip of a small triangle peeked above the horizon line, "I'm not sure my credence can be measured in terms of less or more. Do you want a cigarette?"

Teddy stopped in the middle of a second round of pocket pats, found Chuck watching him, his wry grin etched into his cheeks just below the scar.

"I had them when I boarded," Teddy said.

Chuck looked back over his shoulder. "Government employees. Rob you blind." Chuck shook a cigarette free of his pack of Luckies, handed one to Teddy, and lit it for him with his brass Zippo, the stench of the kerosene climbing over the salt air and finding the back of Teddy's throat. Chuck snapped the lighter closed, then flicked it back open with a snap of his wrist and lit his own.

Teddy exhaled, and the triangle tip of the island disappeared for a moment in the plume of smoke.

"Overseas," Chuck said, "when a weather report dictated if you went to the drop zone with your parachute pack or set off for the beachhead, well, there was much more at stake, wasn't there?"

"True."

"But back home, where's the harm in a little arbitrary faith? That's all I'm saying, boss."

It began to reveal itself to them as more than a triangle tip, the lower sections gradually filling in until the sea stretched out flat again on the other side of it and they could see colors filling in as if by brush stroke—a muted green where the vegetation grew unchecked, a tan strip of shoreline, the dull ochre of cliff face on the northern edge. And at the top, as they churned closer, they began to make out the flat rectangular edges of buildings themselves.

"It's a pity," Chuck said.

"What's that?"

"The price of progress." He placed one foot on the towline and leaned against the rail beside Teddy, and they watched the island attempt to define itself. "With the leaps—and there are leaps going on, don't kid yourself, leaps every day—happening in the field of mental health, a place like this will cease to exist. Barbaric they'll call it twenty years from now. An unfortunate by-product of the bygone Victorian influence. And go it should, they'll say. Incorporation, they'll say. Incorporation will be the order of the day. You are all welcomed into the fold. We will soothe you. Rebuild you. We are all General Marshalls. We are a new society, and there is no place for exclusion. No Elbas."

The buildings had disappeared again behind the trees, but Teddy could make out the fuzzy shape of a conical tower and then hard, jutting angles he took to be the old fort.

"But do we lose our past to assure our future?" Chuck flicked his cigarette out into the foam. "That's the question. What do you lose when you sweep a floor, Teddy? Dust. Crumbs that would otherwise draw ants. But what of the earring she misplaced? Is that in the trash now too?"

Teddy said, "Who's 'she'? Where did 'she' come from, Chuck?"

"There's always a she. Isn't there?"

Teddy heard the whine of the engine change pitch behind them, felt the ferry give a small lurch underfoot, and he could see the fort clearer now atop the southern cliff face as they came around toward the western side of the island. The cannons were gone, but Teddy could make out the turrets easily enough. The land went back into hills behind the fort, and Teddy figured the walls were back there, blurring into the landscape from his current angle, and then Ashecliffe Hospital sat somewhere beyond the bluffs, overlooking the western shore.

"You got a girl, Teddy? Married?" Chuck said.

"Was," Teddy said, picturing Dolores, a look she gave him once on their honeymoon, turning her head, her chin almost touching her bare shoulder, muscles moving under the flesh near her spine. "She died."

Chuck came off the rail, his neck turning pink. "Oh, Jesus."

"It's okay," Teddy said.

"No, no." Chuck held his palm up by Teddy's chest. "It's . . . I'd heard that. I don't know how I could've forgotten. A couple of years ago, wasn't it?"

Teddy nodded.

"Christ, Teddy. I feel like an idiot. Really. I'm so sorry."

Teddy saw her again, her back to him as she walked down the apartment hallway, wearing one of his old uniform shirts, humming as she turned into the kitchen, and a familiar weariness invaded his bones. He would prefer to do just about anything—swim in that water even—rather than speak of Dolores, of the facts of her being on this earth for thirty-one years and then ceasing to be. Just like that. There when he left for work that morning. Gone by the afternoon.

But it was like Chuck's scar, he supposed—the story that had to be dispensed with before they could move on, or otherwise it would always be between them. The hows. The wheres. The whys.

Dolores had been dead for two years, but she came to life at night in his dreams, and he sometimes went full minutes into a new morning thinking she was out in the kitchen or taking her coffee on the front stoop of their apartment on Buttonwood. This was a cruel trick of the mind, yes, but Teddy had long ago accepted the logic of it—waking, after all, was an almost natal state. You surfaced without a history, then spent the blinks and yawns reassembling your past, shuffling the shards into chronological order before fortifying yourself for the present.

What was far crueler were the ways in which a seemingly illogical list of objects could trigger memories of his wife that lodged in his brain like a lit match. He could never predict what one of the objects would be—a shaker of salt, the gait of a strange woman on a crowded street, a bottle of Coca-Cola, a smudge of lipstick on a glass, a throw pillow.

But of all the triggers, nothing was less logical in terms of connective tissue, or more pungent in terms of effect, than water—drizzling from the tap, clattering from the sky, puddled against the sidewalk, or, as now, spread around him for miles in every direction.

He said to Chuck: "There was a fire in our apartment building. I was working. Four people died. She was one of them. The smoke got her, Chuck, not the fire. So she didn't die in pain. Fear? Maybe. But not pain. That's important."

Chuck took another sip from his flask, offered it to Teddy again.

Teddy shook his head. "I quit. After the fire. She used to worry about it, you know? Said all of us soldiers and cops drank too much. So . . ." He could feel Chuck beside him, sinking in embarrassment, and he said, "You learn how to carry something like that, Chuck. You got no choice. Like all the shit you saw in the war. Remember?"

Chuck nodded, his eyes going small with memory for a moment, distant.

"It's what you do," Teddy said softly.

"Sure," Chuck said eventually, his face still flushed.

The dock appeared as if by trick of light, stretching out from the sand, a stick of chewing gum from this distance, insubstantial and gray.

Teddy felt dehydrated from his time at the toilet and maybe a bit exhausted from the last couple of minutes; no matter how much he'd learned to carry it, carry her, the weight could wear him down every now and then. A dull ache settled into the left side of his head, just behind his eye, as if the flat side of an old spoon were pressed there. It was too early to tell if it were merely a minor side effect of the dehydration, the beginnings of a common headache, or the first hint of something worse—the migraines that had plagued him since adolescence and that at various times could come so strongly they could temporarily rob him of vision in one eye, turn light into a hailstorm of hot nails, and had once—only once, thank God—left him partially paralyzed for a day and a half. Migraines, his anyway, never visited during times of pressure or work, only afterward, when all had quieted down, after the shells stopped dropping, after the pursuit was ended. Then, at base camp or barracks or, since the war, in motel rooms or driving home along country highways—they came to do their worst. The trick, Teddy had long since learned, was to stay busy and stay focused. They couldn't catch you if you didn't stop running.

He said to Chuck, "Heard much about this place?"

"A mental hospital, that's about all I know."

"For the criminally insane," Teddy said.

"Well, we wouldn't be here if it weren't," Chuck said.

Teddy caught him smiling that dry grin again. "You never know, Chuck. You don't look a hundred percent stable to me."

"Maybe I'll put a deposit down on a bed while we're here, for the future, make sure they hold a place for me."

"Not a bad idea," Teddy said as the engines cut out for a moment, and the bow swung starboard as they turned with the current and the engines kicked in again and Teddy and Chuck were soon facing the open sea as the ferry backed toward the dock.

"Far as I know," Teddy said, "they specialize in radical approaches."

"Red?" Chuck said.

"Not Red," Teddy said. "Just radical. There's a difference."

"You wouldn't know it lately."

"Sometimes, you wouldn't," Teddy agreed.

"And this woman who escaped?"

Teddy said, "Don't know much about that. She slipped out last night. I got her name in my notebook. I figure they'll tell us everything else."

Chuck looked around at the water. "Where's she going to go? She's going to swim home?"

Teddy shrugged. "The patients here, apparently, suffer a variety of delusions."

"Schizophrenics?"

"I guess, yeah. You won't find your everyday mongoloids in here in any case. Or some guy who's afraid of sidewalk cracks, sleeps too much. Far as I could tell from the file, everyone here is, you know, *really* crazy."

Chuck said, "How many you think are faking it, though? I've always wondered that. You remember all the Section Eights you met in the war? How many, really, did you think were nuts?"

"I served with a guy in the Ardennes—"

"You were there?"

Teddy nodded. "This guy, he woke up one day speaking backward."

"The words or the sentences?"

"Sentences," Teddy said. "He'd say, 'Sarge, today here blood much too is there.' By late afternoon, we found him in a foxhole, hitting his own head with a rock. Just hitting it. Over and over. We were so rattled that it took us a minute to realize he'd scratched out his own eyes."

"You are shitting me."

Teddy shook his head. "I heard from a guy a few years later who ran across the blind guy in a vet hospital in San Diego. Still talking backward, and he had some sort of paralysis that none of the doctors could diagnose the cause of, sat in a wheelchair by the window all day, kept talking about his crops, he had to get to his crops. Thing was, the guy grew up in Brooklyn."

"Well, guy from Brooklyn thinks he's a farmer, I guess he is Section Eight."

"That's one tip-off, sure."

2

DEPUTY WARDEN MCPHERSON met them at the dock. He was young for a man of his rank, and his blond hair was cut a bit longer than the norm, and he had the kind of lanky grace in his movements that Teddy associated with Texans or men who'd grown up around horses.

He was flanked by orderlies, mostly Negroes, a few white guys with deadened faces, as if they hadn't been fed enough as babies, had remained stunted and annoyed ever since.

The orderlies wore white shirts and white trousers and moved in a pack. They barely glanced at Teddy and Chuck. They barely glanced at anything, just moved down the dock to the ferry and waited for it to unload its cargo.

Teddy and Chuck produced their badges upon request and McPherson took his time studying them, looking up from the ID cards to their faces, squinting.

"I'm not sure I've ever seen a U.S. marshal's badge before," he said.

"And now you've seen two," Chuck said. "A big day."

He gave Chuck a lazy grin and flipped the badge back at him.

The beach looked to have been lashed by the sea in recent nights; it was strewn with shells and driftwood, mollusk skeletons and dead fish half eaten by whatever scavengers lived here. Teddy noticed trash that must have blown in from the inner harbor—cans and sodden wads of paper, a single license plate tossed up by the tree line and washed beige and numberless by the sun. The trees were mostly pine and maple, thin and haggard, and Teddy could see some buildings through the gaps, sitting at the top of the rise.

Dolores, who'd enjoyed sunbathing, probably would have loved this place, but Teddy could feel only the constant sweep of the ocean breeze, a warning from the sea that it could pounce at will, suck you down to its floor.

The orderlies came back down the dock with the mail and the medical cases and loaded them onto handcarts, and McPherson signed for the items on a clipboard and handed the clipboard back to one of the ferry guards and the guard said, "We'll be taking off, then."

McPherson blinked in the sun.

"The storm," the guard said. "No one seems to know what it's going to do."

McPherson nodded.

"We'll contact the station when we need a pickup," Teddy said.

The guard nodded. "The storm," he said again.

"Sure, sure," Chuck said. "We'll keep that in mind."

McPherson led them up a path that rose gently through the stand of trees. When they'd cleared the trees, they reached a paved road that crossed their path like a grin, and Teddy could see a house off to both his right and his left. The one to the left was the simpler of the two, a maroon mansarded Victorian with black trim, small windows that gave the appearance of sentinels. The one to the right was a Tudor that commanded its small rise like a castle.

They continued on, climbing a slope that was steep and wild with sea grass before the land greened and softened around them, leveling out up top as the grass grew shorter, gave way to a more traditional lawn that spread back for several hundred yards before coming to a stop at a wall of orange brick that seemed to curve away the length of the island. It was ten feet tall and topped with a single strip of wire, and something about the sight of the wire got to Teddy. He felt a sudden pity for all those people on the other side of the wall who recognized that thin wire for what it was, realized just how badly the world wanted to keep them in. Teddy saw several men in dark blue uniforms just outside the wall, heads down as they peered at the ground.

Chuck said, "Correctional guards at a mental institution. Weird sight, if you don't mind me saying, Mr. McPherson."

"This is a maximum security institution," McPherson said. "We operate under dual charters—one from the Massachusetts Department of Mental Health, the other from the Federal Department of Prisons."

"I understand that," Chuck said. "I've always wondered, though— you guys have much to talk about around the dinner table?"

McPherson smiled and gave a tiny shake of his head.

Teddy saw a man with black hair who wore the same uniform as the rest of the guards, but his was accented by yellow epaulets and a standing collar, and his badge was gold. He was the only one who walked with his head held up, one hand pressed behind his back as he strode among the men, and the stride reminded Teddy of full colonels he'd met in the war, men for whom command was a necessary burden not simply of the military but of God. He carried a small black book pressed to his rib cage, and he nodded in their direction and then walked down the slope from which they'd come, his black hair stiff in the breeze.

"The warden," McPherson said. "You'll meet later."

Teddy nodded, wondering why they didn't meet now, and the warden disappeared on the other side of the rise.

One of the orderlies used a key to open the gate in the center of the wall, and the gate swung wide and the orderlies and their carts went in as two guards approached McPherson and came to a stop on either side of him.

McPherson straightened to his full height, all business now, and said, "I've got to give you guys the basic lay of the land."

"Sure."

"You gentlemen will be accorded all the courtesies we have to offer, all the help we can give. During your stay, however short that may be, you will obey protocol. Is that understood?"

Teddy nodded and Chuck said, "Absolutely."

McPherson fixed his eyes on a point just above their heads. "Dr. Cawley will explain the finer points of protocol to you, I'm sure, but I have to stress the following: unmonitored contact with patients of this institution is forbidden. Is that understood?"

Teddy almost said, Yes, sir, as if he were back in basic, but he stopped short with a simple "Yes."

"Ward A of this institution is the building behind me to my right, the male ward. Ward B, the female ward, is to my left. Ward C is beyond those bluffs directly behind this compound and the staff quarters, housed in what was once Fort Walton. Admittance to Ward C is forbidden without the written consent and physical presence of both the warden and Dr. Cawley. Understood?"

Another set of nods.

McPherson held out one massive palm, as if in supplication to the sun. "You are hereby requested to surrender your firearms."

Chuck looked at Teddy. Teddy shook his head.

Teddy said, "Mr. McPherson, we are duly appointed federal marshals. We are required by government order to carry our firearms at all times."

McPherson's voice hit the air like steel cable. "Executive Order three-nine-one of the Federal Code of Penitentiaries and Institutions for the Criminally Insane states that the peace officer's requirement to bear arms is superseded only by the direct order of his immediate superiors or that of persons entrusted with the care and protection of penal or mental health facilities. Gentlemen, you find yourself under the aegis of that exception. You will not be allowed to pass through this gate with your firearms."

Teddy looked at Chuck. Chuck tilted his head at McPherson's extended palm and shrugged.

Teddy said, "We'd like our exceptions noted for the record."

McPherson said, "Guard, please note the exceptions of Marshals Daniels and Aule."

"Noted, sir."

"Gentlemen," McPherson said.

The guard on McPherson's right opened a small leather pouch.

Teddy pulled back his overcoat and removed the service revolver from his holster. He snapped the cylinder open with a flick of his wrist and then placed the gun in McPherson's hand. McPherson handed it off to the guard, and the guard placed it in his leather pouch and McPherson held out his hand again.

Chuck was a little slower with his weapon, fumbling with the holster snap, but McPherson showed no impatience, just waited until Chuck placed the gun awkwardly in his hand.

McPherson handed the gun to the guard, and the guard added it to the pouch and stepped through the gate.

"Your weapons will be checked into the property room directly outside the warden's office," McPherson said softly, his words rustling like leaves, "which is in the main hospital building in the center of the compound. You will pick them back up on the day of your departure." McPherson's loose, cowboy grin suddenly returned. "Well, that about does it for the official stuff for now. I don't know about y'all, but I am glad to be done with it. What do you say we go see Dr. Cawley?"

And he turned and led the way through the gate, and the gate was closed behind them.

Inside the wall, the lawn swept away from either side of a main path made from the same brick as the wall. Gardeners with manacled ankles tended to the grass and trees and flower beds and even an array of rosebushes that grew along the foundation of the hospital. The gardeners were flanked by orderlies, and Teddy saw other patients in manacles walking the grounds with odd, ducklike steps. Most were men, a few were women.

"When the first clinicians came here," McPherson said, "this was all sea grass and scrub. You should see the pictures. But now . . ."

To the right and left of the hospital stood two identical redbrick colonials with the trim painted bright white, their windows barred, and the panes yellowed by salt and sea wash. The hospital itself was charcoal-colored, its brick rubbed smooth by the sea, and it rose six stories until the dormer windows up top stared down at them.

McPherson said, "Built as the battalion HQ just before the Civil War. They'd had some designs, apparently, to make this a training facility. Then when war seemed imminent, they concentrated on the fort, and then later on transforming this into a POW camp."

Teddy noticed the tower he'd seen from the ferry. The tip of it peeked just above the tree line on the far side of the island.

"What's the tower?"

"An old lighthouse," McPherson said. "Hasn't been used as such since the early 1800s. The Union army posted lookout sentries there, or so I've heard, but now it's a treatment facility."

"For patients?"

He shook his head. "Sewage. You wouldn't believe what ends up in these waters. Looks pretty from the ferry, but every piece of trash in just about every river in this state floats down into the inner harbor, out through the midharbor, and eventually reaches us."

"Fascinating," Chuck said and lit a cigarette, took it from his mouth to suppress a soft yawn as he blinked in the sun.

"Beyond the wall, that way"—he pointed past Ward B—"is the original commander's quarters. You probably saw it on the walk up. Cost a fortune to build at the time, and the commander was relieved of his duties when Uncle Sam got the bill. You should see the place."

"Who lives there now?" Teddy said.

"Dr. Cawley," McPherson said. "None of this would exist if it weren't for Dr. Cawley. And the warden. They created something really unique here."

They'd looped around the back of the compound, met more manacled gardeners and orderlies, many hoeing a dark loam against the rear wall. One of the gardeners, a middle-aged woman with wispy wheat hair gone almost bald on top, stared at Teddy as he passed, and then raised a single finger to her lips. Teddy noticed a dark red scar, thick as licorice, that ran across her throat. She smiled, finger still held to her lips, and then shook her head very slowly at him.

"Cawley's a legend in his field," McPherson was saying as they passed back around toward the front of the hospital. "Top of his class at both Johns Hopkins and Harvard, published his first paper on delusional pathologies at the age of twenty. Has been consulted numerous times by Scotland Yard, MI5, and the OSS."

"Why?" Teddy said.

"Why?"

Teddy nodded. It seemed a reasonable question.

"Well . . ." McPherson seemed at a loss.

"The OSS," Teddy said. "Try them for starters. Why would they consult a psychiatrist?"

"War work," McPherson said.

"Right," Teddy said slowly. "What kind, though?"

"The classified kind," McPherson said. "Or so I'd assume."

"How classified can it be," Chuck said, one bemused eye catching Teddy's, "if we're talking about it?"

McPherson paused in front of the hospital, one foot on the first step. He seemed baffled. He looked off for a moment at the curve of orange wall and then said, "Well, I guess you can ask him. He should be out of his meeting by now."

They went up the stairs and in through a marble foyer, the ceiling arching into a coffered dome above them. A gate buzzed open as they approached it, and they passed on into a large anteroom where an orderly sat at a desk to their right and another across from him to their left and beyond lay a long corridor behind the confines of another gate. They produced their badges again to the orderly by the upper staircase and McPherson signed their three names to a clipboard as the orderly checked their badges and IDs and handed them back. Behind the orderly was a cage, and Teddy could see a man in there wearing a uniform similar to the warden's, keys hanging from their rings on a wall behind him.

They climbed to the second floor and turned into a corridor that smelled of wood soap, the oak floor gleaming underfoot and bathed in a white light from the large window at the far end.

"Lot of security," Teddy said.

McPherson said, "We take every precaution."

Chuck said, "To the thanks of a grateful public, Mr. McPherson, I'm sure."

"You have to understand," McPherson said, turning back to Teddy as they walked past several offices, doors all closed and bearing the names of doctors on small silver plates. "There is no facility like this in the United States. We take only the most damaged patients. We take the ones no other facility can manage."

"Gryce is here, right?" Teddy said.

McPherson nodded. "Vincent Gryce, yes. In Ward C."

Chuck said to Teddy, "Gryce was the one . . . ?"

Teddy nodded. "Killed all his relatives, scalped them, made himself hats."

Chuck was nodding fast. "And wore them into town, right?"

"According to the papers."

They had stopped outside a set of double doors. A brass plate affixed in the center of the right door read CHIEF OF STAFF, DR. J. CAWLEY.

McPherson turned to them, one hand on the knob, and looked at them with an unreadable intensity.

McPherson said, "In a less enlightened age, a patient like Gryce would have been put to death. But here they can study him, define a pathology, maybe isolate the abnormality in his brain that caused him to disengage so completely from acceptable patterns of behavior. If they can do that, maybe we can reach a day where that kind of disengagement can be rooted out of society entirely."

He seemed to be waiting for a response, his hand stiff against the doorknob.

"It's good to have dreams," Chuck said. "Don't you think?"

3

DR. CAWLEY WAS thin to the point of emaciation. Not quite the swimming bones and cartilage Teddy had seen at Dachau, but definitely in need of several good meals. His small dark eyes sat far back in their sockets, and the shadows that leaked from them bled across the rest of his face. His cheeks were so sunken they appeared collapsed, and the flesh around them was pitted with aged acne. His lips and nose were as thin as the rest of him, and his chin appeared squared off to the point of nonexistence. What remained of his hair was as dark as his eyes and the shadows underneath.

He had an explosive smile, however, bright and bulging with a confidence that lightened his irises, and he used it now as he came around the desk to greet them, his hand outstretched.

"Marshal Daniels and Marshal Aule," he said, "glad you could come so quickly."

His hand was dry and statue smooth in Teddy's, and his grip was a shocker, squeezing the bones in Teddy's hand until Teddy could feel the press of it straight up his forearm. Cawley's eyes glittered for a moment, as if to say, Didn't expect that, did you? and then he moved on to Chuck.

He shook Chuck's hand with a "Pleased to meet you, sir," and then the smile shot off his face and he said to McPherson, "That'll be all for now, Deputy Warden. Thank you."

McPherson said, "Yes, sir. A pleasure, gentlemen," and backed out of the room.

Cawley's smile returned, but it was a more viscous version, and it reminded Teddy of the film that formed over soup.

"He's a good man, McPherson. Eager."

"For?" Teddy said, taking a seat in front of the desk.

Cawley's smile morphed again, curling up one side of his face and freezing there for a moment. "I'm sorry?"

"He's eager," Teddy said. "But for what?"

Cawley sat behind the teak desk, spread his arms. "For the work. A moral fusion between law and order and clinical care. Just half a century ago, even less in some cases, the thinking on the kind of patients we deal with here was that they should, at best, be shackled and left in their own filth and waste. They were systematically beaten, as if that could drive the psychosis out. We demonized them. We tortured them. Spread them on racks, yes. Drove screws into their brains. Even drowned them on occasion."

"And now?" Chuck said.

"Now we treat them. Morally. We try to heal, to cure. And if that fails, we at least provide them with a measure of calm in their lives."

"And their victims?" Teddy said.

Cawley raised his eyebrows, waiting.

"These *are* all violent offenders," Teddy said. "Right?"

Cawley nodded. "Quite violent, actually."

"So they've hurt people," Teddy said. "Murdered them in many cases."

"Oh, in most."

"So why does their sense of calm matter in relation to their victims'?"

Cawley said, "Because my job is to treat them, not their victims. I can't help their victims. It's the nature of any life's work that it have limits. That's mine. I can only concern myself with my patients." He smiled. "Did the senator explain the situation?"

Teddy and Chuck shot each other glances as they sat.

Teddy said, "We don't know anything about a senator, Doctor. We were assigned by the state field office."

Cawley propped his elbows on a green desk blotter and clasped his hands together, placed his chin on top of them, and stared at them over the rim of his glasses.

"My mistake, then. So what have you been told?"

"We know a female prisoner is missing." Teddy placed his notebook on his knee, flipped the pages. "A Rachel Solando."

"Patient." Cawley gave them a dead smile.

"Patient," Teddy said. "I apologize. We understand she escaped within the last twenty-four hours."

Cawley's nod was a small tilt of his chin and hands. "Last night. Sometime between ten and midnight."

"And she still hasn't been found," Chuck said.

"Correct, Marshal . . ." He held up an apologetic hand.

"Aule," Chuck said.

Cawley's face narrowed over his hands and Teddy noticed drops of water spit against the window behind him. He couldn't tell whether they were from the sky or the sea.

"And your first name is Charles?" Cawley said.

"Yeah," Chuck said.

"I'd take you for a Charles," Cawley said, "but not necessarily an Aule."

"That's fortunate, I guess."

"How so?"

"We don't choose our names," Chuck said. "So it's nice when someone thinks that one of them, at least, fits."

"Who chose yours?" Cawley said.

"My parents."

"Your surname."

Chuck shrugged. "Who's to tell? We'd have to go back twenty generations."

"Or one."

Chuck leaned forward in his chair. "Excuse me?"

"You're Greek," Cawley said. "Or Armenian. Which?"

"Armenian."

"So Aule was . . ."

"Anasmajian."

Cawley turned his slim gaze on Teddy. "And yourself?"

"Daniels?" Teddy said. "Tenth-generation Irish." He gave Cawley a small grin. "And, yeah, I can trace it back, Doctor."

"But your given first name? Theodore?"

"Edward."

Cawley leaned his chair back, his hands falling free of his chin. He tapped a letter opener against the desk edge, the sound as soft and persistent as snow falling on a roof.

"My wife," he said, "is named Margaret. Yet no one ever calls her that except me. Some of her oldest friends call her Margo, which makes a certain amount of sense, but everyone else calls her Peggy. I've never understood that."

"What?"

"How you get Peggy from Margaret. And yet it's quite common. Or how you get Teddy from Edward. There's no *p* in *Margaret* and no *t* in *Edward*."

Teddy shrugged. "Your first name?"

"John."

"Anyone ever call you Jack?"

He shook his head. "Most people just call me Doctor."

The water spit lightly against the window, and Cawley seemed to review their conversation in his head, his eyes gone shiny and distant, and then Chuck said, "Is Miss Solando considered dangerous?"

"All our patients have shown a proclivity for violence," Cawley said. "It's why they're here. Men and women. Rachel Solando was a war widow. She drowned her three children in the lake behind her house. Took them out there one by one and held their heads under until they died. Then she brought them back into the house and arranged them around the kitchen table and ate a meal there before a neighbor dropped by."

"She kill the neighbor?" Chuck asked.

Cawley's eyebrows rose, and he gave a small sigh. "No. Invited him to sit and have breakfast with them. He declined, naturally, and called the police. Rachel still believes the children are alive, waiting for her. It might explain why she's tried to escape."

"To return home," Teddy said.

Cawley nodded.

"And where's that?" Chuck asked.

"A small town in the Berkshires. Roughly a hundred fifty miles from here." With a tilt of his head, Cawley indicated the window behind him. "To swim that way, you don't reach land for eleven miles. To swim north, you don't reach land until Newfoundland."

Teddy said, "And you've searched the grounds."

"Yes."

"Pretty thoroughly?"

Cawley took a few seconds to answer, played with a silver bust of a horse on the corner of his desk. "The warden and his men and a detail of orderlies spent the night and a good part of the morning scouring the island and every building in the institution. Not a trace. What's even more disturbing is that we can't tell how she got out of her room. It was locked from the outside and its sole window was barred. We've found no indication that the locks were tampered with." He took his eyes off the horse and glanced at Teddy and Chuck. "It's as if she evaporated straight through the walls."

Teddy jotted "evaporated" in his notebook. "And you are sure that she *was* in that room at lights-out."

"Positive."

"How so?"

Cawley moved his hand back from the horse and pressed the call button on his intercom. "Nurse Marino?"

"Yes, Doctor."

"Please tell Mr. Ganton to come in."

"Right away, Doctor."

There was a small table near the window with a pitcher of water and four glasses on top. Cawley went to it and filled three of the glasses. He placed one in front of Teddy and one in front of Chuck, took his own back behind the desk with him.

Teddy said, "You wouldn't have some aspirin around here, would you?"

Cawley gave him a small smile. "I think we could scare some up." He rummaged in his desk drawer, came out with a bottle of Bayer. "Two or three?"

"Three would be nice." Teddy could feel the ache behind his eye begin to pulse.

Cawley handed them across the desk and Teddy tossed them in his mouth, chased them with the water.

"Prone to headaches, Marshal?"

Teddy said, "Prone to seasickness, unfortunately."

Cawley nodded. "Ah. Dehydrated."

Teddy nodded and Cawley opened a walnut cigarette box, held it open to Teddy and Chuck. Teddy took one. Chuck shook his head and produced his own pack, and all three of them lit up as Cawley lifted the window open behind him.

He sat back down and handed a photograph across the desk—a young woman, beautiful, her face blemished by dark rings under the eyes, rings as dark as her black hair. The eyes themselves were too wide, as if something hot were prodding them from inside her head. Whatever she saw beyond that camera lens, beyond the photographer, beyond anything in the known world probably—wasn't fit to be seen.

There was something uncomfortably familiar about her, and then Teddy made the connection—a young boy he'd seen in the camps who wouldn't eat the food they gave him. He sat against a wall in the April sun with that same look in his eyes until his eyelids closed and eventually they added him to the pile at the train station.

Chuck unleashed a low whistle. "My God."

Cawley took a drag on his cigarette. "Are you reacting to her apparent beauty or her apparent madness?"

"Both," Chuck said.

Those eyes, Teddy thought. Even frozen in time, they howled. You wanted to climb inside the picture and say, "No, no, no. It's okay, it's okay. Sssh." You wanted to hold her until the shakes stopped, tell her that everything would be all right.

The office door opened and a tall Negro with thick flecks of gray in his hair entered wearing the white-on-white uniform of an orderly.

"Mr. Ganton," Cawley said, "these are the gentlemen I told you about—Marshals Aule and Daniels."

Teddy and Chuck stood and shook Ganton's hand, Teddy getting a strong whiff of fear from the man, as if he wasn't quite comfortable shaking hands with the law, maybe had a pending warrant or two against him back in the world.

"Mr. Ganton has been with us for seventeen years. He's the head orderly here. It was Mr. Ganton who escorted Rachel to her room last night. Mr. Ganton?"

Ganton crossed his ankles, placed his hands on his knees, and hunched forward a bit, his eyes on his shoes. "There was group at nine o'clock. Then—"

Cawley said, "That's a group therapy session led by Dr. Sheehan and Nurse Marino."

Ganton waited until he was sure Cawley had finished before he began again. "So, yeah. They was in group, and it ended round ten. I escorted Miss Rachel up to her room. She went inside. I locked up from the outside. We do checks every two hours during lights-out. I go back at midnight. I look in, and her bed's empty. I figure maybe she's on the floor. They do that a lot, the patients, sleep on the floor. I open up—"

Cawley again: "Using your keys, correct, Mr. Ganton?"

Ganton nodded at Cawley, looked back at his knees. "I use my keys, yeah, 'cause the door's locked. I go in. Miss Rachel ain't nowhere to be found. I shut the door and check the window and the bars. They locked tight too." He shrugged. "I call the warden." He looked up at Cawley, and Cawley gave him a soft, paternal nod.

"Any questions, gentlemen?"

Chuck shook his head.

Teddy looked up from his notebook. "Mr. Ganton, you said you entered the room and ascertained that the patient wasn't there. What did this entail?"

"Sir?"

Teddy said, "Is there a closet? Space beneath the bed where she could hide?"

"Both."

"And you checked those places."

"Yes, sir."

"With the door still open."

"Sir?"

"You said that you entered the room and looked around and couldn't find the patient. *Then* you shut the door behind you."

"No, I . . . Well . . ."

Teddy waited, took another hit off the cigarette Cawley had given him. It was smooth, richer than his Chesterfields, and the smell of the smoke was different too, almost sweet.

"It took all of five seconds, sir," Ganton said. "No door on the closet. I look there, I look under the bed, and I shut the door. No place she could have been hiding. Room's small."

"Against the wall, though?" Teddy said. "To the right or the left of the door?"

"Nah." Ganton shook his head, and for the first time Teddy thought he glimpsed anger, a sense of primal resentment behind the downcast eyes and the "Yes, sirs" and "No, sirs."

"It's unlikely," Cawley said to Teddy. "I see your point, Marshal, but once you see the room, you'll understand that Mr. Ganton would have been hard-pressed to miss the patient if she were standing *any-where* within its four walls."

"That's right," Ganton said, staring openly at Teddy now, and Teddy could see the man carried a furious pride in his work ethic that Teddy, by questioning, had managed to insult.

"Thank you, Mr. Ganton," Cawley said. "That'll be all for now."

Ganton rose, his eyes lingering on Teddy for another few seconds, and then he said, "Thank you, Doctor," and left the room.

They were quiet for a minute, finishing their cigarettes and then stubbing them out in the ashtrays before Chuck said, "I think we should see the room now, Doctor."

"Of course," Cawley said and came out from behind his desk, a ring of keys in his hand the size of a hubcap. "Follow me."

. . .

IT WAS A tiny room with the door opening inward and to the right, the door cut from steel and the hinges well greased so that it swung hard against the wall on the right. To their left was a short length of wall and then a small wooden closet with a few smocks and drawstring pants hanging on plastic hangers.

"There goes that theory," Teddy admitted.

Cawley nodded. "There would have been no place for her to hide from anyone standing in this doorway."

"Well, the ceiling," Chuck said, and all three of them looked up and even Cawley managed a smile.

Cawley closed the door behind them and Teddy felt the immediate sense of imprisonment in his spine. They might call it a room, but it was a cell. The window hovering behind the slim bed was barred. A small dresser sat against the right wall, and the floor and walls were a white institutional cement. With three of them in the room, there was barely space to move without bumping limbs.

Teddy said, "Who else would have access to the room?"

"At that time of night? Very few would have any reason to be in the ward."

"Sure," Teddy said. "But who would have access?"

"The orderlies, of course."

"Doctors?" Chuck said.

"Well, nurses," Cawley said.

"Doctors don't have keys for this room?" Teddy asked.

"They do," Cawley said with just a hint of annoyance. "But by ten o'clock, the doctors have signed out for the night."

"And turned in their keys?"

"Yes."

"And there's a record of that?" Teddy said.

"I don't follow."

Chuck said, "They have to sign in and out for the keys, Doctor—that's what we're wondering."

"Of course."

"And we could check last night's sign-in log," Teddy said.

"Yes, yes. Of course."

"And that would be kept in the cage we saw on the first floor," Chuck said. "The one with the guard inside of it and the wall of keys behind him?"

Cawley gave him a quick nod.

"And the personnel files," Teddy said, "of the medical staff and the orderlies and the guards. We'll need access to those."

Cawley peered at him as if Teddy's face were sprouting blackflies. "Why?"

"A woman disappears from a locked room, Doctor? She escapes onto a tiny island and no one can find her? I have to at least consider that she had help."

"We'll see," Cawley said.

"We'll *see*?"

"Yes, Marshal. I'll have to speak with the warden and some of the other staff. We'll make a determination of your request based on—"

"Doctor," Teddy said, "it wasn't a request. We're here by order of the government. This is a federal facility from which a dangerous prisoner—"

"Patient."

"A dangerous patient," Teddy said, keeping his voice as even as possible, "has escaped. If you refuse to aid two U.S. marshals, Doctor, in the apprehension of that patient you are, unfortunately—Chuck?"

Chuck said, "Obstructing justice, Doctor."

Cawley looked at Chuck as if he'd been expecting grief from Teddy, but Chuck hadn't been on his radar.

"Yes, well," he said, his voice stripped of life, "all I can say is that I will do all that I can to accommodate your request."

Teddy and Chuck exchanged a small glance, went back to looking at the bare room. Cawley probably wasn't used to questions that continued after he'd shown displeasure with them, so they gave him a minute to catch his breath.

Teddy looked in the tiny closet, saw three white smocks, two pairs of white shoes. "How many shoes are the patients given?"

"Two."

"She left this room barefoot?"

"Yes." He fixed the tie under his lab coat and then pointed at a large sheet of paper lying on the bed. "We found that behind the dresser. We don't know what it means. We were hoping someone could tell us."

Teddy lifted the sheet of paper, turned it over to see that the other side was a hospital eye chart, the letters shrinking and descending in a pyramid. He turned it back over and held it up for Chuck:

THE LAW OF 4

I AM 47

THEY WERE 80

+YOU ARE 3

WE ARE 4

BUT

WHO IS 67?

Teddy didn't even like holding it. The edges of the paper tingled against his fingers.

Chuck said, "Fuck if I know."

Cawley stepped up beside them. "Quite similar to our clinical conclusion."

"We are three," Teddy said.

Chuck peered at the paper. "Huh?"

"We could be the three," Teddy said. "The three of us right now, standing in this room."

Chuck shook his head. "How's she going to predict that?"

Teddy shrugged. "It's a reach."

"Yeah."

Cawley said, "It is, and yet Rachel is quite brilliant in her games. Her delusions—particularly the one that allows her to believe her three children are still alive—are conceived on a very delicate but intricate architecture. To sustain the structure, she employs an elaborate narrative thread to her life that is completely fictitious."

Chuck turned his head slowly, looked at Cawley. "I'd need a degree to understand that, Doctor."

Cawley chuckled. "Think of the lies you tell your parents as a child. How elaborate they are. Instead of keeping them simple to explain why you missed school or forgot your chores, you embellish, you make them fantastical. Yes?"

Chuck thought about it and nodded.

Teddy said, "Sure. Criminals do the same thing."

"Exactly. The idea is to obfuscate. Confuse the listener until they believe out of exhaustion more than any sense of truth. Now consider those lies being told *to* yourself. That's what Rachel does. In four years, she never so much as acknowledged that she was in an institution. As far as she was concerned, she was back home in the Berkshires in her house, and we were deliverymen, milkmen, postal workers, just passing by. Whatever the reality, she used sheer force of will to make her illusions stronger."

"But how does the truth never get through?" Teddy said. "I mean, she's in a mental institution. How does she not notice that from time to time?"

"Ah," Cawley said, "now we're getting into the true horrible beauty of the full-blown schizophrenic's paranoid structure. If you believe, gentlemen, that you are the sole holder of truth, then everyone else must be lying. And if everyone is lying . . ."

"Then any truth they say," Chuck said, "must be a lie."

Cawley cocked his thumb and pointed his finger at him like a gun. "You're getting it."

Teddy said, "And that somehow plays into these numbers?"

"It must. They have to represent something. With Rachel, no thought was idle or ancillary. She had to keep the structure in her head from collapsing, and to do that, she had to be *thinking* always. This"—he tapped the eye chart—"is the structure on paper. This, I sincerely believe, will tell us where she's gone."

For just a moment, Teddy thought it was speaking to him, becoming clearer. It was the first two numbers, he was certain—the "47" and the "80"—he could feel something about them scratching at his brain like the melody of a song he was trying to remember while the radio played a completely different tune. The "47" was the easiest clue. It was right in front of him. It was so simple. It was . . .

And then any possible bridges of logic collapsed, and Teddy felt his mind go white, and he knew it was in flight again—the clue, the connection, the bridge—and he placed the page down on the bed again.

"Insane," Chuck said.

"What's that?" Cawley said.

"Where she's gone," Chuck said. "In my opinion."

"Well, certainly," Cawley said. "I think we can take that as a given."

4

THEY STOOD OUTSIDE the room. The corridor broke off from a staircase in the center. Rachel's door was to the left of the stairs, halfway down on the right-hand side.

"This is the only way off this floor?" Teddy said.

Cawley nodded.

"No roof access?" Chuck said.

Cawley shook his head. "The only way up is from the fire escape. You'll see it on the south side of the building. It has a gate, and the gate is always locked. Staff has keys, of course, but no patients. To get to the roof, she'd have had to go downstairs, outside, use a key, and climb back up top."

"But the roof was checked?"

Another nod. "As were all the rooms in the ward. Immediately. As soon as she was discovered missing."

Teddy pointed at the orderly who sat by a small card table in front of the stairs. "Someone's there twenty-four hours?"

"Yes."

"So, someone was there last night."

"Orderly Ganton, actually."

They walked to the staircase and Chuck said, "So . . . ," and raised his eyebrows at Teddy.

"So," Teddy agreed.

"So," Chuck said, "Miss Solando gets out of her locked room into this corridor, goes down these steps." They went down the steps themselves and Chuck jerked a thumb at the orderly waiting for them by the second-floor landing. "She gets past another orderly here, we don't know how, makes herself invisible or something, goes down this next flight, and comes out into . . ."

They turned down the last flight and were facing a large open room with several couches pressed against the wall, a large folding table in the center with folding chairs, bay windows saturating the space with white light.

"The main living area," Cawley said. "Where most of the patients spend their evenings. Group therapy was held here last night. You'll see the nurses' station is just through that portico there. After lights-out, the orderlies congregate here. They're supposed to be mopping up, cleaning windows and such, but more often than not, we catch them here, playing cards."

"And last night?"

"According to those who were on duty, the card game was in full swing. Seven men, sitting right at the base of the stairs, playing stud poker."

Chuck put his hands on his hips, let out a long breath through his mouth. "She does the invisible thing again, apparently, moves either right or left."

"Right would bring her through the dining area, then into the kitchen, and beyond that is a door that is caged and set with an alarm at nine o'clock at night, once the kitchen staff has left. To the left is the nurses' station and the staff lounge. No door to the outside. The only ways out are that door on the other side of the living area, or back down the corridor behind the staircase. Both had men at their stations last night." Cawley glanced at his watch. "Gentlemen, I have a meeting. If you have any questions, please feel free to ask any of the staff or visit McPherson. He's handled the search thus far. He should have all the information you need. Staff eats at six sharp in the mess hall in the basement of the orderlies' dormitory. After that, we'll assemble here in the staff lounge and you can speak to anyone who was working during last night's incident."

He hurried out the front door, and they watched him until he turned left and disappeared.

Teddy said, "Is there anything about this that *doesn't* feel like an inside job?"

"I'm kind of fond of my invisible theory. She could have the formula in a bottle. You following me? She could be watching us right now, Teddy." Chuck looked over his shoulder quick, then back at Teddy. "Something to think about."

IN THE AFTERNOON they joined the search party and moved inland as the breeze grew swollen, warmer. So much of the island was overgrown, clogged with weeds and thick fields of tall grass threaded with grasping tendrils of ancient oak and green vines covered in thorns. In most places, human passage was impossible even with the machetes some of the guards carried. Rachel Solando wouldn't have had a machete, and even if she had, it seemed the nature of the island to push all comers back to the coast.

The search struck Teddy as desultory, as if no one but he and Chuck truly had his heart in it. The men wound their way along the inner ring above the shoreline with downcast eyes and sullen steps. At one point they rounded a bend on a shelf of black rocks and faced a cliff that towered out past them into the sea. To their left, beyond a stand of moss and thorns and red berries curled into an overgrown mass, lay a small glade that dropped away at the base of some low hills. The hills rose steadily, each one higher than the last, until they gave way to the jagged cliff, and Teddy could see cuts in the hills and oblong holes in the side of the cliff.

"Caves?" he said to McPherson.

He nodded. "A few of them."

"You check 'em?"

McPherson sighed and cupped a match against the wind to light a thin cigar. "She had two pairs of shoes, Marshal. Both found back in her room. How's she going to get through what we just came through, cross over these rocks, and scale that cliff?"

Teddy pointed off past the glade to the lowest of the hills. "She takes the long way, works her way up from the west?"

McPherson placed his own finger beside Teddy's. "See where the glade drops off? That's marshland right there at the tip of your finger. The base of those hills is covered in poison ivy, live oak, sumac, about a thousand different plants, and all of 'em with thorns the size of my dick."

"That mean they're big or little?" This from Chuck, a few steps ahead of them, looking back over his shoulder.

McPherson smiled. "Might be somewhere in between."

Chuck nodded.

"All I'm saying, gentlemen? She would've had no choice but to stick hard to the shoreline, and halfway around in either direction, she would've run out of beach." He pointed at the cliff. "Met one of those."

AN HOUR LATER, on the other side of the island, they met the fence line. Beyond it lay the old fort and the lighthouse, and Teddy could see that the lighthouse had its own fence, penning it in, two guards at the gate, rifles held to their chests.

"Septic processing?" he said.

McPherson nodded.

Teddy looked at Chuck. Chuck raised his eyebrows.

"Septic processing?" Teddy said again.

NO ONE CAME to their table at dinner. They sat alone, damp from the careless spits of rain, that warm breeze that had begun to carry the ocean with it. Outside, the island had begun to rattle in the dark, the breeze turning into a wind.

"A locked room," Chuck said.

"Barefoot," Teddy said.

"Past three interior checkpoints."

"A roomful of orderlies."

"Barefoot," Chuck agreed.

Teddy stirred his food, some kind of shepherd's pie, the meat stringy. "Over a wall with electric security wire."

"Or through a manned gate."

"Out into that." The wind shaking the building, shaking the dark.

"Barefoot."

"No one sees her."

Chuck chewed his food, took a sip of coffee. "Someone dies on this island—it's got to happen, right?—where do they go?"

"Buried."

Chuck nodded. "You see a cemetery today?"

Teddy shook his head. "Probably fenced in somewhere."

"Like the septic plant. Sure." Chuck pushed his tray away, sat back. "Who we speaking to after this?"

"The staff."

"You think they'll be helpful?"

"Don't you?"

Chuck grinned. He lit a cigarette, his eyes on Teddy, his grin turning into a soft laugh, the smoke chugging out in rhythm with it.

TEDDY STOOD IN the center of the room, the staff in a circle around him. He rested his hands on the top of a metal chair, Chuck slouched against a beam beside him, hands in his pockets.

"I assume everyone knows why we're all here," Teddy said. "You had an escape last night. Far as we can tell, the patient vanished. We have no evidence that would allow us to believe the patient left this institution without help. Deputy Warden McPherson, would you agree?"

"Yup. I'd say that's a reasonable assessment at this time."

Teddy was about to speak again when Cawley, sitting in a chair beside the nurse, said, "Could you gentlemen introduce yourselves? Some of my staff have not made your acquaintance."

Teddy straightened to his full height. "U.S. Marshal Edward Daniels. This is my partner, U.S. Marshal Charles Aule."

Chuck gave a small wave to the group, put his hand back in his pocket.

Teddy said, "Deputy Warden, you and your men searched the grounds."

"Sure did."

"And you found?"

McPherson stretched in his chair. "We found no evidence to suggest a woman in flight. No shreds of torn clothing, no footprints, no bent vegetation. The current was strong last night, the tide pushing in. A swim would have been out of the question."

"But she could have tried." This from the nurse, Kerry Marino, a slim woman with a bundle of red hair that she'd loosed from the pile

atop her head and unclenched from another clip just above her verte-
brae as soon as she'd walked into the room. Her cap sat in her lap, and
she finger-combed her hair in a lazy way that suggested weariness but
had every guy in the room sneaking glances at her, the way that weary
finger-combing suggested the need for a bed.

McPherson said, "What was that?"

Marino's fingers stopped moving through her hair and she
dropped them to her lap.

"How do we know she didn't try to swim, end up drowning
instead?"

"She would have washed ashore by now." Cawley yawned into his
fist. "That tide?"

Marino held up a hand as if to say, Oh, excuse me, boys, and said,
"Just thought I'd bring it up."

"And we appreciate it," Cawley said. "Marshal, ask your questions,
please. It's been a long day."

Teddy glanced at Chuck and Chuck gave him a small tilt of the
eyes back. A missing woman with a history of violence at large on a
small island and everyone seemed to just want to get to bed.

Teddy said, "Mr. Ganton has already told us he checked on Miss
Solando at midnight and discovered her missing. The locks to the window grate in her room and the door were not tampered with. Between
ten and twelve last night, Mr. Ganton, was there ever a point where
you didn't have an eye's view of the third-floor corridor?"

Several heads turned to look at Ganton, and Teddy was confused
to see a kind of amused light in some of the faces, as if Teddy were the
third-grade teacher who'd asked a question of the heppest kid in class.

Ganton spoke to his own feet. "Only time my eyes weren't on that
corridor was when I entered her room, found her gone."

"That would have taken thirty seconds."

"More like fifteen." He turned his eyes to Teddy. "It's a small room."

"But otherwise?"

"Otherwise, everyone was locked down by ten. She was the last one in her room. I take up my seat on the landing, I don't see no one for two hours."

"And you never left your post?"

"No, sir."

"Get a cup of coffee, nothing?"

Ganton shook his head.

"All right, people," Chuck said, coming off the pole. "I have to make a huge leap here. I have to say, for the sake of argument only and meaning no disrespect to Mr. Ganton here, let's play with the idea that somehow Miss Solando crawled across the ceiling or something."

Several members of the group chuckled.

"And she gets to the staircase leading down to the second floor. Who's she gotta pass?"

A milk-white orderly with orange hair raised his hand.

"And your name?" Teddy said.

"Glen. Glen Miga."

"Okay, Glen. Were you at your post all night?"

"Uh, yeah."

Teddy said, "Glen."

"Yeah?" He looked up from the hangnail he'd been picking.

"The truth."

Glen looked over at Cawley, then back at Teddy. "Yeah, I was."

"Glen," Teddy said, "come on."

Glen held Teddy's gaze, his eyes beginning to widen, and then he said, "I went to the bathroom."

Cawley leaned forward on his knees. "Who stepped in as your relief?"

"It was a quick piss," Glen said. "A pee, sir. Sorry."

"How long?" Teddy said.

Glen shrugged. "A minute. Tops."

"A minute. You're sure?"

"I'm not a camel."

"No."

"I was in and out."

"You breached protocol," Cawley said. "Christ."

"Sir, I know. I—"

"What time was this?" Teddy said.

"Eleven-thirty. Thereabouts." Glen's fear of Cawley was turning into hate for Teddy. A few more questions, he'd get hostile.

"Thanks, Glen," Teddy said and turned it back to Chuck with a tilt of his head.

"At eleven-thirty," Chuck said, "or thereabouts, was the poker game still in full swing?"

Several heads turned toward one another and then back to Chuck and then one Negro nodded, followed by the rest of the orderlies.

"Who was still sitting in at that point?"

Four Negroes and one white raised their hands.

Chuck zeroed in on the ringleader, the first guy to nod, first one to raise his hand. A round, fleshy guy, his head shaved and shiny under the light.

"Name?"

"Trey, sir. Trey Washington."

"Trey, you were all sitting where?"

Trey pointed at the floor. "Right about here. Center of the room. Looking right at that staircase. Had an eye on the front door, had one on the back."

Chuck walked over by him, craned his head to clock the front and back doors, the staircase. "Good position."

Trey lowered his voice. "Ain't just about the patients, sir. 'Bout the doctors, some of the nurses who don't like us. Ain't supposed to be playing cards. Gotta be able to see who's coming, grab us a mop right quick."

Chuck smiled. "Bet you move fast too."

"You ever seen lightning in August?"

"Yeah."

"Slow compared to me getting on that mop."

That broke the group up, Nurse Marino unable to suppress a smile, and Teddy noticing a few of the Negroes sliding their fingers off each other. He knew then that for the duration of their stay, Chuck would play Good Cop. He had the knack with people, as if he'd be comfortable in any cross section of the population, regardless of color or even language. Teddy wondered how the fuck the Seattle office could have let him go, Jap girlfriend or not.

Teddy, on the other hand, was instinctively alpha male. Once men accepted it, as they'd had to pretty quickly in the war, they got along great with him. Until then, though, there'd be tension.

"Okay, okay." Chuck held up a hand to quiet the laughter, still grinning himself. "So, Trey, you were all at the base of these stairs, playing cards. When did you know something was wrong?"

"When Ike—ah, Mr. Ganton, I mean—he start shouting down, 'Call the warden. We got us a break.' "

"And what time was that?"

"Twelve-oh-two and thirty-nine seconds."

Chuck raised his eyebrows. "You a clock?"

"No, sir, but I trained to look at one the first sign of trouble. Anything might be what you call an 'incident,' we all going to have to fill out an IR, an 'incident re-port.' First thing you get asked on an IR is the time the incident began. You do enough IRs? Gets to be second nature to look at a clock the first hint of trouble."

Several of the orderlies were nodding as he spoke, a few "Uh-huh's" and "That's right's" tumbling out of their mouths as if they were at a church revival.

Chuck gave Teddy a look: Well, how about that?

"So twelve-oh-two," Chuck said.

"And thirty-nine seconds."

Teddy said to Ganton, "Those extra two minutes past midnight, that would be because you checked a few rooms *before* you got to Miss Solando's, right?"

Ganton nodded. "She's the fifth down that hallway."

"Warden arrives on scene when?" Teddy said.

Trey said, "Hicksville—he one o' the guards—he's first through the front door. Was working the gate, I think. He come through at twelve-oh-six and twenty-two seconds. The warden, he come four minutes after that with six men."

Teddy turned to Nurse Marino. "You hear all the commotion and you . . ."

"I lock the nurses' station. I come out into the rec hall at about the same time Hicksville was coming through the front door." She shrugged and lit a cigarette, and several other members of the group took it as a cue, lit up their own.

"And nobody could have gotten by you in the nurses' station."

She propped her chin on the heel of her palm, stared through a sickle-stream of smoke at him. "Gotten by me to where? The door to Hydrotherapy? You go in there, you're locked in a cement box with a lot of tubs, a few small pools."

"That room was checked?"

"It was, Marshal," McPherson said, sounding tired now.

"Nurse Marino," Teddy said, "you were part of the group therapy session last night."

"Yes."

"Anything unusual occur?"

"Define 'unusual.' "

"Excuse me?"

"This is a mental institution, Marshal. For the criminally insane. 'Usual' isn't a big part of our day."

Teddy gave her a nod and a sheepish smile. "Let me rephrase. Anything occur in group last night that was more memorable than, um . . . ?"

"Normal?" she said.

That drew a smile from Cawley, a few stray laughs.

Teddy nodded.

She thought about it for a minute, her cigarette ash growing white and hooked. She noticed it, flicked it off into the ashtray, raised her head. "No. Sorry."

"And did Miss Solando speak last night?"

"A couple of times, I think, yes."

"About?"

Marino looked over at Cawley.

He said, "We're waiving patient confidentiality with the marshals for now."

She nodded, though Teddy could tell she wasn't too fond of the concept.

"We were discussing anger management. We've had a few instances of inappropriate volatility recently."

"What kind?"

"Patients screaming at other patients, fighting, that sort of thing. Nothing out of the norm, just a small upsurge in recent weeks that probably had to do with the heat wave more than anything. So last night we discussed appropriate and inappropriate ways to display anxiety or displeasure."

"Has Miss Solando had any anger issues of late?"

"Rachel? No. Rachel only became agitated when it rained. That was her contribution to group last night. 'I hear rain. I hear rain. It's not here, but it's coming. What can we do about the food?' "

"The food?"

Marino stubbed out her cigarette and nodded. "Rachel hated the food here. She complained constantly."

"For good reason?" Teddy said.

Marino caught herself before a half smile went full. She dropped her eyes. "One could argue the reason was understandable possibly. We don't color reasons or motives in terms of good or bad moral suppositions."

Teddy nodded. "And there was a Dr. Sheehan here last night. He ran group. Is he here?"

No one spoke. Several men stubbed out their cigarettes in the standing ashtrays between chairs.

Eventually, Cawley said, "Dr. Sheehan left on the morning ferry. The one you took on the return trip."

"Why?"

"He'd been scheduled for a vacation for some time."

"But we need to talk to him."

Cawley said, "I have his summation documents in regard to the group session. I have all his notes. He departed the main facility at ten last night, retired to his quarters. In the morning, he left. His vacation had been long overdue and long planned as well. We saw no reason to keep him here."

Teddy looked to McPherson.

"You approved this?"

McPherson nodded.

"It's a state of lockdown," Teddy said. "A patient has escaped. How do you allow anyone to leave during lockdown?"

McPherson said, "We ascertained his whereabouts during the night. We thought it through, couldn't think of any reason to keep him."

"He's a *doctor,*" Cawley said.

"Jesus," Teddy said softly. Biggest breach in standard operating procedure he'd ever encountered at any penal institution and everyone was acting like it was no big deal.

"Where'd he go?"

"Excuse me?"

"On vacation," Teddy said. "Where did he go?"

Cawley looked up at the ceiling, trying to recall. "New York, I believe. The city. It's where his family is from. Park Avenue."

"I'll need a phone number," Teddy said.

"I don't see why—"

"Doctor," Teddy said. "I'll need a phone number."

"We'll get that to you, Marshal." Cawley kept his eyes on the ceiling. "Anything else?"

"You bet," Teddy said.

Cawley's chin came down and he looked across at Teddy.

"I need a phone," Teddy said.

THE PHONE IN the nurses' station gave off nothing but a white hiss of air. There were four more in the ward, locked behind glass, and once the glass was opened, the phones produced the same result.

Teddy and Dr. Cawley walked over to the central switchboard on the first floor of the main hospital building. The operator looked up as they came through the door, a set of black headphones looped around his neck.

"Sir," he said, "we're down. Even radio communication."

Cawley said, "It's not all that bad out."

The operator shrugged. "I'll keep trying. It's not so much what it's doing here, though. It's what kinda weather they're having back on the other side."

"Keep trying," Cawley said. "You get it up and running, you get word to me. This man needs to make a pretty important call."

The operator nodded and turned his back to them, put the headphones back on.

Outside, the air felt like trapped breath.

"What do they do if you don't check in?" Cawley asked.

"The field office?" Teddy said. "They mark it in their nightly reports. Usually twenty-four hours before they start to worry."

Cawley nodded. "Maybe this'll blow over by then."

"Over?" Teddy said. "It hasn't even started yet."

Cawley shrugged and began walking toward the gate. "I'll be having drinks and maybe a cigar or two at my house. Nine o'clock, if you and your partner feel like dropping by."

"Oh," Teddy said. "Can we talk then?"

Cawley stopped, looked back at him. The dark trees on the other side of the wall had begun to sway and whisper.

"We've been talking, Marshal."

CHUCK AND TEDDY walked the dark grounds, feeling the storm in the air swelling hot around them, as if the world were pregnant, distended.

"This is bullshit," Teddy said.

"Yup."

"Rotten to the fucking core."

"I was Baptist, I'd give you an 'Amen, brother.' "

"Brother?"

"How they talk down there. I did a year in Mississippi."

"Yeah?"

"Amen, brother."

Teddy bummed another cigarette off Chuck and lit it.

Chuck said, "You call the field office?"

Teddy shook his head. "Cawley said the switchboard's down." He raised his hand. "The storm, you know."

Chuck spit tobacco off his tongue. "Storm? Where?"

Teddy said, "But you can feel it coming." He looked at the dark sky. "Though, not to where it's taking out their central com'."

"Central com'," Chuck said. "You leave the army yet or you still waiting for your D papers?"

"Switchboard," Teddy said, waving his cigarette at it. "Whatever we're calling it. And their radio too."

"Their fucking radio?" Chuck's eyes bloomed wide. "The *radio,* boss?"

Teddy nodded. "Pretty bleak, yeah. They got us locked down on an island looking for a woman who escaped from a locked room . . ."

"Past four manned checkpoints."

"And a room full of attendants playing poker."

"Scaled a ten-foot brick wall."

"With electric wire up top."

"Swam eleven miles—"

"—against an irate current—"

"—to shore. Irate. I like that. Cold too. What's it, maybe fifty-five degrees in that water?"

"Sixty, tops. Night, though?"

"Back to fifty-five." Chuck nodded. "Teddy, this whole thing, you know?"

Teddy said, "And the missing Dr. Sheehan."

Chuck said, "Struck you as odd too, huh? I wasn't sure. Didn't seem you tore Cawley's asshole quite wide enough, boss."

Teddy laughed, heard the sound of it carry off on the sweep of night air and dissolve in the distant surf, as if it had never been, as if the island and the sea and the salt took what you thought you had and . . .

". . . if we're the cover story?" Chuck was saying.

"What?"

"What if we're the cover story?" Chuck said. "What if we were brought here to help them cross *t*s and dot *i*s?"

"Clarity, Watson."

Another smile. "All right, boss, try and keep up."

"I will, I will."

"Let's say a certain doctor has an infatuation with a certain patient."

"Miss Solando."

"You saw the picture."

"She is attractive."

"Attractive. Teddy, she's a pinup in a GI's locker. So she works our boy, Sheehan . . . You seeing it now?"

Teddy flicked his cigarette into the wind, watching the coals splatter and ignite in the breeze, then streak back past him and Chuck. "And Sheehan gets hooked, decides he can't live without her."

"The operating word being *live*. As a free couple in the real world."

"So they amscray. Off the island."

"Could be at a Fats Domino show as we speak."

Teddy stopped at the far end of the staff dormitories, faced the orange wall. "But why *not* call in the dogs?"

"Well, they did," Chuck said. "Protocol. They had to bring in someone, and in the case of an escape from a place like this, they call in us. But if they're covering up staff involvement, then we're just here to substantiate their story—that they did everything by the book."

"Okay," Teddy said. "But why cover for Sheehan?"

Chuck propped the sole of his shoe against the wall, flexing his knee as he lit a cigarette. "I don't know. Haven't thought that through yet."

"If Sheehan did take her out of here, he greased some palms."

"Had to."

"A lot of them."

"A few attendants, anyway. A guard or two."

"Someone on the ferry. Maybe more than one."

"Unless he didn't leave on the ferry. Could have had his own boat."

Teddy gave it some thought. "Comes from money. Park Avenue, according to Cawley."

"So, there you go—his own boat."

Teddy looked up the wall to the thin wire at the top, the air around them protruding like a bubble pressed against glass.

"Brings up as many questions as it answers," Teddy said after a bit.

"How so?"

"Why those codes in Rachel Solando's room?"

"Well, she *is* crazy."

"Why show it to us, though? I mean, if this is a cover-up, why not make it easier for us to sign off on the reports and go home? 'The attendant fell asleep.' Or 'The lock on the window rusted out and we didn't notice.' "

Chuck pressed his hand to the wall. "Maybe they were lonely. All of them. Needed some company from the outside world."

"Sure. Made up a story so they could bring us here? Have something new to chat about? I'll buy that."

Chuck turned and looked back at Ashecliffe. "Joking aside . . ."

Teddy turned too, and they stood facing it. "Sure . . ."

"Starting to get nervous here, Teddy."

5

"THEY CALLED IT a Great Room," Cawley said as he led them through his parquet foyer to two oak doors with brass knobs the size of pineapples. "I'm serious. My wife found some unsent letters in the attic from the original owner, Colonel Spivey. Going on and on about the Great Room he was building."

Cawley yanked back on one of the pineapples and wrenched the door open.

Chuck let loose a low whistle. Teddy and Dolores had had an apartment on Buttonwood that was the envy of friends because of its size, a central hallway that seemed to go on the length of a football field, and yet that apartment could have folded into this room twice.

The floor was marble, covered here and there by dark Oriental rugs. The fireplace was taller than most men. The drapes alone—three yards of dark purple velvet per window and there were nine windows—had to cost more than Teddy made in a year. Maybe two. A billiards table took up one corner under oil paintings of a man in Union army formal blue, another of a woman in a frilly white dress, a third painting of the man and woman together, a dog at their feet, that same gargantuan fireplace behind them.

"The colonel?" Teddy said.

Cawley followed his gaze, nodded. "Relieved of his command shortly after those paintings were finished. We found them in the basement along with a billiards table, the rugs, most of the chairs. You should see the basement, Marshal. We could fit the Polo Grounds down there."

Teddy smelled pipe tobacco, and he and Chuck turned at the same time, realized there was another man in the room. He sat with his back to them in a high-back wing chair facing the fireplace, one foot extending off the opposite knee, the corner of an open book propped there.

Cawley led them toward the fireplace, gestured at the ring of chairs facing the hearth as he crossed to a liquor cabinet. "Your poison, gentlemen?"

Chuck said, "Rye, if you got it."

"I think I can scare some up. Marshal Daniels?"

"Soda water and some ice."

The stranger looked up at them. "You don't indulge in alcohol?"

Teddy looked down at the guy. A small red head perched like a cherry on top of a chunky body. There was something pervasively delicate about him, a sense Teddy got that he spent far too much time in the bathroom every morning pampering himself with talcs and scented oils.

"And you are?" Teddy said.

"My colleague," Cawley said. "Dr. Jeremiah Naehring."

The man blinked in acknowledgment but didn't offer his hand, so neither did Teddy or Chuck.

"I'm curious," Naehring said as Teddy and Chuck took the two seats that curved away from Naehring's left side.

"That's swell," Teddy said.

"Why you don't drink alcohol. Isn't it common for men in your profession to imbibe?"

Cawley handed him his drink and Teddy stood and crossed to the bookshelves to the right of the hearth. "Common enough," he said. "And yours?"

"Excuse me?"

"Your profession," Teddy said. "I've always heard it's overrun with boozers."

"Not that I've noticed."

"Haven't looked too hard, then, huh?"

"I'm not sure I follow."

"That's, what, cold tea in your glass?"

Teddy turned from the books, watched Naehring glance at his glass, a silkworm of a smile twitching his soft mouth. "Excellent, Marshal. You possess outstanding defense mechanisms. I assume you're quite adept at interrogation."

Teddy shook his head, noticing that Cawley kept little in the way of medical texts, at least in this room. There were a few, but it was mostly novels, a few slim volumes Teddy assumed were poetry, several shelves of histories and biographies.

"No?" Naehring said.

"I'm a federal marshal. We bring them in. That's it. Most times, others handle the interviewing."

"I called it 'interrogation,' you called it 'interviewing.' Yes, Marshal, you do have astonishing defense capabilities." He clicked the bottom of his scotch glass off the table several times as if in applause. "Men of violence fascinate me."

"Men of what?" Teddy strolled over to Naehring's chair, looked down at the little man, and rattled the ice in his glass.

Naehring tilted his head back, took a sip of scotch. "Violence."

"Hell of an assumption to make, Doc." This from Chuck, looking as openly annoyed as Teddy'd ever seen him.

"There's no assumption, no assumption."

Teddy gave his glass one more rattle before he drained it, saw something twitch near Naehring's left eye. "I'd have to agree with my partner," he said and took his seat.

"No." Naehring turned the one syllable into three. "I said you were men of violence. That's not the same as accusing you of being violent men."

Teddy gave him a big smile. "Edify us."

Cawley, behind them, placed a record on the phonograph and the scratch of the needle was followed by stray pops and hisses that reminded Teddy of the phones he'd tried to use. Then a balm of strings and piano replaced the hisses. Something classical, Teddy knew that much. Prussian. Reminding him of cafés overseas and a record collection he'd seen in the office of a subcommandant at Dachau, the man listening to it when he'd shot himself in the mouth. He was still alive when Teddy and four GIs entered the room. Gurgling. Unable to reach the gun for a second shot because it had fallen to the floor. That soft music crawling around the room like spiders. Took him another twenty minutes to die, two of the GIs asking *der Kommandant* if it hurt as they ransacked the room. Teddy had taken a framed photograph off the guy's lap, a picture of his wife and two kids, the guy's eyes going wide and reaching for it as Teddy took it away from him. Teddy stood back and looked from the photo to the guy, back and forth, back and forth, until the guy died. And all the time, that music. Tinkling.

"Brahms?" Chuck asked.

"Mahler." Cawley took the seat beside Naehring.

"You asked for edification," Naehring said.

Teddy rested his elbows on his knees, spread his hands.

"Since the schoolyard," Naehring said, "I would bet neither of you has ever walked away from physical conflict. That's not to suggest you enjoyed it, only that retreat wasn't something you considered an option. Yes?"

Teddy looked over at Chuck. Chuck gave him a small smile, slightly abashed.

Chuck said, "Wasn't raised to run, Doc."

"Ah, yes—raised. And who did raise you?"

"Bears," Teddy said.

Cawley's eyes brightened and he gave Teddy a small nod.

Naehring didn't seem appreciative of humor, though. He adjusted his pants at the knee. "Believe in God?"

Teddy laughed.

Naehring leaned forward.

"Oh, you're serious?" Teddy said.

Naehring waited.

"Ever seen a death camp, Doctor?"

Naehring shook his head.

"No?" Teddy hunched forward himself. "Your English is very good, almost flawless. You still hit the consonants a tad hard, though."

"Is legal immigration a crime, Marshal?"

Teddy smiled, shook his head.

"Back to God, then."

"You see a death camp someday, Doctor, then get back to me with your feelings about God."

Naehring's nod was a slow closing and reopening of his eyelids and then he turned his gaze on Chuck.

"And you?"

"Never saw the camps, myself."

"Believe in God?"

Chuck shrugged. "Haven't given him a lot of thought, one way or the other, in a long time."

"Since your father died, yes?"

Chuck leaned forward now too, stared at the fat little man with his glass-cleaner eyes.

"Your father is dead, yes? And yours as well, Marshal Daniels? In fact, I'll wager that both of you lost the dominant male figure in your lives before your fifteenth birthdays."

"Five of diamonds," Teddy said.

"I'm sorry?" Hunching ever forward.

"Is that your next parlor trick?" Teddy said. "You tell me what card I'm holding. Or, no, wait—you cut a nurse in half, pull a rabbit from Dr. Cawley's head."

"These are not parlor tricks."

"How about this," Teddy said, wanting to pluck that cherry head right off those lumpy shoulders. "You teach a woman how to walk through walls, levitate over a building full of orderlies and penal staff, and float across the sea."

Chuck said, "That's a good one."

Naehring allowed himself another slow blink that reminded Teddy of a house cat after it's been fed.

"Again, your defense mechanisms are—"

"Oh, here we go."

"—impressive. But the issue at hand—"

"The issue at hand," Teddy said, "is that this facility suffered about nine flagrant security breaches last night. You've got a missing woman and no one's looking for—"

"We're looking."

"Hard?"

Naehring sat back, glanced over at Cawley in such a way that Teddy wondered which of them was really in charge.

Cawley caught Teddy's look and the underside of his jaw turned slightly pink. "Dr. Naehring, among other capacities, serves as chief liaison to our board of overseers. I asked him here in that capacity tonight to address your earlier requests."

"Which requests were those?"

Naehring stoked his pipe back to life with a cupped match. "We will not release personnel files of our clinical staff."

"Sheehan," Teddy said.

"Anyone."

"You're cock-blocking us, essentially."

"I'm not familiar with that term."

"Consider traveling more."

"Marshal, continue your investigation and we'll help where we can, but—"

"No."

"Excuse me?" Cawley leaning forward now, all four of them with hunched shoulders and extended heads.

"No," Teddy repeated. "This investigation is over. We'll return to the city on the first ferry. We'll file our reports and the matter will be turned over, I can only assume, to Hoover's boys. But we're out of this."

Naehring's pipe stayed hovering in his hand. Cawley took a pull on his drink. Mahler tinkled. Somewhere in the room a clock ticked. Outside, the rain had grown heavy.

Cawley placed his empty glass on the small table beside his chair.

"As you wish, Marshal."

IT WAS POURING when they left Cawley's house, the rain clattering against the slate roof and the brick patio, the black roof of the waiting car. Teddy could see it slicing through the blackness in slanted sheets of silver. It was only a few steps from Cawley's porch to the car, but they got drenched just the same, and then McPherson came around the front and hopped behind the wheel and moisture splattered the dashboard as he shook it free of his head and put the Packard in gear.

"Nice night." His voice rose over the slapping wiper blades and the drumming rain.

Teddy looked back through the rear window, could see the blurry forms of Cawley and Naehring on the porch watching them go.

"Not fit for man or beast," McPherson said as a thin branch, torn from its mother trunk, floated past the windshield.

Chuck said, "How long you worked here, McPherson?"

"Four years."

"Ever had a break before?"

"Hell no."

"How about a breach? You know, someone gets missing for an hour or two?"

McPherson shook his head. "Not even that. You'd have to be, well, fucking crazy. Where can you go?"

"How about Dr. Sheehan?" Teddy said. "You know him?"

"Sure."

"How long has he been here?"

"I think a year before me."

"So five years."

"Sounds right."

"Did he work with Miss Solando much?"

"Not that I know of. Dr. Cawley was her primary psychotherapist."

"Is that common for the chief of staff to be the primary on a patient's case?"

McPherson said, "Well . . ."

They waited, and the wipers continued to slap, and the dark trees bent toward them.

"It depends," McPherson said, waving at the guard as the Packard rolled through the main gate. "Dr. Cawley does a lot of primary work with the Ward C patients, of course. And then, yeah, there are a few in the other wards whose casework he assumes."

"Who besides Miss Solando?"

McPherson pulled up outside the male dormitory. "You don't mind if I don't come around to open your doors, do you? You get some sleep. I'm sure Dr. Cawley will answer all your questions in the morning."

"McPherson," Teddy said as he opened his door.

McPherson looked back over the seat at him.

"You're not very good at this," Teddy said.

"Good at what?"

Teddy gave him a grim smile and stepped out into the rain.

THEY SHARED A room with Trey Washington and another orderly named Bibby Luce. The room was a good size, with two sets of bunk beds and a small sitting area where Trey and Bibby were playing cards when they came in. Teddy and Chuck dried their hair with white towels from a stack someone had left for them on the top bunk, and then they pulled up chairs and joined the game.

Trey and Bibby played penny-ante, and cigarettes were deemed an acceptable substitute if anyone ran short of coins. Teddy strung all three of them along on a hand of seven-card, came away with five bucks and eighteen cigarettes on a club flush, pocketed the cigarettes, and played conservative from that point on.

Chuck turned out to be the real player, though, jovial as ever, impossible to read, amassing a pile of coins and cigarettes and eventually bills, glancing down at the end of it all as if surprised at how such a fat pile got in front of him.

Trey said, "You got yourself some of them X-ray eyes, Marshal?"

"Lucky, I guess."

"Booshit. Motherfucker that lucky? He got hisself some voodoo working."

Chuck said, "Maybe some motherfucker shouldn't tug his earlobe."

"Huh?"

"You tug your earlobe, Mr. Washington. Every time you got less than a full house." He pointed at Bibby. "And this motherfucker—"

All three of them burst out laughing.

"He . . . he—no, wait a minute, wait—he . . . he gets all squirrelly-eyed, starts looking at everybody's chips just before he bluffs. When he's got a hot hand, though? He's all serene and inward-looking."

Trey ripped the air with his loudest guffaw and slapped the table. "What about Marshal Daniels? How's he give himself away?"

Chuck grinned. "I'm going to rat out my partner? No, no, no."

"Ooooh!" Bibby pointed across the table at them both.

"Can't do it."

"I see, I see," Trey said. "It's a *white man* kinda thing."

Chuck's face darkened and he stared at Trey until the room was sucked dry of air.

Trey's Adam's apple bobbed, and he started to raise a hand in apology, and Chuck said, "Absolutely. What else would it be?" and the grin that broke across his face was river-size.

"Mother-*fucker*!" Trey slapped his hand off Chuck's fingers.

"Motherfucker!" Bibby said.

"Mutha-fucka," Chuck said, and then all three of them giggled like little girls.

Teddy thought of trying it, decided he'd fail, a white man trying to sound hep. And yet Chuck? Chuck could pull it off somehow.

"SO WHAT GAVE me away?" Teddy asked Chuck as they lay in the dark. Across the room, Trey and Bibby were locked in a snoring competition and the rain had gone soft in the last half an hour, as if it were catching its breath, awaiting reinforcements.

"At cards?" Chuck said from the lower bunk. "Forget it."

"No. I want to know."

"You thought you were pretty good up till now, didn't you? Admit it."

"I didn't think I was *bad*."

"You're not."

"You cleaned my clock."

"I won a few bucks."

"Your daddy was a gambler, that it?"

"My daddy was a prick."

"Oh, sorry."

"Not your fault. Yours?"

"My daddy?"

"No, your uncle. Of course, your daddy."

Teddy tried to picture him in the dark, could only see his hands, welted with scars.

"He was a stranger," Teddy said. "To everyone. Even my mother. Hell, I doubt *he* knew who he was. He was his boat. When he lost the boat, he just drifted away."

Chuck didn't say anything and after a while Teddy figured he'd fallen asleep. He could suddenly see his father, all of him, sitting in that chair on the days there'd been no work, the man swallowed by the walls, ceilings, rooms.

"Hey, boss."

"You still up?"

"We really going to pack it in?"

"Yeah. You surprised?"

"I'm not blaming you. I just, I dunno . . ."

"What?"

"I never quit anything before."

Teddy lay quiet for a bit. Finally, he said, "We haven't heard the truth once. We got no way through to it and we got nothing to fall back on, nothing to make these people talk."

"I know, I know," Chuck said. "I agree with the logic."

"But?"

"But I never quit anything before is all."

"Rachel Solando didn't slip barefoot out of a locked room without help. A lot of help. The whole institution's help. My experience? You can't break a whole society that doesn't want to hear what you have to say. Not if there's only two of us. Best-case scenario—the threat worked and Cawley's sitting up in his mansion right now, rethinking his whole attitude. Maybe in the morning . . ."

"So you're bluffing."

"I didn't say that."

"I just played cards with you, boss."

They lay in silence, and Teddy listened to the ocean for a while.

"You purse your lips," Chuck said, his voice beginning to garble with sleep.

"What?"

"When you're holding a good hand. You only do it for a second, but you always do it."

"Oh."

"'Night, boss."

"'Night."

6

SHE COMES DOWN the hallway toward him.

Dolores, karats of anger in her eyes, Bing Crosby crooning "East Side of Heaven" from somewhere in the apartment, the kitchen, maybe. She says, "Jesus, Teddy. Jesus *Christ.*" She's holding an empty bottle of JTS Brown in her hand. His empty bottle. And Teddy realizes she's found one of his stashes.

"Are you ever sober? Are you ever fucking sober anymore? Answer me."

But Teddy can't. He can't speak. He's not even sure where his body is. He can see her and she keeps coming down that long hallway toward him, but he can't see his physical self, can't even feel it. There's a mirror at the other end of the hall behind Dolores, and he's not reflected in it.

She turns left into the living room and the back of her is charred, smoldering a bit. The bottle is no longer in her hand, and small ribbons of smoke unwind from her hair.

She stops at a window. "Oh, look. They're so pretty like that. Floating."

Teddy is beside her at the window, and she's no longer burned, she's soaking wet, and he can see himself, his hand as he places it on her shoulder, the fingers draping over her collarbone, and she turns her head and gives his fingers a quick kiss.

"What did you do?" he says, not even sure why he's asking.

"Look at them out there."

"Baby, why you all wet?" he says, but isn't surprised when she doesn't answer.

The view out the window is not what he expects. It's not the view they had from the apartment on Buttonwood, but the view of another place they stayed once, a cabin. There's a small pond out there with small logs floating in it, and Teddy notices how smooth they are, turning almost imperceptibly, the water shivering and gone white in places under the moon.

"That's a nice gazebo," she says. "So white. You can smell the fresh paint."

"It is nice."

"So," Dolores says.

"Killed a lot of people in the war."

"Why you drink."

"Maybe."

"She's here."

"Rachel?"

Dolores nods. "She never left. You almost saw it. You almost did."

"The Law of Four."

"It's code."

"Sure, but for what?"

"She's here. You can't leave."

He wraps his arms around her from behind, buries his face in the side of her neck. "I'm not going to leave. I love you. I love you so much."

Her belly springs a leak and the liquid flows through his hands.

"I'm bones in a box, Teddy."

"No."

"I am. You have to wake up."

"You're here."

"I'm not. You have to face that. She's here. You're here. He's here too. Count the beds. He's here."

"Who?"

"Laeddis."

The name crawls through his flesh and climbs over his bones.

"No."

"Yes." She bends her head back, looks up at him. "You've known."

"I haven't."

"Yes, you have. You can't leave."

"You're tense all the time." He kneads her shoulders, and she lets out a soft moan of surprise that gives him a hard-on.

"I'm not tense anymore," she says. "I'm home."

"This isn't home," he says.

"Sure it is. My home. She's here. He's here."

"Laeddis."

"Laeddis," she says. Then: "I need to go."

"No." He's crying. "No. Stay."

"Oh, God." She leans back into him. "Let me go. Let me go."

"Please don't go." His tears spill down her body and mix with her pouring belly. "I need to hold you just a little longer. A little longer. Please."

She lets loose a small bubble of a sound—half sigh, half howl, so torn and beautiful in its anguish—and she kisses his knuckles.

"Okay. Hold tight. Tight as you can."

And he holds his wife. He holds her and holds her.

FIVE O'CLOCK IN the morning, the rain dropping on the world, and Teddy climbed off the top bunk and took his notebook from his coat. He sat at the table where they'd played poker and opened the notebook to the page where he'd transcribed Rachel Solando's Law of 4.

Trey and Bibby continued to snore as loud as the rain. Chuck slept quietly, on his stomach, one fist tucked close to his ear, as if it were whispering secrets.

Teddy looked down at the page. It was simple once you knew how to read it. A child's code, really. It was still code, though, and it took Teddy until six to break it.

He looked up, saw Chuck watching him from the lower bunk, Chuck's chin propped up on his fist.

"We leaving, boss?"

Teddy shook his head.

"Ain't nobody leaving in this shit," Trey said, climbing out of his bunk, pulling up the window shade on a drowning landscape the color of pearl. "No how."

The dream was harder to hold suddenly, the smell of her evaporating with the ascent of the shade, a dry cough from Bibby, Trey stretching with a loud, long yawn.

Teddy wondered, and not for the first time, not by a long shot, if this was the day that missing her would finally be too much for him. If he could turn back the years to that morning of the fire and replace her body with his own, he would. That was a given. That had always been a given. But as the years passed, he missed her more, not less, and his need for her became a cut that would not scar over, would not stop leaking.

I held her, he wanted to say to Chuck and Trey and Bibby. I held her as Bing Crosby crooned from the kitchen radio and I could smell her and the apartment on Buttonwood and the lake where we stayed that summer and her lips grazed my knuckles.

I held her. This world can't give me that. This world can only give me reminders of what I don't have, can never have, didn't have for long enough.

We were supposed to grow old together, Dolores. Have kids. Take walks under old trees. I wanted to watch the lines etch themselves into your flesh and know when each and every one of them appeared. Die together.

Not this. Not this.

I held her, he wanted to say, and if I knew for certain that all it would take to hold her again would be to die, then I couldn't raise the gun to my head fast enough.

Chuck was staring at him, waiting.

Teddy said, "I broke Rachel's code."

"Oh," Chuck said, "is that all?"

DAY TWO

Laeddis

7

CAWLEY MET THEM in the foyer of Ward B. His clothes and face were drenched and he looked like a man who'd spent the night on a bus stop bench.

Chuck said, "The trick, Doctor, is to sleep when you lie down."

Cawley wiped his face with a handkerchief. "Oh, is that the trick, Marshal? I knew I was forgetting something. Sleep, you say. Right." They climbed the yellowed staircase, nodded at the orderly posted at the first landing.

"And how was Dr. Naehring this morning?" Teddy asked.

Cawley gave him a weary rise and fall of his eyebrows. "I apologize for that. Jeremiah is a genius, but he could use some social polishing. He has this idea for a book about the male warrior culture throughout history. He's constantly bringing his obsession into conversations, trying to fit people into his preconceived models. Again, I'm sorry."

"You guys do that a lot?"

"What's that, Marshal?"

"Sit around over drinks and, um, probe people?"

"Occupational hazard, I guess. How many psychiatrists does it take to screw in a lightbulb?"

"I don't know. How many?"

"Eight."

"Why?"

"Oh, stop overanalyzing it."

Teddy caught Chuck's eyes and they both laughed.

"Shrink humor," Chuck said. "Who would've guessed?"

"You know what the state of the mental health field is these days, gentlemen?"

"Not a clue," Teddy said.

"Warfare," Cawley said and yawned into his damp handkerchief. "Ideological, philosophical, and yes, even psychological warfare."

"You're doctors," Chuck said. "You're supposed to play nice, share your toys."

Cawley smiled and they passed the orderly on the second-floor landing. From somewhere below, a patient screamed, and the echo fled up the stairs toward them. It was a plaintive howl, and yet Teddy could hear the hopelessness in it, the certainty it carried that whatever it longed for was not going to be granted.

"The old school," Cawley said, "believes in shock therapy, partial lobotomies, spa treatments for the most docile patients. Psychosurgery is what we call it. The new school is enamored of psychopharmacology. It's the future, they say. Maybe it is. I don't know."

He paused, a hand on the banister, midway between the second floor and the third, and Teddy could feel his exhaustion as a living, broken thing, a fourth body in the stairwell with them.

"How does psychopharmacology apply?" Chuck asked.

Cawley said, "A drug has just been approved—lithium is its name— that relaxes psychotic patients, tames them, some would say. Manacles will become a thing of the past. Chains, handcuffs. Bars even, or so the optimists say. The old school, of course, argues that nothing will replace psychosurgery, but the new school is stronger, I think, and it will have money behind it."

"Money from where?"

"Pharmaceutical companies, of course. Buy stock now, gentlemen, and you'll be able to retire to your own island. New schools, old schools. My god, I do rant sometimes."

"Which school are you?" Teddy asked gently.

"Believe it or not, Marshal, I believe in talk therapy, basic interpersonal skills. I have this radical idea that if you treat a patient with respect and listen to what he's trying to tell you, you just might reach him."

Another howl. Same woman, Teddy was pretty sure. It slid between them on the stairs and seemed to spike Cawley's attention.

"But *these* patients?" Teddy said.

Cawley smiled. "Well, yes, many of these patients need to be medicated and some need to be manacled. No argument. But it's a slippery slope. Once you introduce the poison into the well, how do you ever get it out of the water?"

"You don't," Teddy said.

He nodded. "That's right. What should be the last resort gradually becomes standard response. And, I know, I'm mixing my metaphors. Sleep," he said to Chuck. "Right. I'll try that next time."

"I've heard it works wonders," Chuck said, and they headed up the final flight.

In Rachel's room, Cawley sat heavily on the edge of her bed and Chuck leaned against the door. Chuck said, "Hey. How many surrealists does it take to screw in a lightbulb?"

Cawley looked over at him. "I'll bite. How many?"

"Fish," Chuck said and let loose a bright bark of a laugh.

"You'll grow up someday, Marshal," Cawley said. "Won't you?"

"I've got my doubts."

Teddy held the sheet of paper in front of his chest and tapped it to get their attention. "Take another look."

THE LAW OF 4

I AM 47

THEY WERE 80

+YOU ARE 3

WE ARE 4

BUT

WHO IS 67?

After a minute, Cawley said, "I'm too tired, Marshal. It's all gibberish to me right now. Sorry."

Teddy looked at Chuck. Chuck shook his head.

Teddy said, "It was the plus sign that got me going, made me look at it again. Look at the line under 'They were eighty.' We're supposed to add the two lines. What do you get?"

"A hundred and twenty-seven."

"One, two, and seven," Teddy said. "Right. Now you add three. But it's separated. She wants us to keep the integers apart. So you have one plus two plus seven plus three. What's that give you?"

"Thirteen." Cawley sat up on the bed a bit.

Teddy nodded. "Does thirteen have any particular relevance to Rachel Solando? Was she born on the thirteenth? Married on it? Killed her kids on the thirteenth?"

"I'd have to check," Cawley said. "But thirteen is often a significant number to schizophrenics."

"Why?"

He shrugged. "The same way it is to many people. It's a harbinger of bad luck. Most schizophrenics live in a state of fear. It's the common bonding element in the disease. So most schizophrenics are also deeply superstitious. Thirteen plays into that."

"That makes sense, then," Teddy said. "Look at the next number. Four. Add one plus three you get four. But one and three on their own?"

"Thirteen." Chuck came off the wall and cocked his head at the sheet of paper.

"And the last number," Cawley said. "Sixty-seven. Six and seven equals thirteen."

Teddy nodded. "It's not the 'law of four.' It's the law of thirteen. There are thirteen letters in the name Rachel Solando."

Teddy watched both Cawley and Chuck count it up in their heads. Cawley said, "Go on."

"Once we've accepted that, Rachel leaves a whole lot of bread crumbs. The code follows the most rudimentary principle of number-to-letter assignation. One equals *A*. Two equals *B*. You with me?"

Cawley nodded, followed by Chuck a few seconds later.

"The first letter of her name is *R*. Numerical assignation of *R* is eighteen. *A* is one. *C* is three. *H* is eight. *E* is five. *L* is twelve. Eighteen, one, three, eight, five, and twelve. Add 'em up, guys, and what do you get?"

"Jesus," Cawley said softly.

"Forty-seven," Chuck said, his eyes gone wide, staring at the sheet of paper over Teddy's chest.

"That's the 'I,' " Cawley said. "Her first name. I get that now. But what about 'they'?"

"Her last name," Teddy said. "It's theirs."

"Whose?"

"Her husband's family and their ancestors. It's not hers, not by birth. Or it refers to her children. In either case, it doesn't really matter, the whys. It's her last name. Solando. Take the letters and add up their numerical assignations and, yeah, trust me, you come up with eighty."

Cawley came off the bed, and both he and Chuck stood in front of Teddy to look at the code draped over his chest.

Chuck looked up after a while, into Teddy's eyes. "What're you— fucking Einstein?"

"Have you broken code before, Marshal?" Cawley said, eyes still on the sheet of paper. "In the war?"

"No."

"So how did you . . . ?" Chuck said.

Teddy's arms were tired from holding up the sheet. He placed it on the bed.

"I don't know. I do a lot of crosswords. I like puzzles." He shrugged.

Cawley said, "But you were Army Intelligence overseas, right?"

Teddy shook his head. "Regular army. You, though, Doctor, you were OSS."

Cawley said, "No. I did some consulting."

"What kind of consulting?"

Cawley gave him that sliding smile of his, gone almost as soon as it appeared. "The never-talk-about-it kind."

"But this code," Teddy said, "it's pretty simple."

"Simple?" Chuck said. "You've explained it, and my head still hurts."

"But for you, Doctor?"

Cawley shrugged. "What can I tell you, Marshal? I wasn't a code breaker."

Cawley bent his head and stroked his chin as he turned his attention back to the code. Chuck caught Teddy's eyes, his own filled with question marks.

Cawley said, "So we've figured out—well, you have, Marshal—the forty-seven and the eighty. We've ascertained that all clues are permutations of the number thirteen. What about the 'three'?"

"Again," Teddy said, "it either refers to us, in which case she's clairvoyant . . ."

"Not likely."

"Or it refers to her children."

"I'll buy that."

"Add Rachel to the three . . ."

"And you get the next line," Cawley said. " 'We are four.' "

"So who's sixty-seven?"

Cawley looked at him. "You're not being rhetorical?"

Teddy shook his head.

Cawley ran his finger down the right side of the paper. "None of the numbers add up to sixty-seven?"

"Nope."

Cawley ran a palm over the top of his head and straightened. "And you have no theories?"

Teddy said, "It's the one I can't break. Whatever it refers to isn't anything I'm familiar with, which makes me think it's something on this island. You, Doctor?"

"Me, what?"

"Have any theories?"

"None. I wouldn't have gotten past the first line."

"You said that, yeah. Tired and all."

"Very tired, Marshal." He said it with his gaze fixed on Teddy's face, and then he crossed to the window, watched the rain sluice down it, the sheets so thick they walled off the land on the other side. "You said last night that you'd be leaving."

"First ferry out," Teddy said, riding the bluff.

"There won't be one today. I'm pretty sure of that."

"So tomorrow, then. Or the next day," Teddy said. "You still think she's out there? In this?"

"No," Cawley said. "I don't."

"So where?"

He sighed. "I don't know, Marshal. It's not my specialty."

Teddy lifted the sheet of paper off the bed. "This is a template. A guide for deciphering future codes. I'd bet a month's salary on it."

"And if it is?"

"Then she's not trying to escape, Doctor. She brought us here. I think there's more of these."

"Not in this room," Cawley said.

"No. But maybe in this building. Or maybe out on the island."

Cawley sucked the air of the room into his nostrils, steadying one hand against the windowsill, the man all but dead on his feet, making Teddy wonder what really had kept him up last night.

"She *brought* you here?" Cawley said. "To what end?"

"You tell me."

Cawley closed his eyes and stayed silent for so long that Teddy began to wonder if he'd fallen asleep.

He opened his eyes again, looked at both of them. "I've got a full day. I've got staff meetings, budget meetings with the overseers, emergency maintenance meetings in case this storm really hits us. You'll be happy to know I've arranged for you both to speak with all of the patients who were in group therapy with Miss Solando the night she disappeared. Those interviews are scheduled to begin in fifteen minutes. Gentlemen, I appreciate you being here. I do. I'm jumping through as many hoops as I can, whether it appears so or not."

"Then give me Dr. Sheehan's personnel file."

"I can't do that. I absolutely cannot." He leaned his head back against the wall. "Marshal, I've got the switchboard operator trying his number on a steady basis. But we can't reach anyone right now. For all we know, the whole eastern seaboard is underwater. Patience, gentle-men. That's all I'm asking. We'll find Rachel, or we'll find out what happened to her." He looked at his watch. "I'm late. Is there anything else, or can it wait?"

THEY STOOD UNDER an awning outside the hospital, the rain sweeping across their field of vision in sheets the size of train cars.

"You think he knows what sixty-seven means?" Chuck said.

"Yup."

"You think he broke the code before you did?"

"I think he was OSS. I think he's got a gift or two in that department."

Chuck wiped his face, flicked his fingers toward the pavement. "How many patients they got here?"

"It's small," Teddy said.

"Yeah."

"What, maybe twenty women, thirty guys?"

"Not many."

"No."

"Not quite sixty-seven anyway."

Teddy turned, looked at him. "But . . . ," he said.

"Yeah," Chuck said. "But."

And they looked off at the tree line and beyond, at the top of the fort pressed back behind the squall, gone fuzzy and indistinct like a charcoal sketch in a smoky room.

Teddy remembered what Dolores had said in the dream—Count the beds.

"How many they got up there, you think?"

"I don't know," Chuck said. "We'll have to ask the helpful doctor."

"Oh, yeah, he just screams 'helpful,' don't he?"

"Hey, boss."

"Yeah."

"In your life, have you ever come across this much wasted federal space?"

"How so?"

"Fifty patients in these two wards? What do you think these buildings could hold? A couple hundred more?"

"At least."

"And the staff-to-patient ratio. It's like two-to-one favoring staff. You ever seen anything like that?"

"I gotta say no to that one."

They looked at the grounds sizzling underwater.

"What the fuck is this place?" Chuck said.

THEY HELD THE interviews in the cafeteria, Chuck and Teddy sitting at a table in the rear. Two orderlies sat within shouting distance, and Trey Washington was in charge of leading the patients to them and then taking them away when they were through.

The first guy was a stubbled wreck of tics and eye blinks. He sat hunched into himself like a horseshoe crab, scratching his arms, and refused to meet their eyes.

Teddy looked down at the top page in the file Cawley had provided—just thumbnail sketches from Cawley's own memory, not the actual patient files. This guy was listed first and his name was Ken Gage and he was in here because he'd attacked a stranger in the aisle of a corner grocery store, beat the victim on the head with a can of peas, all the time saying, in a very subdued voice, "Stop reading my mail."

"So, Ken," Chuck said, "how you doing?"

"I got a cold. I got a cold in my feet."

"Sorry to hear that."

"It hurts to walk, yeah." Ken scratched around the edges of a scab on his arm, delicately at first, as if tracing a moat for it.

"Were you in group therapy the night before last?"

"I got a cold in my feet and it hurts to walk."

"You want some socks?" Teddy tried. He noticed the two orderlies looking over at them, snickering.

"Yeah, I want some socks, I want some socks, I want some socks." Whispering it, head down and bobbing a bit.

"Well, we'll get you some in a minute. We just need to know if you were—"

"It's just so cold. In my feet? It's cold and it hurts to walk."

Teddy looked over at Chuck. Chuck smiled at the orderlies as the sound of their giggles floated to the table.

"Ken," Chuck said. "Ken, can you look at me?"

Ken kept his head down, bobbing a bit more. His fingernail tore open the scab and a small line of blood seeped into the hairs of his arm.

"Ken?"

"I can't walk. Not like this, not like this. It's so cold, cold, cold."

"Ken, come on, look at me."

Ken brought his fists down on the table.

Both orderlies stood and Ken said, "It shouldn't hurt. It shouldn't. But they want it to. They fill the air with cold. They fill my kneecaps."

The orderlies crossed to their table, looked over Ken at Chuck. The white one said, "You guys about done, or you want to hear more about his feet?"

"My feet are cold."

The black orderly raised an eyebrow. "It's okay, Kenny. We'll take you to Hydro, warm you right up."

The white one said, "I been here five years. Topic don't change."

"Ever?" Teddy said.

"It hurts to walk."

"Ever," the orderly said.

"Hurts to walk 'cause they put cold in my feet . . ."

THE NEXT ONE, Peter Breene, was twenty-six, blond, and pudgy. A knuckle-cracker and a nail-biter.

"What are you here for, Peter?"

Peter looked across the table at Teddy and Chuck with eyes that seemed permanently damp. "I'm scared all the time."

"Of what?"

"Things."

"Okay."

Peter propped his left ankle up on his right knee, gripped the ankle, and leaned forward. "It sounds stupid, but I'm afraid of watches. The ticking. It gets in your head. Rats terrify me."

"Me too," Chuck said.

"Yeah?" Peter brightened.

"Hell, yeah. Squeaky bastards. I get the piss-shivers just looking at one."

"Don't go out past the wall at night, then," Peter said. "They're everywhere."

"Good to know. Thanks."

"Pencils," Peter said. "The lead, you know? The scratch-scratch on the paper. I'm afraid of you."

"Me?"

"No," Peter said, pointing his chin at Teddy. "Him."

"Why?" Teddy asked.

He shrugged. "You're big. Mean-looking crew cut. You can handle yourself. Your knuckles are scarred. My father was like that. He didn't have the scars. His hands were smooth. But he was mean-looking. My brothers too. They used to beat me up."

"I'm not going to beat you up," Teddy said.

"But you could. Don't you see? You have that power. And I don't. And that makes me vulnerable. Being vulnerable makes me scared."

"And when you get scared?"

Peter gripped his ankle and rocked back and forth, his bangs falling down his forehead. "She was nice. I didn't mean anything. But she scared me with her big breasts, the way her can moved in that white dress, coming to our house every day. She'd look at me like . . . You know the smile you give a child? She'd give me that smile. And she was *my* age. Oh, okay, maybe a few years older, but still, in her twenties. And she had so much sexual knowledge. It was apparent in her eyes. She liked to be naked. She'd sucked cock. And then she asks *me* if she can have a glass of water. She's alone in the kitchen with *me,* as if that's no big deal?"

Teddy tilted the file so Chuck could see Cawley's notes:

> Patient assaulted his father's nurse with a broken glass. Victim critically injured, permanently scarred. Patient in denial over his responsibility for the act.

"It's only because she scared me," Peter said. "She wanted me to pull out my thing so she could laugh at it. Tell me how I'd never be with a woman, never have children of my own, never be a man? Because, otherwise, I mean you know this, you can see it in my face— I wouldn't hurt a fly. It's not in me. But when I'm scared? Oh, the mind."

"What about it?" Chuck's voice was soothing.

"You ever think about it?"

"Your mind?"

"*The* mind," he said. "Mine, yours, anyone's. It's an engine essentially. That's what it is. A very delicate, intricate motor. And it's got all these pieces, all these gears and bolts and hinges. And we don't even know what half of them do. But if just one gear slips, just *one* . . . Have you thought about that?"

"Not recently."

"You should. It's just like a car. No different. One gear slips, one bolt cracks, and the whole system goes haywire. Can you live knowing that?" He tapped his temple. "That it's all trapped in here and you can't *get to it* and you don't really control it. But it controls you, doesn't it? And if it decides one day that it doesn't feel like coming to work?" He leaned forward, and they could see tendons straining in his neck. "Well, then you're pretty much good and fucked, aren't you?"

"Interesting perspective," Chuck said.

Peter leaned back in his chair, suddenly listless. "That's what scares me most."

Teddy, whose migraines gave him a bit of insight into the lack of control one had over one's mind, would cede a point to Peter on the general concept, but mostly he just wanted to pick the little shit up by his throat, slam him against one of the ovens in the back of the cafeteria, and ask him about that poor nurse he'd carved up.

Do you even remember her name, Pete? What do you think she feared? Huh? *You.* That's what. Trying to do an honest day's work, make a living. Maybe she had kids, a husband. Maybe they were trying to save enough to put one of those kids through college someday, give him a better life. A small dream.

But, no, some rich prick's fucked-up mama's boy of a son decides she can't have that dream. Sorry, but no. No normal life for you, miss. Not ever again.

Teddy looked across the table at Peter Breene, and he wanted to punch him in the face so hard that doctors would never find all the bones in his nose. Hit him so hard the sound would never leave his head.

Instead, he closed the file and said, "You were in group therapy the night before last with Rachel Solando. Correct?"

"Yes, I sure was, sir."

"You see her go up to her room?"

"No. The men left first. She was still sitting there with Bridget Kearns and Leonora Grant and that nurse."

"That nurse?"

Peter nodded. "The redhead. Sometimes I like her. She seems genuine. But other times, you know?"

"No," Teddy said, keeping his voice as smooth as Chuck's had been, "I don't."

"Well, you've *seen* her, right?"

"Sure. What's her name again?"

"She doesn't need a name," Peter said. "Woman like that? No name for her. Dirty Girl. That's her name."

"But, Peter," Chuck said, "I thought you said you liked her."

"When did I say that?"

"Just a minute ago."

"Uh-uh. She's trash. She's squishy-squishy."

"Let me ask you something else."

"Dirty, dirty, dirty."

"Peter?"

Peter looked up at Teddy.

"Can I ask you something?"

"Oh, sure."

"Did anything unusual happen in group that night? Did Rachel Solando say anything or do anything out of the ordinary?"

"She didn't say a word. She's a mouse. She just sat there. She killed her kids, you know. Three of them. You believe that? What kind of person does that sort of thing? Sick fucking people in this world, sirs, if you don't mind me mentioning."

"People have problems," Chuck said. "Some are deeper than others. Sick, like you said. They need help."

"They need gas," Peter said.

"Excuse me?"

"Gas," Peter said to Teddy. "Gas the retards. Gas the killers. Killed her own kids? Gas the bitch."

They sat silent, Peter glowing as if he'd illuminated the world for them. After a while, he patted the table and stood.

"Good to meet you, gents. I'll be getting back."

Teddy used a pencil to doodle on the file cover, and Peter stopped, looked back at him.

"Peter," Teddy said.

"Yeah?"

"I—"

"Could you stop that?"

Teddy scratched his initials into the cardboard in long, slow strokes. "I was wondering if—"

"Could you please, please . . . ?"

Teddy looked up, still pulling the pencil down the file cover. "Which?"

"—*stop that?*"

"What?" Teddy looked at him, looked down at the file. He lifted the pencil, cocked an eyebrow.

"Yes. Please. That."

Teddy dropped the pencil on the cover. "Better?"

"Thank you."

"Do you know a patient, Peter, by the name of Andrew Laeddis?"

"No."

"No? No one here by that name?"

Peter shrugged. "Not in Ward A. He could be in C. We don't mingle with them. They're fucking nuts."

"Well, thank you, Peter," Teddy said, and picked up the pencil and went back to doodling.

AFTER PETER BREENE, they interviewed Leonora Grant. Leonora was convinced that she was Mary Pickford and Chuck was Douglas Fairbanks and Teddy was Charlie Chaplin. She thought that the cafeteria was an office on Sunset Boulevard and they were here to discuss a public stock offering in United Artists. She kept caressing the back of Chuck's hand and asking who was going to record the minutes.

In the end, the orderlies had to pull her hand from Chuck's wrist while Leonora cried, *"Adieu, mon chéri. Adieu."*

Halfway across the cafeteria, she broke free of the orderlies, came charging back across the floor toward them, and grabbed Chuck's hand.

She said, "Don't forget to feed the cat."

Chuck looked in her eyes and said, "Noted."

After that, they met Arthur Toomey, who kept insisting they call him Joe. Joe had slept through group therapy that night. Joe, it turned out, was a narcoleptic. He fell asleep twice on them, the second time for the day, more or less.

Teddy was feeling the place in the back of his skull by that point. It was making his hair itch, and while he felt sympathy for all the patients except for Breene, he couldn't help wonder how anyone could stand working here.

Trey came ambling back in with a small woman with blond hair and a face shaped like a pendant. Her eyes pulsed with clarity. And not the clarity of the insane, but the everyday clarity of an intelligent woman in a less-than-intelligent world. She smiled and gave them each a small, shy wave as she sat.

Teddy checked Cawley's notes—Bridget Kearns.

"I'll never get out of here," she said after they'd been sitting there for a few minutes. She smoked her cigarettes only halfway before stubbing them out, and she had a soft, confident voice, and a little over a decade ago she'd killed her husband with an ax.

"I'm not sure I should," she said.

"Why's that?" Chuck said. "I mean, excuse me for saying it, Miss Kearns—"

"Mrs."

"Mrs. Kearns. Excuse me, but you seem, well, normal to me."

She leaned back in her chair, as at ease as anyone they'd met in this place, and gave a soft chuckle. "I suppose. I wasn't when I first came here. Oh my god. I'm glad they didn't take pictures. I've been diagnosed as a manic-depressive, and I have no reason to doubt that. I do have my dark days. I suppose everyone does. The difference is that most people don't kill their husbands with an ax. I've been told I have deep, unresolved conflicts with my father, and I'll agree to that too. I doubt I'd go out and kill someone again, but you can never tell." She pointed the tip of her cigarette in their direction. "I think if a man beats you and fucks half the women he sees and no one will help you, axing him isn't the least understandable thing you can do."

She met Teddy's eyes and something in her pupils—a schoolgirl's shy giddiness, perhaps—made him laugh.

"What?" she said, laughing with him.

"Maybe you *shouldn't* get out," he said.

"You say that because you're a man."

"You're damn right."

"Well then, I don't blame you."

It was a relief to laugh after Peter Breene, and Teddy wondered if he was actually flirting a bit too. With a mental patient. An ax murderer. *This is what it's come to, Dolores.* But he didn't feel altogether bad about it, as if after these two long dark years of mourning he was maybe entitled to a little harmless repartee.

"What would I do if I did get out?" Bridget said. "I don't know what's out in that world anymore. Bombs, I hear. Bombs that can turn whole cities to ash. And televisions. That's what they call them, isn't it? There's a rumor each ward will get one, and we'll be able to see plays on this box. I don't know that I'd like that. Voices coming from a box. Faces from a box. I hear enough voices and see enough faces every day. I don't need more noise."

"Can you tell us about Rachel Solando?" Chuck asked.

She paused. It was more like a hitch, actually, and Teddy watched her eyes turn up slightly, as if she were searching her brain for the right file, and Teddy scribbled "lies" in his notepad, curling his wrist over the word as soon as he was done.

Her words came more carefully and smelled of rote.

"Rachel is nice enough. She keeps to herself. She talks about rain a lot, but mostly she doesn't talk at all. She believed her kids were alive. She believed she was still living in the Berkshires and that we were all neighbors and postmen, deliverymen, milkmen. She was hard to get to know."

She spoke with her head down, and when she finished, she couldn't meet Teddy's eyes. Her glance bounced off his face, and she studied the tabletop and lit another cigarette.

Teddy thought about what she'd just said, realized the description of Rachel's delusions was almost word for word what Cawley had said to them yesterday.

"How long was she here?"

"Huh?"

"Rachel. How long was she in Ward B with you?"

"Three years? About that, I think. I lose track of time. It's easy to do that in this place."

"And where was she before that?" Teddy asked.

"Ward C, I heard. She transferred over, I believe."

"But you're not sure."

"No. I . . . Again, you lose track."

"Sure. Anything unusual happen the last time you saw her?"

"No."

"That was in group."

"What?"

"The last time you saw her," Teddy said. "It was in group therapy the night before last."

"Yeah, yeah." She nodded several times and shaved some ash off against the rim of the ashtray. "In group."

"And you all went up to your rooms together?"

"With Mr. Ganton, yes."

"What was Dr. Sheehan like that night?"

She looked up, and Teddy saw confusion and maybe some terror in her face. "I don't know what you mean."

"Was Dr. Sheehan there that night?"

She looked at Chuck, then over at Teddy, sucked her upper lip against her teeth. "Yeah. He was there."

"What's he like?"

"Dr. Sheehan?"

Teddy nodded.

"He's okay. He's nice. Handsome."

"Handsome?"

"Yeah. He's . . . not hard on the eyes, as my mother used to say."

"Did he ever flirt with you?"

"No."

"Come on to you?"

"No, no, no. Dr. Sheehan's a good doctor."

"And that night?"

"That night?" She gave it some thought. "Nothing unusual happened that night. We spoke about, um, anger management? And Rachel complained about the rain. And Dr. Sheehan left just before the group broke up, and Mr. Ganton led us up to our rooms, and we went to bed, and that was it."

In his notebook, Teddy wrote "coached" underneath "lies" and closed the cover.

"That was it?"

"Yes. And the next morning Rachel was gone."

"The next morning?"

"Yeah. I woke up and heard that she'd escaped."

"But that night? Around midnight—you heard it, right?"

"Heard what?" Stubbing out her cigarette, waving at the smoke that wafted up in its wake.

"The commotion. When she was discovered missing."

"No. I—"

"There was shouting, yelling, guards running in from everywhere, alarms sounding."

"I thought it was a dream."

"A dream?"

She nodded fast. "Sure. A nightmare." She looked at Chuck. "Could I get a glass of water?"

"You bet." Chuck stood and looked around, saw a stack of glasses in the rear of the cafeteria beside a steel dispenser.

One of the orderlies half rose from his seat. "Marshal?"

"Just getting some water. It's okay."

Chuck crossed to the machine, selected a glass, and took a few seconds to decide which nozzle produced milk and which produced water.

As he lifted the nozzle, a thick knob that looked like a metal hoof, Bridget Kearns grabbed Teddy's notebook and pen. She looked at him, holding him with her eyes, and flipped to a clean page, scribbled something on it, then flipped the cover closed and slid the notebook and pen back to him.

Teddy gave her a quizzical look, but she dropped her eyes and idly caressed her cigarette pack.

Chuck brought the water back and sat down. They watched Bridget drain half the glass and then say, "Thank you. Do you have any more questions? I'm kind of tired."

"You ever meet a patient named Andrew Laeddis?" Teddy asked.

Her face showed no expression. None whatsoever. It was as if it had turned to alabaster. Her hands stayed flat on the tabletop, as if removing them would cause the table to float to the ceiling.

Teddy had no clue as to why, but he'd swear she was on the verge of weeping.

"No," she said. "Never heard of him."

"YOU THINK SHE was coached?" Chuck said.

"Don't you?"

"Okay, it sounded a little forced."

They were in the breezeway that connected Ashecliffe to Ward B, impervious to the rain now, the drip of it on their skin.

"A little? She used the exact same words Cawley used in some cases. When we asked what the topic was about in group, she paused and then she said 'anger management?' Like she wasn't sure. Like she was taking a quiz and she'd spent last night cramming."

"So what's that mean?"

"Fuck if I know," Teddy said. "All I got are questions. Every half an hour, it's like there're thirty more."

"Agreed," Chuck said. "Hey, here's a question for you—who's Andrew Laeddis?"

"You caught that, huh?" Teddy lit one of the cigarettes he'd won in poker.

"You asked every patient we talked to."

"Didn't ask Ken or Leonora Grant."

"Teddy, they didn't know what planet they were on."

"True."

"I'm your partner, boss."

Teddy leaned back against the stone wall and Chuck joined him. He turned his head, looked at Chuck.

"We just met," he said.

"Oh, you don't trust me."

"I trust you, Chuck. I do. But I'm breaking the rules here. I asked for this case specifically. The moment it came over the wire in the field office."

"So?"

"So my motives aren't exactly impartial."

Chuck nodded and lit his own cigarette, took some time to think about it. "My girl, Julie—Julie Taketomi, that's her name—she's as American as I am. Doesn't speak a word of Japanese. Hell, her parents go back two generations in this country. But they put her in a camp and then . . ." He shook his head and then flicked his cigarette into the rain and pulled up his shirt, exposed the skin over his right hip. "Take a look, Teddy. See my other scar."

Teddy looked. It was long and dark as jelly, thick as his thumb.

"I didn't get this one in the war, either. Got it working for the marshals. Went through a door in Tacoma. The guy we were after sliced me with a sword. You believe that? A fucking sword. I spent three weeks in the hospital while they sewed my intestines back together. For the U.S. Marshals Service, Teddy. For my country. And then they run me out of my home district because I'm in love with an American woman with Oriental skin and eyes?" He tucked his shirt back in. "Fuck them."

"If I didn't know you better," Teddy said after a bit, "I'd swear you really love that woman."

"Die for her," Chuck said. "No regrets about it, either."

Teddy nodded. No purer feeling in the world that he knew of.

"Don't let that go, kid."

"I *won't,* Teddy. That's the point. But you gotta tell me why we're here. Who the hell is Andrew Laeddis?"

Teddy dropped the butt of his cigarette to the stone walk and ground it out with his heel.

Dolores, he thought, I've got to tell him. I can't do this alone.

If after all my sins—all my drinking, all the times I left you alone for too long, let you down, broke your heart—if I can ever make up for any of that, this might be the time, the last opportunity I'll ever have.

I want to do right, honey. I want to atone. You, of all people, would understand that.

"Andrew Laeddis," he said to Chuck, and the words clogged in his dry throat. He swallowed, got some moisture into his mouth, tried again . . .

"Andrew Laeddis," he said, "was the maintenance man in the apartment building where my wife and I lived."

"Okay."

"He was also a firebug."

Chuck took that in, studied Teddy's face.

"So . . ."

"Andrew Laeddis," Teddy said, "lit the match that caused the fire—"

"Holy fuck."

"—that killed my wife."

8

TEDDY WALKED OVER to the edge of the breezeway and stuck his head out from under the roof to douse his face and hair. He could see her in the drops. Dissolving on impact.

She hadn't wanted him to go to work that morning. In that final year of her life, she'd grown inexplicably skittish, prone to insomnia that left her tremor-filled and addled. She'd tickled him after the alarm had gone off, then suggested they close the shutters and block out the day, never leave the bed. When she hugged him, she held on too tightly and for too long, and Teddy could feel the bones in her arms crush into his neck.

As he took his shower, she came to him, but he was too rushed, already late, and as had so often been the case in those days, hungover. His head simultaneously soggy and filled with spikes. Her body like sandpaper when she pressed it against his. The water from the shower as hard as BBs.

"Just stay," she said. "One day. What difference will one day make?"

He tried to smile as he lifted her gently out of the way and reached for the soap. "Honey, I can't."

"Why not?" She ran her hand between his legs. "Here. Give me the soap. I'll wash it for you." Her palm sliding under his testicles, her teeth nipping his chest.

He tried not to push her. He gripped her shoulders as gently as he could and lifted her back a step or two. "Come on," he said. "I've really got to go."

She laughed some more, tried to nuzzle him again, but he could see her eyes growing hard with desperation. To be happy. To not be left alone. To have the old days back—before he worked too much, drank too much, before she woke up one morning and the world seemed too bright, too loud, too cold.

"Okay, okay." She leaned back so he could see her face as the water bounced off his shoulders and misted her body. "I'll make a deal with you. Not the whole day, baby. Not the whole day. Just an hour. Just be an hour late."

"I'm already—"

"One hour," she said, stroking him again, her hand soapy now. "One hour and then you can go. I want to feel you inside of me." She raised herself up on her toes to kiss him.

He gave her a quick peck on the lips and said, "Honey, I can't," and turned his face to the shower spray.

"Will they call you back up?" she said.

"Huh?"

"To fight."

"That piss-ant country? Honey, that war will be over before I could lace my boots."

"I don't know," she said. "I don't even know why we're there. I mean—"

"Because the NKPA doesn't get weaponry like that from nowhere, honey. They got it from Stalin. We have to prove that we learned from Munich, that we should have stopped Hitler then, so we'll stop Stalin and Mao. Now. In Korea."

"You'd go."

"If they called me up? I'd have to. But they won't, honey."

"How do you know?"

He shampooed his hair.

"You ever wonder why they hate us so much? The Communists?" she said. "Why can't they leave us alone? The world's going to blow up and I don't even know why."

"It's not going to blow up."

"It is. You read the papers and—"

"Stop reading the papers, then."

Teddy rinsed the shampoo from his hair and she pressed her face to his back and her hands snaked around his abdomen. "I remember the first time I saw you at the Grove. In your uniform."

Teddy hated when she did this. Memory Lane. She couldn't adapt to the present, to who they were now, warts and all, so she drove winding lanes into the past to warm herself.

"You were so handsome. And Linda Cox said, 'I saw him first.' But you know what I said?"

"I'm late, honey."

"Why would I say *that*? No. I said, 'You might have seen him first, Linda, but I'll see him last.' She thought you looked mean up close, but I said, 'Honey, have you looked in his eyes? There's nothing mean there.' "

Teddy shut off the shower and turned, noticed that his wife had managed to get some of his soap on her. Smudges of lather splattered her flesh.

"You want me to turn it back on?"

She shook her head.

He wrapped a towel around his waist and shaved at the sink, and Dolores leaned against the wall as the soap dried white on her body and watched him.

"Why don't you dry off?" Teddy said. "Put a robe on?"

"It's gone now," she said.

"It's not gone. Looks like white leeches stuck all over you."

"Not the soap," she said.

"What, then?"

"The Cocoanut Grove. Burned to the ground while you were over there."

"Yeah, honey, I heard that."

"Over there," she sang lightly, trying to lighten the mood. "Over there . . ."

She'd always had the prettiest voice. The night he'd returned from the war, they'd splurged on a room at the Parker House, and after they'd made love, he heard her sing for the first time from the bathroom as he lay in bed—"Buffalo Girls" with the steam creeping out from under the door.

"Hey," she said.

"Yeah?" He caught the reflection of the left side of her body in the mirror. Most of the soap had dried on her skin and something about it annoyed him. It suggested violation in a way he couldn't put his finger on.

"Do you have somebody else?"

"What?"

"Do you?"

"The fuck are you talking about? I *work,* Dolores."

"I'm touching your dick in the—"

"Don't say that word. Jesus Christ."

"—shower and you don't even get hard?"

"Dolores." He turned from the mirror. "You were talking about bombs. The end of the world."

She shrugged, as if that had no relevance to this current conversation. She propped her foot back against the wall and used a finger to wipe the water off her inner thigh. "You don't fuck me anymore."

"Dolores, I'm serious—you don't talk like that in this house."

"So I've gotta assume you're fucking her."

"I'm not fucking anyone, and could you stop saying that word?"

"Which word?" She placed a hand over her dark pubic hair. "Fucking?"

"Yes." He raised one hand. He went back to shaving with the other.

"So that's a bad word?"

"You know it is." He pulled the razor up his throat, heard the scratch of hairs through the foam.

"So what's a good word?"

"Huh?" He dipped the razor, shook it.

"What word about my body won't cause you to make a fist?"

"I didn't make a fist."

"You did."

He finished his throat, wiped the razor on a facecloth. He laid the flat of it below his left sideburn. "No, honey. I didn't." He caught her left eye in the mirror.

"What should I say?" She ran one hand through her upper hair and one through her lower. "I mean, you can lick it and you can kiss it and you can fuck it. You can watch a baby come out of it. But you can't say it?"

"Dolores."

"Cunt," she said.

The razor slid so far through Teddy's skin he suspected it hit jaw bone. It widened his eyes and lit up the entire left side of his face, and then some shaving cream dripped into the wound and eels exploded through his head and the blood poured into the white clouds and water in the sink.

She came to him with a towel, but he pushed her away and sucked air through his teeth and felt the pain burrowing into his eyes, scorching his brain, and he bled into the sink and he felt like crying. Not from the pain. Not from the hangover. But because he didn't know what was happening to his wife, to the girl he'd first danced with at the Cocoanut Grove. He didn't know what she was becoming or what the world was becoming with its lesions of tiny, dirty wars and furious hatreds and spies in Washington, in Hollywood, gas masks in schoolhouses, cement bomb shelters in basements. And it was, somehow, all connected—his wife, this world, his drinking, the war he'd fought because he honestly believed it would end all this . . .

He bled into the sink and Dolores said, "I'm sorry, I'm sorry, I'm sorry," and he took the towel the second time she offered it but couldn't touch her, couldn't look at her. He could hear the tears in her voice and he knew there were tears in her eyes and on her face, and he hated how fucked up and obscene the world and everything in it had become.

IN THE PAPER, he'd been quoted as saying the last thing he told his wife was that he loved her.

A lie.

The last thing he really said?

Reaching for the doorknob, a third towel pressed to his jaw, her eyes searching his face:

"Jesus, Dolores, you've got to get yourself together. You've got responsibilities. Think about those sometimes—okay?—and get your fucking head right."

Those were the last words his wife heard from him. He'd closed the door and walked down the stairs, paused on the last step. He thought of going back. He thought of going back up the stairs and into the apartment and somehow making it right. Or, if not right, at least softer.

Softer. That would have been nice.

THE WOMAN WITH the licorice scar across her throat came waddling down the breezeway toward them, her ankles and wrists enchained, an orderly on each elbow. She looked happy and made duck sounds and tried to flap her elbows.

"What did she do?" Chuck said.

"This one?" the orderly said. "This here Old Maggie. Maggie Moonpie, we call her. She just going to Hydro. Can't take no chances with her, though."

Maggie stopped in front of them, and the orderlies made a half-hearted attempt to keep her moving, but she shoved back with her elbows and dug her heels against the stone, and one of the orderlies rolled his eyes and sighed.

"She gone proselytize now, hear?"

Maggie stared up into their faces, her head cocked to the right and moving like a turtle sniffing its way out of its shell.

"I am the way," she said. "I am the light. And I will not bake your fucking pies. I will not. Do you understand?"

"Sure," Chuck said.

"You bet," Teddy said. "No pies."

"You've been here. You'll stay here." Maggie sniffed the air. "It's your future and your past and it cycles like the moon cycles around the earth."

"Yes, ma'am."

She leaned in close and sniffed them. First Teddy, then Chuck.

"They keep secrets. That's what feeds this hell."

"Well, that and pies," Chuck said.

She smiled at him, and for a moment it seemed as if someone lucid entered her body and passed behind her pupils.

"Laugh," she said to Chuck. "It's good for the soul. Laugh."

"Okay," Chuck said. "I will, ma'am."

She touched his nose with a hooked finger. "I want to remember you that way—laughing."

And then she turned away and started walking. The orderlies fell into step and they walked down the breezeway and through a side door into the hospital.

Chuck said, "Fun girl."

"Kind you'd bring home to Mom."

"And then she'd kill Mom and bury her in an outhouse, but still . . ." Chuck lit a cigarette. "Laeddis."

"Killed my wife."

"You said that. How?"

"He was a firebug."

"Said that too."

"He was also the maintenance man in our building. Got in a fight with the owner. The owner fired him. At the time, all we knew was that the fire was arson. *Someone* had set it. Laeddis was on a list of suspects, but it took them a while to find him, and once they did, he'd shored up an alibi. Hell, I wasn't even sure it was him."

"What changed your mind?"

"A year ago, I open the paper and there he is. Burned down a schoolhouse where he'd been working. Same story—they fired him and he came back, lit it in the basement, primed the boiler so it would explode. Exact same M.O. Identical. No kids in the schoolhouse, but the principal was there, working late. She died. Laeddis went to trial, claimed he heard voices, what have you, and they committed him to Shattuck. Something happened there—I don't know what—but he was transferred here six months ago."

"But no one's seen him."

"No one in Ward A or B."

"Which suggests he's in C."

"Yup."

"Or dead."

"Possibly. One more reason to find the cemetery."

"Let's say he isn't dead, though."

"Okay . . ."

"If you find him, Teddy, what are you going to do?"

"I don't know."

"Don't bullshit me, boss."

A pair of nurses came toward them, heels clicking, bodies pressed close to the wall to avoid the rain.

"You guys are *wet,*" one of them said.

"*All* wet?" Chuck said, and the one closest to the wall, a tiny girl with short black hair, laughed.

Once they'd passed, the black-haired nurse looked back over her shoulder at them. "You marshals always so flirty?"

"Depends," Chuck said.

"On?"

"Quality of personnel."

That stopped both of them for a moment, and then they got it, and the black-haired nurse buried her face in the other one's shoulder, and they burst out laughing and walked to the hospital door.

Christ, how Teddy envied Chuck. His ability to believe in the words he spoke. In silly flirtations. In his easy-GI's penchant for quick, meaningless wordplay. But most of all for the weightlessness of his charm.

Charm had never come easily to Teddy. After the war, it had come harder still. After Dolores, not at all.

Charm was the luxury of those who still believed in the essential rightness of things. In purity and picket fences.

"You know," he said to Chuck, "the last morning I was with my wife, she spoke about the Cocoanut Grove fire."

"Yeah?"

"That's where we met. The Grove. She had this rich roommate and I was let in because they gave a serviceman's discount. It was just before I shipped out. Danced with her all night. Even the foxtrot."

Chuck craned his neck out from the wall, looked into Teddy's face. "You doing the foxtrot? I'm trying to picture it, but . . ."

"Hey, hoss," Teddy said, "if you'd seen my wife that night? You would have hopped around the floor like a bunny if she asked."

"So you met her at the Cocoanut Grove."

Teddy nodded. "And then it burned down while I was in—Italy? Yeah, I was in Italy then—and she found that fact, I dunno, meaningful, I guess. She was terrified of fire."

"But she died in a fire," Chuck said softly.

"Beats all, don't it?" Teddy bit back against an image of her from that last morning, lifting her leg against the bathroom wall, naked, her body splattered with dead white foam.

"Teddy?"

Teddy looked at him.

Chuck spread his hands. "I'll back you on this. No matter what. You want to find Laeddis and kill him? That's jake with me."

"Jake." Teddy smiled. "I haven't heard that since—"

"But, boss? I need to know what to expect. I'm serious. We got to get our shit straight or we'll end up in some new Kefauver Hearing or something. Everyone's looking these days, you know? Looking in at all of us. Watching. World gets smaller every minute." Chuck pushed back at the stand of bushy hair over his forehead. "I think you know about this place. I think you know shit you haven't told me. I think you came here to do damage."

Teddy fluttered a hand over his heart.

"I'm serious, boss."

Teddy said, "We're wet."

"So?"

"My point. Care if we get wetter?"

THEY LEFT THROUGH the gate and walked the shore. The rain blanketed everything. Waves the size of houses hit the rocks. They flared high and then shattered to make way for new ones.

"I don't want to kill him," Teddy shouted over the roar.

"No?"

"No."

"Not sure I believe you."

Teddy shrugged.

"It was *my* wife?" Chuck said. "I'd kill him twice."

"I'm tired of killing," Teddy said. "In the war? I lost track. How's that possible, Chuck? But I did."

"Still. Your wife, Teddy."

They found an outcropping of sharp, black stones that rose off the beach toward the trees, and they climbed inland.

"Look," Teddy said once they'd reached a small plateau and a circle of high trees that blocked some of the rain, "I still put the job first.

We find what happened to Rachel Solando. And if I meet up with Laeddis while I'm doing it? Great. I'll tell him I know he killed my wife. I'll tell him I'll be waiting on the mainland when he gets released. I'll tell him free air isn't something he breathes as long as I'm alive."

"And that's all?" Chuck said.

"That's all."

Chuck wiped his eyes with his sleeve, pushed his hair off his forehead. "I don't believe you. I just don't."

Teddy looked off to the south of the ring of trees, saw the top of Ashecliffe, its watchful dormers.

"And don't you think Cawley knows why you're really here?"

"I'm *really* here for Rachel Solando."

"But fuck, Teddy, if the guy who killed your wife was committed here, then—"

"He wasn't *convicted* for it. There's nothing to tie me and him to each other. Nothing."

Chuck sat down on a stone jutting out of the field, lowered his head to the rain. "The graveyard, then. Why don't we see if we can find that, now that we're out here? We see a 'Laeddis' headstone, we know half the battle's over."

Teddy looked off at the ring of trees, the black depth of them. "Fine."

Chuck stood. "What did she say to you, by the way?"

"Who?"

"The patient." Chuck snapped his fingers. "Bridget. She sent me for water. She said something to you, I know it."

"She didn't."

"She didn't? You're lying. I know she—"

"She wrote it," Teddy said and patted the pockets of his trench coat for his notebook.

He found it eventually in his inside pocket and started to flip through it.

Chuck began to whistle and clop his feet into the soft earth in a goose step.

When he reached the page, Teddy said, "Adolf, enough."

Chuck came over. "You find it?"

Teddy nodded, turned the notebook so that Chuck could see the page, the single word written there, tightly scrawled and already beginning to bleed in the rain:

run

9

THEY FOUND THE stones about a half mile inland as the sky rushed toward darkness under slate-bottomed clouds. They came over soggy bluffs where the sea grass was lank and slick in the rain, and they were both covered in mud from clawing and stumbling their way up.

A field lay below them, as flat as the undersides of the clouds, bald except for a stray bush or two, some heavy leaves tossed in by the storm, and a multitude of small stones that Teddy initially assumed had come with the leaves, riding the wind. He paused halfway down the far side of the bluff, though, gave them another look.

They were spread across the field in small, tight piles, each pile separated from the one closest to it by about six inches, and Teddy put his hand on Chuck's shoulder and pointed at them.

"How many piles do you count?"

Chuck said, "What?"

Teddy said, "Those rocks. You see 'em?"

"Yeah."

"They're piled separately. How many do you count?"

Chuck gave him a look like the storm had found his head. "They're rocks."

"I'm serious."

Chuck gave him a bit more of that look and then turned his attention to the field. After a minute, he said, "I count ten."

"Me too."

The mud gave way under Chuck's foot and he slipped, flailed back with an arm that Teddy caught and held until Chuck righted himself.

"Can we go down?" Chuck said and gave Teddy a mild grimace of annoyance.

They worked their way down and Teddy went to the stone piles and saw that they formed two lines, one above the other. Some piles were much smaller than others. A few contained only three or four stones while others had more than ten, maybe even twenty.

Teddy walked between the two lines and then stopped and looked over at Chuck and said, "We miscounted."

"How?"

"Between these two piles here?" Teddy waited for him to join him and then they were looking down at it. "That's one stone right there. Its own single pile."

"In this wind? No. It fell from one of the other stacks."

"It's equidistant to the other piles. Half a foot to the left of that one, half a foot to the right of that one. And in the next row, the same thing occurs again twice. Single stones."

"So?"

"So, there're thirteen piles of rock, Chuck."

"You think *she* left this. You really do."

"I think someone did."

"Another code."

Teddy squatted by the rocks. He pulled his trench coat over his head and extended the flaps of it in front of his body to protect his notebook from the rain. He moved sideways like a crab and paused at each pile to count the number of stones and write it down. When he was finished, he had thirteen numbers: 18-1-4-9-5-4-23-1-12-4-19-14-5.

"Maybe it's a combination," Chuck said, "for the world's biggest padlock."

Teddy closed the notebook and placed it in his pocket. "Good one."

"Thank you, thank you," Chuck said. "I'll be appearing twice nightly in the Catskills. Please come out, won't you?"

Teddy pulled the trench coat back off his head and stood, and the rain pounded him again and the wind had found its voice.

They walked north with the cliffs off to the right and Ashecliffe shrouded to their left somewhere in the smash of wind and rain. It grew measurably worse in the next half hour, and they pressed their shoulders together in order to hear each other talk and listed like drunks.

"Cawley asked you if you were Army Intelligence. Did you lie to him?"

"I did and I didn't," Teddy said. "I received my discharge from regular army."

"How'd you enter, though?"

"Out of basic, I was sent to radio school."

"And from there?"

"A crash course at War College and then, yeah, Intel'."

"So how'd you end up in regulation brown?"

"I fucked up." Teddy had to shout it against the wind. "I blew a decoding. Enemy position coordinates."

"How bad?"

Teddy could still hear the noise that had come over the radio. Screams, static, crying, static, machine gun fire followed by more screams and more crying and more static. And a boy's voice, in the near background of all that noise, saying, "You see where the rest of me went?"

"About half a battalion," Teddy shouted into the wind. "Served 'em up like meat loaf."

There was nothing but the gale in his ears for a minute, and then Chuck yelled, "I'm sorry. That's horrible."

They crested a knoll and the wind up top nearly blew them back off it, but Teddy gripped Chuck's elbow and they surged forward, heads down, and they walked that way for some time, bowing their heads and bodies into the wind, and they didn't even notice the headstones at first. They kept trudging along with the rain filling their eyes and then Teddy bumped into a slate stone that tipped backward and was wrenched from its hole by the wind and lay flat on its back looking up at him.

JACOB PLUGH

BOSUN'S MATE

1832–1858

A tree broke to their left, and the crack of it sounded like an ax through a tin roof, and Chuck yelled, "Jesus Christ," and parts of the tree were picked up by the wind and shot past their eyes.

They moved into the graveyard with their arms up around their faces and the dirt and leaves and pieces of trees gone alive and electric, and they fell several times, almost blinded by it, and Teddy saw a fat charcoal shape ahead and started pointing, his shouts lost to the wind.

A chunk of something passed so close to his head he could feel it kiss his hair and they ran with the wind battering their legs and the earth rising up and chunking against their knees.

A mausoleum. The door was steel but broken at the hinges, and weeds sprouted from the foundation. Teddy pulled the door back and the wind tore into him, banged him to his left with the door, and he fell to the ground and the door rose off its broken lower hinge and yowled and then slammed back against the wall. Teddy slipped in the mud and rose to his feet and the wind battered his shoulders and he dropped to one knee and saw the black doorway facing him and he plunged forward through the muck and crawled inside.

"You ever see anything like this?" Chuck said as they stood in the doorway and watched the island whirl itself into a rage. The wind was thick with dirt and leaves, tree branches and rocks and always the rain, and it squealed like a pack of boar and shredded the earth.

"Never," Teddy said, and they stepped back from the doorway.

Chuck found a pack of matches that was still dry in the inside pocket of his coat and he lit three at once and tried to block the wind with his body and they saw that the cement slab in the center of the room was empty of a coffin or a body, either moved or stolen in the years since it had been interred. There was a stone bench built into the wall on the other side of the slab, and they walked to it as the matches went out. They sat down and the wind continued to sweep past the doorway and hammer the door against the wall.

"Kinda pretty, though, huh?" Chuck said. "Nature gone crazy, the color of that sky . . . You see the way that headstone did a backflip?"

"I gave it a nudge, but, yeah, that was impressive."

"Wow." Chuck squeezed his pants cuffs until there were puddles under his feet, fluttered his soaked shirt against his chest. "Guess we should have stayed closer to home base. We might have to ride this out. Here."

Teddy nodded. "I don't know enough about hurricanes, but I get the feeling it's just warming up."

"That wind changes direction? That graveyard's going to be coming in here."

"I'd still rather be in here than out there."

"Sure, but seeking high ground in a hurricane? How fucking smart are we?"

"Not very."

"It was so *fast*. One second it was just heavy rain, the next second we're Dorothy heading to Oz."

"That was a tornado."

"Which?"

"In Kansas."

"Oh."

The squealing rose in pitch and Teddy could hear the wind find the thick stone wall behind him, pounding on it like fists until he could feel tiny shudders of impact in his back.

"Just warming up," he repeated.

"What do you suppose all the crazies are doing about now?"

"Screaming back at it," he said.

They sat silent for a while and each had a cigarette. Teddy was reminded of that day on his father's boat, of his first realization that nature was indifferent to him and far more powerful, and he pictured the wind as something with a hawk's face and hooked beak as it swooped over the mausoleum and cawed. An angry thing that turned waves into towers and chewed houses into matchsticks and could lift him in its grasp and throw him to China.

"I was in North Africa in 'forty-two," Chuck said. "Went through a couple of sandstorms. Nothing like this, though. Then again, you forget. Maybe it was as bad."

"I can take this," Teddy said. "I mean, I wouldn't walk out into what's going on now, start strolling around, but it beats the cold. The Ardennes, Jesus, your breath froze coming out of your mouth. To this day, I can feel it. So cold my fingers felt like they were on fire. How do you figure that?"

"North Africa, we had the heat. Guys dropping from it. Just standing there one minute, on the deck the next. Guys had coronaries from it. I shot this guy and his skin was so soft from the heat, he actually turned and watched the bullet fly out the other side of his body." Chuck tapped the bench with his finger. "Watched it fly," he said softly. "I swear to God."

"Only guy you ever killed?"

"Up close. You?"

"I was the opposite. Killed a lot, saw most of them." Teddy leaned his head back against the wall, looked up at the ceiling. "If I ever had a son, I don't know if I'd let him go to war. Even a war like that where we had no choice. I'm not sure that should be asked of anyone."

"What?"

"Killing."

Chuck raised a knee to his chest. "My parents, my girlfriend, some of my friends who couldn't pass the physical, they all ask, you know?"

"Yeah."

"What was it *like*? That's what they want to know. And you want to say, 'I don't know what it was like. It happened to someone else. I was just watching it from above or something.'" He held out his hands. "I can't explain it any better. Did that make a bit of sense?"

Teddy said, "At Dachau, the SS guards surrendered to us. Five hundred of them. Now there were reporters there, but they'd seen all the bodies piled up at the train station too. They could smell exactly what we were smelling. They looked at us and they wanted us to do what we did. And we sure as hell wanted to do it. So we executed every one of those fucking Krauts. Disarmed them, leaned them against walls, executed them. Machine-gunned over three hundred men at one time. Walked down the line putting bullets into the head of anyone still breathing. A war crime if ever there was one. Right? But, Chuck, that was the *least* we could have done. Fucking reporters were clapping. The camp prisoners were so happy they were weeping. So we handed a few of the storm troopers over to them. And they tore them to shreds. By the end of that day, we'd removed five hundred souls from the face of the earth. Murdered 'em all. No self-defense, no warfare came into it. It was homicide. And yet, there was no gray area. They deserved so much worse. So, fine—but how do you live with that? How do you tell the wife and the parents and the kids that you've done this thing? You've executed unarmed people? You've killed boys? Boys with guns and uniforms, but boys just the same? Answer is—You can't tell 'em. They'll never understand. Because what you did was for the right reason. But what you *did* was also wrong. And you'll never wash it off."

After a while, Chuck said, "At least it was for the right reason. You ever look at some of these poor bastards come back from Korea? They still don't know why they were there. We stopped Adolf. We saved millions of lives. Right? We did something, Teddy."

"Yeah, we did," Teddy admitted. "Sometimes that's enough."

"It's gotta be. Right?"

An entire tree swept past the door, upside down, its roots sprouting upward like horns.

"You see that?"

"Yeah. It's gonna wake up in the middle of the ocean, say, 'Wait a *second*. This isn't right.' "

" 'I'm supposed to be over there.' "

" 'Took me years to get that hill looking the way I wanted it.' "

They laughed softly in the dark and watched the island race by like a fever dream.

"So how much do you really know about this place, boss?"

Teddy shrugged. "I know some. Not nearly enough. Enough to scare me."

"Oh, great. You're scared. What's a normal mortal supposed to feel, then?"

Teddy smiled. "Abject terror?"

"Okay. Consider me terrified."

"It's known as an experimental facility. I told you—radical therapy. Its funding comes partially from the Commonwealth, partially from the Bureau of Federal Penitentiaries, but mostly from a fund set up in 'fifty-one by HUAC."

"Oh," Chuck said. "Terrific. Fighting the Commies from an island in Boston Harbor. How *does* one go about doing that?"

"They experiment on the mind. That's my guess. Write down what they know, turn it over to Cawley's old OSS buddies in the CIA maybe. I dunno. You ever heard of phencyclidine?"

Chuck shook his head.

"LSD? Mescaline?"

"Nope and nope."

"They're hallucinogens," Teddy said. "Drugs that cause you to hallucinate."

"All right."

"In even minimal doses, strictly sane people—you or I—would start seeing things."

"Upside-down trees flying past our door?"

"Ah, there's the rub. If we're both seeing it, it's not a hallucination. Everyone sees different things. Say you looked down right now and your arms had turned to cobras and the cobras were rising up, opening their jaws to eat your head?"

"I'd say that would be a hell of a bad day."

"Or those raindrops turned into flames? A bush became a charging tiger?"

"An even worse day. I should've never left the bed. But, hey, you're saying a drug could make you think shit like that was really happening?"

"Not just 'could.' Will. Given the right dosage, you *will* start to hallucinate."

"Those are some drugs."

"Yeah, they are. A lot of these drugs? Their effect is supposedly identical to what it's like to be a severe schizophrenic. What's his name, Ken, that guy. The cold in his feet. He believes that. Leonora Grant, she wasn't seeing you. She was seeing Douglas Fairbanks."

"Don't forget—Charlie Chaplin too, my friend."

"I'd do an imitation, but I don't know what he sounds like."

"Hey, not bad, boss. You can open for me in the Catskills."

"There have been documented cases of schizophrenics tearing their own faces off because they believed their hands were something else, animals or whatever. They see things that aren't there, hear voices no one else hears, jump from perfectly sound roofs because they think the building's on fire, and on and on. Hallucinogens cause similar delusions."

Chuck pointed a finger at Teddy. "You're suddenly speaking with a lot more erudition than usual."

Teddy said, "What can I tell you? I did some homework. Chuck, what do you think would happen if you gave hallucinogens to people with extreme schizophrenia?"

"No one would do that."

"They do it, and it's legal. Only humans get schizophrenia. It doesn't happen to rats or rabbits or cows. So how are you going to test cures for it?"

"On humans."

"Give that man a cigar."

"A cigar that's *just* a cigar, though, right?"

Teddy said, "If you like."

Chuck stood and placed his hands on the stone slab, looked out at the storm. "So they're giving schizophrenics drugs that make them even more schizophrenic?"

"That's one test group."

"What's another?"

"People who don't have schizophrenia are given hallucinogens to see how their brains react."

"Bullshit."

"This is a matter of public record, buddy. Attend a psychiatrists' convention someday. I have."

"But you said it's legal."

"It's legal," Teddy said. "So was eugenics research."

"But if it's legal, we can't do anything about it."

Teddy leaned into the slab. "No argument. I'm not here to arrest anyone just yet. I was sent to gather information. That's all."

"Wait a minute—sent? Christ, Teddy, how fucking deep are we here?"

Teddy sighed, looked over at him. "Deep."

"Back up." Chuck held up a hand. "From the top. How'd you get involved in all this?"

"It started with Laeddis. A year ago," Teddy said. "I went to Shattuck under the pretense of wanting to interview him. I made up a bullshit story about how a known associate of his was wanted on a federal warrant and I thought Laeddis could shed some light on his whereabouts. Thing was, Laeddis wasn't there. He'd been transferred to Ashecliffe. I call over here, but they claim to have no record of him."

"And?"

"And that gets me curious. I make some phone calls to some of the psych hospitals in town and everyone is aware of Ashecliffe but no one wants to talk about it. I talk to the warden at Renton Hospital for the Criminally Insane. I'd met him a couple times before and I say,

'Bobby, what's the big deal? It's a hospital and it's a prison, no differ-ent from your place,' and he shakes his head. He says, 'Teddy, that place is something else entirely. Something classified. Black bag. Don't go out there.' "

"But you do," Chuck said. "And I get assigned to go with you."

"That wasn't part of the plan," Teddy said. "Agent in charge tells me I have to take a partner, I take a partner."

"So you've just been waiting for an excuse to come out here?"

"Pretty much," Teddy said. "And, hell, I couldn't bet it would ever happen. I mean, even if there was a patient break, I didn't know if I'd be in town when it happened. Or if someone else would be assigned to it. Or, hell, a million 'ifs.' I got lucky."

"Lucky? Fuck."

"What?"

"It's not luck, boss. Luck doesn't work that way. The world doesn't work that way. You think you just *happened* to get assigned to this detail?"

"Sure. Sounds a little crazy, but—"

"When you first called Ashecliffe about Laeddis, did you ID yourself?"

"Of course."

"Well then—"

"Chuck, it was a full year ago."

"So? You don't think they keep tabs? Particularly in the case of a patient they claim to have no record of?"

"Again—twelve months ago."

"Teddy, Jesus." Chuck lowered his voice, placed the flats of his palms on the slab, took a long breath. "Let's say they are doing some bad shit here. What if they've been onto you since before you ever stepped foot on this island? What if *they* brought *you* here?"

"Oh, bullshit."

"Bullshit? Where's Rachel Solando? Where's one shred of evidence that she ever existed? We've been shown a picture of *a* woman and a file anyone could have fabricated."

"But, Chuck—even if they made her up, even if they staged this whole thing, there's still no way they could have predicted that I would be assigned to the case."

"You've made inquiries, Teddy. You've looked into this place, asked around. They got an electrified fence around a septic processing facility. They got a ward inside a fort. They got under a hundred patients in a facility that could hold three hundred. This place is fucking scary, Teddy. No other hospital wants to talk about it, and that doesn't tell you something? You got a chief of staff with OSS ties, funding from a slush fund created by HUAC. Everything about this place screams 'government ops.' And you're surprised by the possibility that instead of you looking at them for the past year, they've been looking at you?"

"How many times do I have to say it, Chuck: how could they know I'd be assigned to Rachel Solando's case?"

"Are you fucking thick?"

Teddy straightened, looked down at Chuck.

Chuck held up a hand. "Sorry, sorry. I'm nervous, okay?"

"Okay."

"All I'm saying, boss, is that they knew you'd jump at any excuse to come here. Your wife's killer is here. All they had to do was pretend someone escaped. And then they knew you'd pole-vault your way across that harbor if you had to."

The door ripped free of its sole hinge and smashed back into the doorway, and they watched it hammer the stone and then lift into the air and shoot out above the graveyard and disappear in the sky.

Both of them stared at the doorway, and then Chuck said, "We *both* saw that, right?"

"They're using human beings as guinea pigs," Teddy said. "Doesn't that bother you?"

"It terrifies me, Teddy. But how do you know this? You say you were sent to gather information. Who sent you?"

"In our first meeting with Cawley, you heard him ask about the senator?"

"Yeah."

"Senator Hurly, Democrat, New Hampshire. Heads up a subcommittee on public funding for mental health affairs. He saw what kind of money was being funneled to this place, and he didn't like it. Now, I'd come across a guy named George Noyce. Noyce spent time here. In Ward C. He was off the island two weeks when he walked into a bar in Attleboro and began stabbing people. Strangers. In jail, he starts talking about dragons in Ward C. His lawyer wants to claim insanity. If ever there was a case for it, it's this guy. He's bonkers. But Noyce fires his lawyer, goes in front of the judge, and pleads guilty, pretty much begs to be sent to a prison, any prison, just not a hospital. Takes him about a year in prison, but his mind starts coming back, and eventually, he starts telling stories about Ashecliffe. Stories that sound crazy, but the senator thinks they're maybe not as crazy as everyone else assumes."

Chuck sat up on the slab and lit a cigarette, smoked it for a bit as he considered Teddy.

"But how'd the senator know to find you and how'd you both manage to find Noyce?"

For a moment, Teddy thought he saw lights arcing through the eruptions outside.

"It actually worked the other way around. Noyce found me and I found the senator. It was Bobby Farris, the warden at Renton. He called me one morning and asked if I was still interested in Ashecliffe. I said sure, and he told me about this convict down in Dedham who was making all this noise about Ashecliffe. So I go to Dedham a few times, talk to Noyce. Noyce says when he was in college, he got a bit tense one year around exams time. Shouted at a teacher, put his fist through a window in his dorm. He ends up talking to somebody in the psych department. Next thing you know, he agrees to be part of a test so he can make a little pocket change. A year later, he's out of college, a full-fledged schizophrenic, raving on street corners, seeing things, the whole nine yards."

"Now this is a kid who started out normal . . ."

Teddy saw lights again flaring through the storm and he walked nearer to the door, stared out. Lightning? It would make sense, he supposed, but he hadn't seen any before this.

"Normal as pecan pie. Maybe had some—what do they call it here?—'anger management issues,' but all in all, perfectly sane. A year later, he's out of his mind. So he sees this guy in Park Square one day, thinks it's the professor who first recommended he see someone in the psych department. Long story short—it ain't, but Noyce fucks him up pretty bad. Gets sent to Ashecliffe. Ward A. But he's not there long. He's a pretty violent guy by this time, and they send him to Ward C. They fill him up with hallucinogens and they step back and watch as the dragons come to eat him and he goes crazy. A little crazier than they hoped, I guess, because in the end, just to calm him down, they performed surgery."

"Surgery," Chuck said.

Teddy nodded. "A transorbital lobotomy. Those are fun, Chuck. They zap you with electroshock and then they go in through your eye with, get this, an ice pick. I'm not kidding. No anesthesia. They poke around here and there and take a few nerve fibers out of your brain, and then that's it, it's over. Piece of cake."

Chuck said, "The Nuremberg Code prohibits—"

"—experimenting on humans purely in the interest of science, yes. I thought we had a case based on Nuremberg too. So did the senator. No go. Experimentation is allowable if it's used to directly attack a patient's malady. So as long as a doctor can say, 'Hey, we're just trying to help the poor bastard, see if these drugs can induce schizophrenia and these drugs over here can stop it'—then they're legally in the clear."

"Wait a second, wait a second," Chuck said. "You said this Noyce had a trans, um—"

"A transorbital lobotomy, yeah."

"But if the point of that, however medieval, is to calm someone down, how's he manage to go fuck some guy up in Park Square?"

"Obviously, it didn't take."

"Is that common?"

Teddy saw the arcing lights again, and this time he was pretty sure he could hear the whine of an engine behind all that squealing.

"Marshals!" The voice was weak on the wind, but they both heard it.

Chuck swung his legs over the end of the slab and jumped off and joined Teddy at the doorway and they could see headlights at the far end of the cemetery and they heard the squawk of a megaphone and a screech of feedback and then:

"Marshals! If you are out here, please signal us. This is Deputy Warden McPherson. Marshals!"

Teddy said, "How about that? They found us."

"It's an island, boss. They'll always find us."

Teddy met Chuck's eyes and nodded. For the first time since they'd met, he could see fear in Chuck's eyes, his jaw trying to tighten against it.

"It's going to be okay, partner."

"Marshals! Are you out here?"

Chuck said, "I don't know."

"I do," Teddy said, though he didn't. "Stick with me. We're walking out of this fucking place, Chuck. Make no mistake about it."

And they stepped out of the doorway and into the cemetery. The wind hit their bodies like a team of linemen but they stayed on their feet, locking arms and gripping the other's shoulder as they stumbled toward the light.

10

"ARE YOU FUCKING crazy?"

This from McPherson, shouting into the wind, as the jeep hurtled down a makeshift trail along the western edge of the cemetery.

He was in the passenger seat, looking back at them with red eyes, all vestiges of Texas country boy charm washed away in the storm. The driver hadn't been introduced to them. Young kid, lean face, and pointed chin were about all Teddy could make out under the hood of his rain slicker. Drove that jeep like a professional, though, tearing through scrub brush and the storm's debris like it wasn't even there.

"This has just been upgraded from a tropical storm to a hurricane. Winds are coming in at around a hundred miles an hour right now. By midnight, they're expected to hit a hundred fifty. And you guys go strolling off in it?"

"How do you know it was upgraded?" Teddy said.

"Ham radio, Marshal. We expect to lose that within a couple of hours too."

"Of course," Teddy said.

"We could have been shoring up the compound right now, but instead we were looking for you." He slapped the back of his seat, then turned forward, done with them.

The jeep bounced over a rise and for a moment Teddy saw only sky, felt nothing underneath the wheels, and then the tires hit dirt and they spun through a sharp curve that dipped steeply with the trail and Teddy could see the ocean off their left, the water churning with explosions that bloomed white and wide like mushroom clouds.

The jeep tore down through a rise of small hills and then burst into a stand of trees, Teddy and Chuck holding on to the seats as they banged off each other in the back, and then the trees were behind them and they were facing the back of Cawley's mansion, crossing a quarter acre of wood chips and pine needles before they hit the access road and the driver pushed out of low gear and roared toward the main gate.

"We're taking you to see Dr. Cawley," McPherson said, looking back at them. "He just can't wait to talk to you guys."

"And here I thought my mother was back in Seattle," Chuck said.

THEY SHOWERED IN the basement of the staff dormitory and were given clothes from the orderlies' stockpile. Their own clothes were sent to the hospital laundry, and Chuck combed his hair back in the bathroom and looked at his white shirt and white pants and said, "Would you like to see a wine list? Our special tonight is beef Wellington. It's quite good."

Trey Washington stuck his head in the bathroom. He seemed to be biting back on a smile as he appraised their new clothes and then he said, "I'm to bring you to Dr. Cawley."

"How much trouble we in?"

"Oh, a bit, I'd expect."

"GENTLEMEN," CAWLEY SAID as they entered the room, "good to see you."

He seemed in a magnanimous mood, his eyes bright, and Teddy and Chuck left Trey at the door as they entered a boardroom on the top floor of the hospital.

The room was filled with doctors, some in white lab coats, some in suits, all sitting around a long teak table with green-shaded banker's lamps in front of their chairs and dark ashtrays that smoldered with cigarettes or cigars, the sole pipe belonging to Naehring, who sat at the head of the table.

"Doctors, these are the federal marshals we discussed. Marshals Daniels and Aule."

"Where are your clothes?" one man asked.

"Good question," Cawley said, enjoying the hell out of this, in Teddy's opinion.

"We were out in the storm," Teddy said.

"Out in that?" The doctor pointed at the tall windows. They'd been crisscrossed with heavy tape and they seemed to breathe slightly, exhaling into the room. The panes drummed with fingertips of rain, and the entire building creaked under the press of wind.

"Afraid so," Chuck said.

"If you could take a seat, gentlemen," Naehring said. "We're just finishing up."

They found two seats at the end of the table.

"John," Naehring said to Cawley, "we need a consensus on this."

"You know where I stand."

"And I think we all respect that, but if neuroleptics can provide the necessary decrease in five-HT imbalances of serotonin, then I don't feel we have much choice. We have to continue the research. This first test patient, this, uh, Doris Walsh, fits all the criteria. I don't see a problem there."

"I'm just worried about the cost."

"Far less than surgery and you know that."

"I'm talking about the damage risks to the basal ganglia and the cerebral cortex. I'm talking about early studies in Europe that have shown risks of neurological disruption similar to those caused by encephalitis and strokes."

Naehring dismissed the objection with a raised hand. "All those in favor of Dr. Brotigan's request, please raise your hands."

Teddy watched every hand at the table except Cawley's and one other man's hit the air.

"I'd say that's a consensus," Naehring said. "We'll petition the board, then, for funding on Dr. Brotigan's research."

A young guy, must have been Brotigan, gave a nod of thanks to each end of the table. Lantern-jawed, all-American, smooth-cheeked. He struck Teddy as the kind of guy who needed watching, too secure in his own fulfillment of his parents' wildest dreams.

"Well, then," Naehring said and closed the binder in front of him as he looked down the table at Teddy and Chuck, "how are things, Marshals?"

Cawley rose from his seat and fixed a cup of coffee for himself at the sideboard. "Rumor has it you were both found in a mausoleum."

There were several soft chuckles from the table, doctors raising fists to mouths.

"You know a better place to sit out a hurricane?" Chuck said.

Cawley said, "Here. Preferably in the basement."

"We hear it may hit land at a hundred fifty miles an hour."

Cawley nodded, his back to the room. "This morning, Newport, Rhode Island, lost thirty percent of its homes."

Chuck said, "Not the Vanderbilts, I pray."

Cawley took his seat. "Provincetown and Truro got hit this afternoon. No one knows how bad because the roads are out and so is radio communication. But it looks to be heading right at us."

"Worst storm to hit the eastern seaboard in thirty years," one of the doctors said.

"Turns the air to pure static electricity," Cawley said. "That's why the switchboard went to hell last night. That's why the radios have been so-so at best. If it gives us a direct hit, I don't know what's going to be left standing."

"Which is why," Naehring said, "I repeat my insistence that all Blue Zone patients be placed in manual restraints."

"Blue Zone?" Teddy said.

"Ward C," Cawley said. "Patients who have been deemed a danger to themselves, this institution, and the general public at large." He turned to Naehring. "We can't do that. If that facility floods, they'll drown. You know that."

"It would take a lot of flooding."

"We're in the ocean. About to get hit with hurricane winds of a hundred and fifty miles per hour. A 'lot of flooding' seems distinctly possible. We double up the guards. We account for every Blue Zone patient at all times. No exceptions. But we cannot lock them to their beds. They're already locked down in cells, for Christ's sake. It's overkill."

"It's a gamble, John." This was said quietly by a brown-haired man in the middle of the table. Along with Cawley, he'd been the only abstaining vote on whatever they'd been discussing when Teddy and Chuck first entered. He clicked a ballpoint pen repeatedly and his gaze was given to the tabletop, but Teddy could tell from his tone that he was friends with Cawley. "It's a real gamble. Let's say the power fails."

"There's a backup generator."

"And if that goes? Those cells will open."

"It's an island," Cawley said. "Where's anyone going to go? It's not like they can catch a ferry, scoot over to Boston, and wreak havoc. If they're in manual restraints and that facility floods, gentlemen, they'll all die. That's twenty-four human beings. If, god forbid, anything happens in the compound? To the other forty-two? I mean, good Christ. Can you live with that? I can't."

Cawley looked up and down the table, and Teddy suddenly felt a capacity for compassion coming from him that he'd barely sensed before. He had no idea why Cawley had allowed them into this meeting, but he was starting to think the man didn't have many friends in the room.

"Doctor," Teddy said, "I don't mean to interrupt."

"Not at all, Marshal. We brought you here."

Teddy almost said: no kidding?

"When we spoke this morning about Rachel Solando's code—"

"Everyone's familiar with what the marshal's talking about?"

"The Law of Four," Brotigan said with a smile Teddy wanted to take a pair of pliers to. "I just love that."

Teddy said, "When we talked this morning you said you had no theories about the final clue."

" 'Who is sixty-seven?' " Naehring said. "Yes?"

Teddy nodded and then leaned back in his chair, waiting.

He found everyone looking back down the table at him, baffled.

"You honestly don't see it," Teddy said.

"See what, Marshal?" This from Cawley's friend, and Teddy took a look at his lab coat, saw that his name was Miller.

"You have sixty-six patients here."

They stared back at him like birthday-party children waiting for the clown's next bouquet.

"Forty-two patients, combined, in Wards A and B. Twenty-four in Ward C. That's sixty-six."

Teddy could see the realization dawn on a few faces, but the majority still looked dumbfounded.

"Sixty-six patients," Teddy said. "That suggests that the answer to 'Who is sixty-seven?' is that there's a sixty-seventh patient here."

Silence. Several of the doctors looked across the table at one another.

"I don't follow," Naehring said eventually.

"What's not to follow? Rachel Solando was suggesting that there's a sixty-seventh patient."

"But there isn't," Cawley said, his hands held out in front of him on the table. "It's a great idea, Marshal, and it would certainly crack the code if it were true. But two plus two never equals five even if you want it to. If there are only sixty-six patients on the island, then the question referring to a sixty-seventh is moot. You see what I mean?"

"No," Teddy said, keeping his voice calm. "I'm not quite with you on this one."

Cawley seemed to choose his words carefully before he spoke, as if picking the simplest ones. "If, say, this hurricane weren't going on, we would have received two new patients this morning. That would put our total at sixty-eight. If a patient, God forbid, died in his sleep last night, that would put our total at sixty-five. The total can change day by day, week by week, depending on a number of variables."

"But," Teddy said, "as of the night Miss Solando wrote her code . . ."

"There were sixty-six, including her. I'll grant you that, Marshal. But that's still one short of sixty-seven, isn't it? You're trying to put a round peg into a square hole."

"But that was her point."

"I realize that, yes. But her point was fallacious. There is no sixty-seventh patient here."

"Would you permit my partner and me to go through the patient files?"

That brought a round of frowns and offended looks from the table.

"Absolutely not," Naehring said.

"We can't do that, Marshal. I'm sorry."

Teddy lowered his head for a minute, looked at his silly white shirt and matching pants. He looked like a soda jerk. Probably appeared as authoritative. Maybe he should serve scoops of ice cream to the room, see if he could get to them that way.

"We can't access your staff files. We can't access your patient files. How are we supposed to find your missing patient, gentlemen?"

Naehring leaned back in his chair, cocked his head.

Cawley's arm froze, a cigarette half lifted to his lips.

Several of the doctors whispered to one another.

Teddy looked at Chuck.

Chuck whispered, "Don't look at me. I'm baffled."

Cawley said, "The warden didn't tell you?"

"We've never spoken to the warden. We were picked up by McPherson."

"Oh," Cawley said, "my goodness."

"What?"

Cawley looked around at the other doctors, his eyes wide.

"What?" Teddy repeated.

Cawley let a rush of air out of his mouth and looked back down the table at them.

"We found her."

"You what?"

Cawley nodded and took a drag off his cigarette. "Rachel Solando. We found her this afternoon. She's here, gentlemen. Right out that door and down the hall."

Teddy and Chuck both looked over their shoulders at the door.

"You can rest now, Marshals. Your quest is over."

11

CAWLEY AND NAEHRING led them down a black-and-white-tiled corridor and through a set of double doors into the main hospital ward. They passed a nurses' station on their left and turned right into a large room with long fluorescent bulbs and U-shaped curtain rods hanging from hooks in the ceiling, and there she was, sitting up on a bed in a pale green smock that ended just above her knees, her dark hair freshly washed and combed back off her forehead.

"Rachel," Cawley said, "we've dropped by with some friends. I hope you don't mind."

She smoothed the hem of the smock under her thighs and looked at Teddy and Chuck with a child's air of expectation.

There wasn't a mark on her.

Her skin was the color of sandstone. Her face and arms and legs were unblemished. Her feet were bare, and the skin was free of scratches, untouched by branches or thorns or rocks.

"How can I help you?" she asked Teddy.

"Miss Solando, we came here to—"

"Sell something?"

"Ma'am?"

"You're not here to sell something, I hope. I don't want to be rude, but my husband makes all those decisions."

"No, ma'am. We're not here to sell anything."

"Well, that's fine, then. What can I do for you?"

"Could you tell me where you were yesterday?"

"I was here. I was home." She looked at Cawley. "Who are these men?"

Cawley said, "They're police officers, Rachel."

"Did something happen to Jim?"

"No," Cawley said. "No, no. Jim's fine."

"Not the children." She looked around. "They're right out in the yard. They didn't get into any mischief, did they?"

Teddy said, "Miss Solando, no. Your children aren't in any trouble. Your husband's fine." He caught Cawley's eye and Cawley nodded in approval. "We just, um, we heard there was a known subversive in the area yesterday. He was seen on your street passing out Communist literature."

"Oh, dear Lord, no. To children?"

"Not as far as we know."

"But in this neighborhood? On this street?"

Teddy said, "I'm afraid so, ma'am. I was hoping you could account for your whereabouts yesterday so we'd know if you ever crossed paths with the gentleman in question."

"Are you accusing me of being a Communist?" Her back came off the pillows and she bunched the sheet in her fists.

Cawley gave Teddy a look that said: You dug the hole. You dig your way out.

"A Communist, ma'am? You? What man in his right mind would

think that? You're as American as Betty Grable. Only a blind man could miss that."

She unclenched one hand from the sheet, rubbed her kneecap with it. "But I don't look like Betty Grable."

"Only in your obvious patriotism. No, I'd say you look more like Teresa Wright, ma'am. What was that one she did with Joseph Cotton, ten—twelve years ago?"

"*Shadow of a Doubt*. I've *heard* that," she said, and her smile managed to be gracious and sensual at the same time. "Jim fought in that war. He came home and said the world was free now because Americans fought for it and the whole world saw that the American way was the only way."

"Amen," Teddy said. "I fought in that war too."

"Did you know my Jim?"

"'Fraid not, ma'am. I'm sure he's a fine man. Army?"

She crinkled her nose at that. "Marines."

"Semper fi," Teddy said. "Miss Solando, it's important we know every move this subversive made yesterday. Now you might not have even seen him. He's a sneaky one. So we need to know what *you* did so that we can match that against what we know about where he was, so we can see if you two may have ever passed each other."

"Like ships in the night?"

"Exactly. So you understand?"

"Oh, I do." She sat up on the bed and tucked her legs underneath her, and Teddy felt her movements in his stomach and groin.

"So if you could walk me through your day," he said.

"Well, let's see. I made Jim and the children their breakfast and then I packed Jim's lunch and Jim left, and then I sent the children off to school and then I decided to take a long swim in the lake."

"You do that often?"

"No," she said, leaning forward and laughing, as if he'd made a pass at her. "I just, I don't know, I felt a little kooky. You know how you do sometimes? You just feel a little kooky?"

"Sure."

"Well, that's how I felt. So I took off all my clothes and swam in the lake until my arms and legs were like logs, they were so heavy, and then I came out and dried off and put my clothes right back on and took a long walk along the shore. And I skipped some stones and built several small sand castles. Little ones."

"You remember how many?" Teddy asked and felt Cawley staring at him.

She thought about it, eyes tilted toward the ceiling. "I do."

"How many?"

"Thirteen."

"That's quite a few."

"Some were very small," she said. "Teacup-size."

"And then what did you do?"

"I thought about you," she said.

Teddy saw Naehring glance over at Cawley from the other side of the bed. Teddy caught Naehring's eye, and Naehring held up his hands, as surprised as anyone.

"Why me?" Teddy said.

Her smile exposed white teeth that were nearly clamped together except for a tiny red tip of tongue pressed in between. "Because you're my Jim, silly. You're my soldier." She rose on her knees and reached out and took Teddy's hand in hers, caressed it. "So rough. I love your calluses. I love the bump of them on my skin. I miss you, Jim. You're never home."

"I work a lot," Teddy said.

"Sit." She tugged his arm.

Cawley nudged him forward with a glance, so Teddy allowed himself to be led to the bed. He sat beside her. Whatever had caused that howl in her eyes in the photograph had fled from her, at least tem-porarily, and it was impossible, sitting this close, not to be fully aware of how beautiful she was. The overall impression she gave was liquid—dark eyes that shone with a gaze as clear as water, languid uncoilings of her body that made her limbs appear to swim through air, a face that was softly overripe in the lips and chin.

"You work too much," she said and ran her fingers over the space just below his throat, as if she were smoothing a kink in the knot of his tie.

"Gotta bring home the bacon," Teddy said.

"Oh, we're fine," she said, and he could feel her breath on his neck. "We've got enough to get by."

"For now," Teddy said. "I'm thinking about the future."

"Never seen it," Rachel said. "'Member what my poppa used to say?"

"I've forgotten."

She combed the hair along his temple with her fingers. " 'Future's something you put on layaway,' he'd say. 'I pay cash.' " She gave him a soft giggle and leaned in so close that he could feel her breasts against the back of his shoulder. "No, baby, we've got to live for today. The here and now."

It was something Dolores used to say. And the lips and hair were both similar, enough so that if Rachel's face got much closer, he could be forgiven for thinking he was talking to Dolores. They even had the same tremulous sensuality, Teddy never sure—even after all their years together—if his wife was even aware of its effect.

He tried to remember what he was supposed to ask her. He knew he was supposed to get her back on track. Have her tell him about her day yesterday, that was it, what happened after she walked the shore and built the castles.

"What did you do after you walked the lake?" he said.

"You know what I did."

"No."

"Oh, you want to hear me say it? Is that it?"

She leaned in so that her face was slightly below his, those dark eyes staring up, and the air that escaped her mouth climbed into his.

"You don't remember?"

"I don't."

"Liar."

"I'm serious."

"You're not. If you forgot that, James Solando, you are in for some trouble."

"So, tell me," Teddy whispered.

"You just want to hear it."

"I just want to hear it."

She ran her palm down his cheekbone and along his chin, and her voice was thicker when she spoke:

"I came back still wet from the lake and you licked me dry."

Teddy placed his hands on her face before she could close the distance between them. His fingers slid back along her temples, and he could feel the dampness from her hair against his thumbs and he looked into her eyes.

"Tell me what else you did yesterday," he whispered, and he saw something fighting against the water-clarity in her eyes. Fear, he was pretty sure. And then it sprouted onto her upper lip and the skin between her eyebrows. He could feel tremors in her flesh.

She searched his face and her eyes widened and widened and flicked from side to side in their sockets.

"I buried you," she said.

"No, I'm right here."

"I buried you. In an empty casket because your body was blown all over the North Atlantic. I buried your dog tags because that's all they could find. Your body, your beautiful body, that was burned up and eaten by sharks."

"Rachel," Cawley said.

"Like meat," she said.

"No," Teddy said.

"Like black meat, burned beyond tenderness."

"No, that wasn't me."

"They killed Jim. My Jim's dead. So who the fuck are you?"

She wrenched from his grip and crawled up the bed to the wall and then turned to look back at him.

"Who the fuck is that?" She pointed at Teddy and spit at him.

Teddy couldn't move. He stared at her, at the rage filling her eyes like a wave.

"You were going to fuck me, sailor? Is that it? Put your dick inside me while my children played in the yard? Was that your plan? You get the hell out of here! You hear me? You get the hell out of—"

She lunged for him, one hand raised over her head, and Teddy jumped from the bed and two orderlies swooped past him with thick leather belts draped over their shoulders and caught Rachel under the arms and flipped her back onto the bed.

Teddy could feel the shakes in his body, the sweat springing from his pores, and Rachel's voice blew up through the ward:

"You rapist! You cruel fucking rapist! My husband will come and cut your throat open! You hear me? He will cut your fucking head off and we'll drink the blood! We'll bathe ourselves in it, you sick fucking bastard!"

One orderly lay across her chest and the other one grasped her ankles in a massive hand and they slid the belts through metal slots in the bedrails and crossed them over Rachel's chest and ankles and pulled them through slots on the other side, pulled them taut and then slid the flaps through buckles, and the buckles made a snap as they locked, and the orderlies stepped back.

"Rachel," Cawley said, his voice gentle, paternal.

"You're all fucking rapists. Where are my babies? Where are my babies? You give me back my babies, you sick sons-a-bitches! You give me my babies!"

She let loose a scream that rode up Teddy's spine like a bullet, and she surged against her restraints so hard the gurney rails clattered, and Cawley said, "We'll come check on you later, Rachel."

She spit at him and Teddy heard it hit the floor and then she screamed again and there was blood on her lip from where she must have bitten it, and Cawley nodded at them and started walking and they fell into step behind him, Teddy looking back over his shoulder to see Rachel watching him, looking him right in the eye as she arched her shoulders off the mattress and the cords in her neck bulged and her lips were slick with blood and spittle as she shrieked at him, shrieked like she'd seen all the century's dead climb through her window and walk toward her bed.

CAWLEY HAD A bar in his office, and he went to it as soon as they entered, crossing to the right, and that's where Teddy lost him for a moment. He vanished behind a film of white gauze, and Teddy thought:

No, not now. Not now, for Christ's sake.

"Where'd you find her?" Teddy said.

"On the beach near the lighthouse. Skipping stones into the ocean."

Cawley reappeared, but only because Teddy shifted his head to the left as Cawley continued on to the right. As Teddy turned his head, the gauze covered a built-in bookcase and then the window. He rubbed his right eye, hoping against all evidence, but it did no good, and then he felt it along the left side of his head—a canyon filled with lava cut through the skull just below the part in his hair. He'd thought it was Rachel's screams in there, the furious noise, but it was more than that, and the pain erupted like a dozen dagger points pushed slowly into his cranium, and he winced and raised his fingers to his temple.

"Marshal?" He looked up to see Cawley on the other side of his desk, a ghostly blur to his left.

"Yeah?" Teddy managed.

"You're deathly pale."

"You okay, boss?" Chuck was beside him suddenly.

"Fine," Teddy managed, and Cawley placed his scotch glass down on the desk, and the sound of it was like a shotgun report.

"Sit down," Cawley said.

"I'm okay," Teddy said, but the words made their way down from his brain to his tongue on a spiked ladder.

Cawley's bones cracked like burning wood as he leaned against the desk in front of Teddy. "Migraine?"

Teddy looked up at the blur of him. He would have nodded, but past experience had taught him never to nod during one of these. "Yeah," he managed.

"I could tell by the way you're rubbing your temple."

"Oh."

"You get them often?"

"Half-dozen . . ." Teddy's mouth dried up and he took a few seconds to work some moisture back into his tongue. ". . . times a year."

"You're lucky," Cawley said. "In one respect anyway."

"How's that?"

"A lot of migraine sufferers get cluster migraines once a week or so." His body made that burning-wood sound again as he came off the desk and Teddy heard him unlock a cabinet.

"What do you get?" he asked Teddy. "Partial vision loss, dry mouth, fire in the head?"

"Bingo."

"All the centuries we've studied the brain, and no one has a clue where they come from. Can you believe that? We know they attack the parietal lobe usually. We know they cause a clotting of the blood. It's infinitesimal as these things go, but have it occur in something as delicate and small as the brain, and you will get explosions. All this time, though, all this study, and we know no more about the cause or much of the long-term effects than we do about how to stop the common cold."

Cawley handed him a glass of water and put two yellow pills in his hand. "These should do the trick. Knock you out for an hour or two, but when you come to, you should be fine. Clear as a bell."

Teddy looked down at the yellow pills, the glass of water that hung in a precarious grip.

He looked up at Cawley, tried to concentrate with his good eye because the man was bathed in a light so white and harsh that it flew off his shoulders and arms in shafts.

Whatever you do, a voice started to say in Teddy's head . . .

Fingernails pried open the left side of his skull and poured a shaker of thumbtacks in there, and Teddy hissed as he sucked his breath in.

"Jesus, boss."

"He'll be fine, Marshal."

The voice tried again: Whatever you do, Teddy . . .

Someone hammered a steel rod through the field of thumbtacks, and Teddy pressed the back of his hand to his good eye as tears shot from it and his stomach lurched.

. . . don't take those pills.

His stomach went fully south, sliding across into his right hip as flames licked the sides of the fissure in his head, and if it got any worse, he was pretty sure he'd bite straight through his tongue.

Don't take those fucking pills, the voice screamed, running back and forth down the burning canyon, waving a flag, rallying the troops.

Teddy lowered his head and vomited onto the floor.

"Boss, boss. You okay?"

"My, my," Cawley said. "You do get it bad."

Teddy raised his head.

Don't . . .

His cheeks were wet with his own tears.

. . . take . . .

Someone had inserted a blade lengthwise into the canyon now.

. . . those . . .

The blade had begun to saw back and forth.

. . . pills.

Teddy gritted his teeth, felt his stomach surge again. He tried to concentrate on the glass in his hand, noticed something odd on his thumb, and decided it was the migraine playing tricks with his perception.

don'ttakethosepills.

Another long pull of the sawteeth across the pink folds of his brain, and Teddy had to bite down against a scream and he heard Rachel's screams in there too with the fire and he saw her looking into his eyes and felt her breath on his lips and felt her face in his hands as his thumbs caressed her temples and that fucking saw went back and forth through his head—

don'ttakethosefuckingpills

—and he slapped his palm up to his mouth and felt the pills fly back in there and he chased them with water and swallowed, felt them slide down his esophagus and he gulped from the glass until it was empty.

"You're going to thank me," Cawley said.

Chuck was beside him again and he handed Teddy a handkerchief and Teddy wiped his forehead with it and then his mouth and then he dropped it to the floor.

Cawley said, "Help me get him up, Marshal."

They lifted Teddy out of the chair and turned him and he could see a black door in front of him.

"Don't tell anyone," Cawley said, "but there's a room through there where I steal my naps sometimes. Oh, okay, once a day. We're going to put you in there, Marshal, and you'll sleep this off. Two hours from now, you'll be fit as a fiddle."

Teddy saw his hands draping off their shoulders. They looked funny—his hands hanging like that just over his sternum. And the thumbs, they both had that optical illusion on them. What the fuck was it? He wished he could scratch the skin, but Cawley was opening the door now, and Teddy took one last look at the smudges on both thumbs.

Black smudges.

Shoe polish, he thought as they led him into the dark room.

How the hell did I get shoe polish on my thumbs?

12

THEY WERE THE worst dreams he'd ever had.

They began with Teddy walking through the streets of Hull, streets he had walked countless times from childhood to manhood. He passed his old schoolhouse. He passed the small variety store where he'd bought gum and cream sodas. He passed the Dickerson house and the Pakaski house, the Murrays, the Boyds, the Vernons, the Constantines. But no one was home. No one was anywhere. It was empty, the entire town. And dead quiet. He couldn't even hear the ocean, and you could always hear the ocean in Hull.

It was terrible—his town, and everyone gone. He sat down on the seawall along Ocean Avenue and searched the empty beach and he sat and waited but no one came. They were all dead, he realized, long dead and long gone. He was a ghost, come back through the centuries to his ghost town. It wasn't here any longer. He wasn't here any longer. There was no here.

He found himself in a great marble hall next, and it was filled with people and gurneys and red IV bags and he immediately felt better. No matter where this was, he wasn't alone. Three children—two boys and a girl—crossed in front of him. All three wore hospital smocks, and the girl was afraid. She clutched her brothers' hands. She said, "She's here. She'll find us."

Andrew Laeddis leaned in and lit Teddy's cigarette. "Hey, no hard feelings, right, buddy?"

Laeddis was a grim specimen of humanity—a gnarled cord of a body, a gangly head with a jutting chin that was twice as long as it should have been, misshapen teeth, sprouts of blond hair on a scabby, pink skull—but Teddy was glad to see him. He was the only one he knew in the room.

"Got me a bottle," Laeddis said, "if you want to have a toot later." He winked at Teddy and clapped his back and turned into Chuck and that seemed perfectly normal.

"We've gotta go," Chuck said. "Clock's ticking away here, my friend."

Teddy said, "My town's empty. Not a soul."

And he broke into a run because there she was, Rachel Solando, shrieking as she ran through the ballroom with a cleaver. Before Teddy could reach her, she'd tackled the three children, and the cleaver went up and down and up and down, and Teddy froze, oddly fascinated, knowing there was nothing he could do at this point, those kids were dead.

Rachel looked up at him. Her face and neck were speckled with blood. She said, "Give me a hand."

Teddy said, "What? I could get in trouble."

She said, "Give me a hand and I'll be Dolores. I'll be your wife. She'll come back to you."

So he said, "Sure, you bet," and helped her. They lifted all three children at once somehow and carried them out through the back door and down to the lake and they carried them into the water. They didn't throw them. They were gentle. They lay them on the water and the children sank. One of the boys rose back up, a hand flailing, and Rachel said, "It's okay. He can't swim."

They stood on the shore and watched the boy sink, and she put her arm around Teddy's waist and said, "You'll be my Jim. I'll be your Dolores. We'll make new babies."

That seemed a perfectly just solution, and Teddy wondered why he'd never thought of it before.

He followed her back into Ashecliffe and they met up with Chuck and the three of them walked down a long corridor that stretched for a mile. Teddy told Chuck: "She's taking me to Dolores. I'm going home, buddy."

"That's great!" Chuck said. "I'm glad. I'm never getting off this island."

"No?"

"No, but it's okay, boss. It really is. I belong here. This is my home."

Teddy said, "My home is Rachel."

"Dolores, you mean."

"Right, right. What did I say?"

"You said Rachel."

"Oh. Sorry about that. You really think you belong here?"

Chuck nodded. "I've never left. I'm never going to leave. I mean, look at my hands, boss."

Teddy looked at them. They looked perfectly fine to him. He said as much.

Chuck shook his head. "They don't fit. Sometimes the fingers turn into mice."

"Well, then I'm glad you're home."

"Thanks, boss." He slapped his back and turned into Cawley and

Rachel had somehow gotten far ahead of them and Teddy started walking double-time.

Cawley said, "You can't love a woman who killed her children."

"I can," Teddy said, walking faster. "You just don't understand."

"What?" Cawley wasn't moving his legs, but he was keeping pace with Teddy just the same, gliding. "What don't I understand?"

"I can't be alone. I can't face that. Not in this fucking world. I need her. She's my Dolores."

"She's Rachel."

"I know that. But we've got a deal. She'll be my Dolores. I'll be her Jim. It's a good deal."

"Uh-oh," Cawley said.

The three children came running back down the corridor toward them. They were soaking wet and they were screaming their little heads off.

"What kind of mother does that?" Cawley said.

Teddy watched the children run in place. They'd gotten past him and Cawley, and then the air changed or something because they ran and ran but never moved forward.

"Kills her kids?" Cawley said.

"She didn't mean to," Teddy said. "She's just scared."

"Like me?" Cawley said, but he wasn't Cawley anymore. He was Peter Breene. "She's scared, so she kills her kids and that makes it okay?"

"No. I mean, yes. I don't like you, Peter."

"What're you going to do about it?"

Teddy placed his service revolver to Peter's temple.

"You know how many people I've executed?" Teddy said, and there were tears streaming down his face.

"Well, don't," Peter said. "Please."

Teddy pulled the trigger, saw the bullet come out the other side of

Breene's head, and the three kids had watched the whole thing and they were screaming like crazy now and Peter Breene said, "Dammit," and leaned against the wall, holding his hand over the entrance wound. "In front of the children?"

And they heard her. A shriek that came out of the darkness ahead of them. Her shriek. She was coming. She was up there somewhere in the dark and she was running toward them full tilt and the little girl said, "Help us."

"I'm not your daddy. It's not my place."

"I'm going to call you Daddy."

"Fine," Teddy said with a sigh and took her hand.

They walked the cliffs overlooking the Shutter Island shore and then they wandered into the cemetery and Teddy found a loaf of bread and some peanut butter and jelly and made them sandwiches in the mausoleum and the little girl was so happy, sitting on his lap, eating her sandwich, and Teddy took her out with him into the graveyard and pointed out his father's headstone and his mother's headstone and his own:

EDWARD DANIELS

BAD SAILOR

1920–1957

"Why are you a bad sailor?" the girl asked.

"I don't like water."

"I don't like water, either. That makes us friends."

"I guess it does."

"You're already dead. You got a whatchamacallit."

"A headstone."

"Yeah."

"I guess I am, then. There was no one in my town."

"I'm dead too."

"I know. I'm sorry about that."

"You didn't stop her."

"What could I do? By the time I reached her, she'd already, you know . . ."

"Oh, boy."

"What?"

"Here she comes again."

And there was Rachel walking into the graveyard by the headstone Teddy had knocked over in the storm. She took her time. She was so beautiful, her hair wet and dripping from the rain, and she'd traded in the cleaver for an ax with a long handle and she dragged it beside her and said, "Teddy, come on. They're mine."

"I know. I can't give them to you, though."

"It'll be different this time."

"How?"

"I'm okay now. I know my responsibilities. I got my head right."

Teddy wept. "I love you so much."

"And I love you, baby. I do." She came up and kissed him, really kissed him, her hands on his face and her tongue sliding over his and a low moan traveling up her throat and into his mouth as she kissed him harder and harder and he loved her so much.

"Now give me the girl," she said.

He handed the girl to her and she held the girl in one arm and picked up the ax in the other and said, "I'll be right back. Okay?"

"Sure," Teddy said.

He waved to the girl, knowing she didn't understand. But it was for her own good. He knew that. You had to make tough decisions when you were an adult, decisions children couldn't possibly understand. But you made them for the children. And Teddy kept waving, even though the girl wouldn't wave back as her mother carried her toward the mausoleum and the little girl stared at Teddy, her eyes beyond hope for rescue, resigned to this world, this sacrifice, her mouth still smeared with peanut butter and jelly.

"OH, JESUS!" TEDDY sat up. He was crying. He felt he'd wrenched himself awake, tore his brain into consciousness just to get out of that dream. He could feel it back there in his brain, waiting, its doors wide open. All he had to do was close his eyes and tip his head back toward the pillow and he'd topple right back into it.

"How are you, Marshal?"

He blinked several times into the darkness. "Who's there?"

Cawley turned on a small lamp. It stood beside his chair in the corner of the room. "Sorry. Didn't mean to startle you."

Teddy sat up on the bed. "How long have I been here?"

Cawley gave him a smile of apology. "The pills were a little stronger than I thought. You've been out for four hours."

"Shit." Teddy rubbed his eyes with the heels of his hands.

"You were having nightmares, Marshal. Serious nightmares."

"I'm in a mental institution on an island in a hurricane," Teddy said.

"Touché," Cawley said. "I was here a month before I had a decent night's sleep. Who's Dolores?"

Teddy said, "What?" and swung his legs off the side of the bed.

"You kept saying her name."

"My mouth is dry."

Cawley nodded and turned his body in the chair, lifted a glass of water off the table beside him. He handed it across to Teddy. "A side effect, I'm afraid. Here."

Teddy took the glass and drained it in a few gulps.

"How's the head?"

Teddy remembered why he was in this room in the first place and took a few moments to take stock. Vision clear. No more thumbtacks in his head. Stomach a little queasy, but not too bad. A mild ache in the right side of his head, like a three-day-old bruise, really.

"I'm okay," he said. "Those were some pills."

"We aim to please. So who's Dolores?"

"My wife," Teddy said. "She's dead. And, yes, Doctor, I'm still coming to terms with it. Is that okay?"

"It's perfectly fine, Marshal. And I'm sorry for your loss. She died suddenly?"

Teddy looked at him and laughed.

"What?"

"I'm not really in the mood to be psychoanalyzed, Doc."

Cawley crossed his legs at the ankles and lit a cigarette. "And I'm not trying to fuck with your head, Marshal. Believe it or not. But something happened in that room tonight with Rachel. It wasn't just her. I'd be negligent in my duties as her therapist if I didn't wonder what kind of demons you're carrying around."

"What happened in that room?" Teddy said. "I was playing the part she wanted me to."

Cawley chuckled. "Know thyself, Marshal. Please. If we'd left you two alone, you're telling me we would have come back to find you both fully clothed?"

Teddy said, "I'm an officer of the law, Doctor. Whatever you think you saw in there, you didn't."

Cawley held up a hand. "Fine. As you say."

"As I say," Teddy said.

He sat back and smoked and considered Teddy and smoked some more and Teddy could hear the storm outside, could feel the press of it against the walls, feel it pushing through gaps under the roof, and Cawley remained silent and watchful, and Teddy finally said:

"She died in a fire. I miss her like you . . . If I was underwater, I wouldn't miss oxygen that much." He raised his eyebrows at Cawley. "Satisfied?"

Cawley leaned forward and handed Teddy a cigarette and lit it for him. "I loved a woman once in France," he said. "Don't tell my wife, okay?"

"Sure."

"I loved this woman the way you love . . . well, nothing," he said, a note of surprise in his voice. "You can't compare that kind of love to anything, can you?"

Teddy shook his head.

"It's its own unique gift." Cawley's eyes followed the smoke from his cigarette, his gaze gone out of the room, over the ocean.

"What were you doing in France?"

He smiled, shook a playful finger at Teddy.

"Ah," Teddy said.

"Anyway, this woman was coming to meet me one night. She's hurrying, I guess. It's a rainy night in Paris. She trips. That's it."

"She what?"

"She tripped."

"And?" Teddy stared at him.

"And nothing. She tripped. She fell forward. She hit her head. She died. You believe that? In a war. All the ways you'd think a person could die. She tripped."

Teddy could see the pain in his face, even after all these years, the stunned disbelief at being the butt of a cosmic joke.

"Sometimes," Cawley said quietly, "I make it a whole three hours without thinking of her. Sometimes I go whole weeks without remembering her smell, that look she'd give me when she knew we'd find time to be alone on a given night, her hair—the way she played with it when she was reading. Sometimes . . ." Cawley stubbed out his cigarette. "Wherever her soul went—if there was a portal, say, under her body and it opened up as she died and that's where she went? I'd go back to Paris tomorrow if I knew that portal would open, and I'd climb in after her."

Teddy said, "What was her name?"

"Marie," Cawley said, and the saying of it took something from him.

Teddy took a draw on the cigarette, let the smoke drift lazily back out of his mouth.

"Dolores," he said, "she tossed in her sleep a lot, and her hand, seven times out of ten, I'm not kidding, would flop right into my face. Over my mouth and nose. Just *whack* and there it was. I'd remove it, you know? Sometimes pretty roughly. I'm having a nice sleep and, bang, now I'm awake. Thanks, honey. Sometimes, though, I'd leave it there. Kiss it, smell it, what have you. Breathe her in. If I could have that hand back over my face, Doc? I'd sell the world."

The walls rumbled, the night shook with wind.

Cawley watched Teddy the way you'd watch children on a busy street corner. "I'm pretty good at what I do, Marshal. I'm an egotist, I admit. My IQ is off the charts, and ever since I was a boy, I could read people. Better than anyone. I say what I'm about to say meaning no offense, but have you considered that you're suicidal?"

"Well," Teddy said, "I'm glad you didn't mean to offend me."

"But have you considered it?"

"Yeah," Teddy said. "It's why I don't drink anymore, Doctor."

"Because you know that—"

"—I'd have eaten my gun a long time ago, if I did."

Cawley nodded. "At least you're not deluding yourself."

"Yeah," Teddy said, "at least I got that going for me."

"When you leave here," Cawley said, "I can give you some names. Damn good doctors. They could help you."

Teddy shook his head. "U.S. marshals don't go to head doctors. Sorry. But if it ever leaked, I'd be pensioned out."

"Okay, okay. Fair enough. But, Marshal?"

Teddy looked up at him.

"If you keep steering your current course, it's not a matter of if. It's a matter of when."

"You don't know that."

"Yes. Yes, I do. I specialize in grief trauma and survivor's guilt. I suffer from the same, so I specialize in the same. I saw you look into Rachel Solando's eyes a few hours ago and I saw a man who wants to die. Your boss, the agent in charge at the field office? He told me you're the most decorated man he has. Said you came back from the war with enough medals to fill a chest. True?"

Teddy shrugged.

"Said you were in the Ardennes and part of the liberating force at Dachau."

Another shrug.

"And then your wife is killed? How much violence, Marshal, do you think a man can carry before it breaks him?"

Teddy said, "Don't know, Doc. Kind of wondering, myself."

Cawley leaned across the space between them and clapped Teddy on the knee. "Take those names from me before you leave. Okay? I'd like to be sitting here five years from now, Marshal, and know you're still in the world."

Teddy looked down at the hand on his knee. Looked up at Cawley.

"I would too," he said softly.

13

HE MET BACK up with Chuck in the basement of the men's dormitory, where they'd assembled cots for everyone while they rode out the storm. To get here, Teddy had come through a series of underground corridors that connected all the buildings in the compound. He'd been led by an orderly named Ben, a hulking mountain of jiggling white flesh, through four locked gates and three manned checkpoints, and from down here you couldn't even tell the world stormed above. The corridors were long and gray and dimly lit, and Teddy wasn't all that fond of how similar they were to the corridor in his dream. Not nearly as long, not filled with sudden banks of darkness, but ball-bearing gray and cold just the same.

He felt embarrassed to see Chuck. He'd never had a migraine attack that severe in public before, and it filled him with shame to remember vomiting on the floor. How helpless he'd been, like a baby, needing to be lifted from the chair.

But as Chuck called, "Hey, boss!" from the other side of the room, it surprised him to realize what a relief it was to be reunited with him. He'd asked to go on this investigation alone and been declined. At the time, it had pissed him off, but now, after two days in this place, after the mausoleum and Rachel's breath in his mouth and those fucking dreams, he had to admit he was glad not to be alone on this.

They shook hands and he remembered what Chuck had said to him in the dream—"I'm never getting off this island"—and Teddy felt a sparrow's ghost pass through the center of his chest and flap its wings.

"How you doing, boss?" Chuck clapped his shoulder.

Teddy gave him a sheepish grin. "I'm better. A little shaky, but all in all, okay."

"Fuck," Chuck said, lowering his voice and stepping away from two orderlies smoking cigarettes against a support column. "You had me scared, boss. I thought you were having a heart attack or a stroke or something."

"Just a migraine."

"Just," Chuck said. He lowered his voice even further and they walked to the beige cement wall on the south side of the room, away from the other men. "I thought you were faking it at first, you know, like you had some plan to get to the files or something."

"I wish I was that smart."

He looked in Teddy's eyes, his own glimmering, pushing forward. "It got me thinking, though."

"You didn't."

"I did."

"What'd you do?"

"I told Cawley I'd sit with you. And I did. And after a while, he got a call and he left the office."

"You went after his files?"

Chuck nodded.

"What did you find?"

Chuck's face dropped. "Well, not much actually. I couldn't get into the file cabinets. He had some locks I've never seen before. And I've picked a lot of locks. I could've picked these, but I would have left marks. You know?"

Teddy nodded. "You did the right thing."

"Yeah, well . . ." Chuck nodded at a passing orderly and Teddy had the surreal sensation that they'd been transported into an old Cagney movie, cons on the yard plotting their escape. "I did get into his desk."

"You what?"

Chuck said, "Crazy, huh? You can slap my wrist later."

"Slap your wrist? Give you a medal."

"No medal. I didn't find much, boss. Just his calendar. Here's the thing, though—yesterday, today, tomorrow, and the next day were all blocked off, you know? He bordered them in black."

"The hurricane," Teddy said. "He'd heard it was coming."

Chuck shook his head. "He wrote across the four boxes. You know what I mean? Like you'd write 'Vacation on Cape Cod.' Following me?"

Teddy said, "Sure."

Trey Washington ambled on over to them, a ratty stogie in his mouth, his head and clothes drenched with rain. "Ya'll getting clandestine over here, Marshals?"

"You bet," Chuck said.

"You been out there?" Teddy said.

"Oh, yeah. Brutal now, Marshals. We were sandbagging the whole compound, boarding up all the windows. Shit. Motherfuckers falling all over themselves out there." Trey relit his cigar with a Zippo and turned to Teddy. "You okay, Marshal? Word around the campfire was you had some sort of attack."

"What sort of attack?"

"Oh, now, you'd be here all night, you tried to get every version of the story."

Teddy smiled. "I get migraines. Bad ones."

"Had an aunt used to get 'em something awful. Lock herself up in a bedroom, shut off the light, pull the shades, you wouldn't see her for twenty-four hours."

"She's got my sympathy."

Trey puffed his cigar. "Well, she long dead and all now, but I'll pass it upstairs in my prayers tonight. She was a mean woman anyway, headache or not. Used to beat me and my brother with a hickory stick. Sometimes for nothing. I'd say, 'Auntie, what I do?' She say, 'I don't know, but you *thinking* about doing something terrible.' What you do with a woman like that?"

He truly seemed to be waiting for an answer, so Chuck said, "Run faster."

Trey let out a low "Heh, heh, heh" around his cigar. "Ain't that the truth. Yes, sir." He sighed. "I'm gone go dry off. We'll see you later."

"See you."

The room was filling up with men coming in from the storm, shaking the moisture off black slickers and black forest ranger hats, coughing, smoking, passing around the not-so-secret flasks.

Teddy and Chuck leaned against the beige wall and spoke in flat tones while facing the room.

"So the words on the calendar . . ."

"Yeah."

"Didn't say 'Vacation on Cape Cod.' "

"Nope."

"What'd they say?"

" 'Patient sixty-seven.' "

"That's it?"

"That's it."

"That's enough, though, huh?"

"Oh, yeah. I'd say so."

HE COULDN'T SLEEP. He listened to the men snore and huff and inhale and exhale, some with faint whistles, and he heard some talk in their sleep, heard one say, "You shoulda told me. That's all. Just said the words . . ." Heard another say, "I got popcorn in my throat." Some kicked the sheets and some rolled over and back again and some rose long enough to slap their pillows before dropping back to the mattresses. After a while, the noise achieved a kind of comfortable rhythm that reminded Teddy of a muffled hymn.

The outside was muffled too, but Teddy could hear the storm scrabble along the ground and thump against the foundation, and he wished there were windows down here, if only so he could see the flash of it, the weird light it must be painting on the sky.

He thought of what Cawley had said to him.

It's not a matter of if. It's a matter of when.

Was he suicidal?

He supposed he was. He couldn't remember a day since Dolores's death when he hadn't thought of joining her, and it sometimes went further than that. Sometimes he felt as if continuing to live was an act of cowardice. What was the point of buying groceries, of filling the Chrysler tank, of shaving, putting on socks, standing in yet another line, picking a tie, ironing a shirt, washing his face, combing his hair, cashing a check, renewing his license, reading the paper, taking a piss, eating—alone, always alone—going to a movie, buying a record, paying bills, shaving again, washing again, sleeping again, waking up again . . .

. . . if none of it brought him closer to her?

He knew he was supposed to move on. Recover. Put it behind him. His few stray friends and few stray relatives had said as much, and he knew that if he were on the outside looking in, he would tell that other Teddy to buck up and suck in your gut and get on with the rest of your life.

But to do that, he'd have to find a way to put Dolores on a shelf, to allow her to gather dust in the hope that enough dust would accumulate to soften his memory of her. Mute her image. Until one day she'd be less a person who had lived and more the dream of one.

They say, Get over her, you have to get over her, but get over to what? To this fucking life? How am I going to get you out of my mind? It hasn't worked so far, so how am I supposed to do that? How am I supposed to let you go, that's all I'm asking. I want to hold you again, smell you, and, yes too, I just want you to fade. To please, please fade . . .

He wished he'd never taken those pills. He was wide awake at three in the morning. Wide awake and hearing her voice, the dusk in it, the faint Boston accent that didn't reveal itself on the *a* and *r*, so much as the *e* and *r* so that Dolores loved him in a whispered *foreva and eva*. He smiled in the dark, hearing her, seeing her teeth, her eyelashes, the lazy carnal appetite in her Sunday-morning glances.

That night he'd met her at the Cocoanut Grove. The band playing a big, brassy set and the air gone silver with smoke and everyone dressed to the nines—sailors and soldiers in their best dress whites, dress blues, dress grays, civilian men in explosive floral ties and double-breasted suits with handkerchief triangles pressed smartly into the pockets, sharp-brimmed fedoras propped on the tables, and the women, the women were everywhere. They danced even as they walked to the powder room. They danced moving from table to table and they spun on their toes as they lit cigarettes and snapped open their compacts, glided to the bar and threw back their heads to laugh, and their hair was satin-shiny and caught the light when they moved.

Teddy was there with Frankie Gordon, another sergeant from Intel, and a few other guys, all of them shipping out in a week, but he dumped Frankie the moment he saw her, left him in midsentence and walked down to the dance floor, lost her for a minute in the throng between them, everyone pushing to the sides to make space for a sailor and a blonde in a white dress as the sailor spun her across his back and then shot her above his head in a twirl and caught her coming back down, dipped her toward the floor as the throng broke out in applause and then Teddy caught the flash of her violet dress again.

It was a beautiful dress and the color had been the first thing to catch his eye. But there were a lot of beautiful dresses there that night, too many to count, so it wasn't the dress that held his attention but the way she wore it. Nervously. Self-consciously. Touching it with a hint of apprehension. Adjusting and readjusting it. Palms pressing down on the shoulder pads.

It was borrowed. Or rented. She'd never worn a dress like that before. It terrified her. So much so that she couldn't be sure if men and women looked at her out of lust, envy, or pity.

She'd caught Teddy watching as she fidgeted and pulled her thumb back out from the bra strap. She dropped her eyes, the color rushing up from her throat, and then looked back up and Teddy held her eyes and smiled and thought, I feel stupid in this getup too. Willing that thought across the floor. And maybe it worked, because she smiled back, less a flirtatious smile than a grateful one, and Teddy left Frankie Gordon right there and then, Frankie talking about feed stores in Iowa or something, and by the time he passed through the sweaty siege of dancers, he realized he had nothing to say to her. What was he going to say? Nice dress? Can I buy you a drink? You have beautiful eyes?

She said, "Lost?"

His turn to spin. He found himself looking down at her. She was a small woman, no more than five four in heels. Outrageously pretty. Not in a tidy way, like so many of the other women in there with perfect noses and hair and lips. There was something unkempt about her face, eyes maybe a bit too far apart, lips that were so wide they seemed messy on her small face, a chin that was uncertain.

"A bit," he said.

"Well, what are you looking for?"

He said it before he could think to stop himself: "You."

Her eyes widened and he noticed a flaw, a speckle of bronze, in the left iris, and he felt horror sweep through his body as he realized he'd blown it, come off as a Romeo, too smooth, too full of himself.

You.

Where the fuck did he come up with that one? What the fuck was he—?

"Well," she said . . .

He wanted to run. He couldn't bear to look at her another second.

". . . at least you didn't have to walk far."

He felt a goofy grin break across his face, felt himself reflected in her eyes. A goof. An oaf. Too happy to breathe.

"No, miss, I guess I didn't."

"My God," she said, leaning back to look at him, her martini glass pressed to her upper chest.

"What?"

"You're as out of place here as I am, aren't you, soldier?"

LEANING IN THE cab window as she sat in the back with her friend Linda Cox, Linda hunching forward to give the driver an address, and Teddy said, "Dolores."

"Edward."

He laughed.

"What?"

He held up a hand. "Nothing."

"No. What?"

"No one calls me Edward but my mother."

"Teddy, then."

He loved hearing her say the word.

"Yes."

"Teddy," she said again, trying it out.

"Hey. What's your last name?" he said.

"Chanal."

Teddy cocked an eyebrow at that.

She said, "I know. It doesn't go with the rest of me at all. Sounds so highfalutin."

"Can I call you?"

"You got a head for numbers?"

Teddy smiled. "Actually . . ."

"Winter Hill six-four-three-four-six," she said.

He'd stood on the sidewalk as the cab pulled away, and the memory of her face just an inch from his—through the cab window, on the dance floor—nearly short-circuited his brain, almost drove her name and number right out of there.

He thought: so this is what it feels like to love. No logic to it—he barely knew her. But there it was just the same. He'd just met the woman he'd known, somehow, since before he was born. The measure of every dream he'd never dared indulge.

Dolores. She was thinking of him now in the dark backseat, feeling him as he was feeling her.

Dolores.

Everything he'd ever needed, and now it had a name.

. . .

TEDDY TURNED OVER on his cot and reached down to the floor, searched around until he found his notebook and a box of matches. He lit the first match off his thumb, held it above the page he'd scribbled on in the storm. He went through four matches before he'd ascribed the appropriate letters to the numbers:

18—1—4—9—5—4—19—1—12—4—23—14—5
R—A—D—I—E—D—S—A—L—D—W—N—E

Once that was done, though, it didn't take long to unscramble the code. Another two matches, and Teddy was staring at the name as the flame winnowed its way down the wood toward his fingers:

Andrew Laeddis.

As the match grew hotter, he looked over at Chuck, sleeping two cots over, and he hoped his career wouldn't suffer. It shouldn't. Teddy would take all the blame. Chuck should be fine. He had that aura about him in general—no matter what happened, Chuck would emerge unscathed.

He looked back at the page, got one last glimpse before the match blew itself out.

Going to find you today, Andrew. If I don't owe Dolores my life, I owe her that much, at least.

Going to find you.

Going to kill you dead.

DAY THREE

Patient Sixty-Seven

14

THE TWO HOMES outside the wall—the warden's and Cawley's—
took direct hits. Half of Cawley's roof was gone, the tile flung all over
the hospital grounds like a lesson in humility. A tree had gone through
the warden's living room window, through the plywood nailed there
for protection, roots and all in the middle of his house.

The compound was strewn with shells and tree branches and an
inch and a half of water. Cawley's tile, a few dead rats, scores of soggy
apples, all of it gritty with sand. The foundation of the hospital looked
like someone had taken a jackhammer to it, and Ward A had lost four
windows and several sections of flashing were curled back like pom-
padours on the roof. Two of the staff cottages had been turned into
sticks, and a few others lay on their sides. The nurse and orderly dormitories had lost several windows and suffered some water damage
between them. Ward B had been spared, not a mark on it. All up and
down the island, Teddy could see trees with their tops snapped off, the
naked wood pointing up like spears.

The air was dead again, thick and sullen. The rain fell in a tired, steady drizzle. Dead fish covered the shore. When they'd first come out into the morning, a single flounder lay flapping and puffing in the breezeway, one sad, swollen eye looking back toward the sea.

Teddy and Chuck watched McPherson and a guard rock a jeep off its side. When they turned the ignition, it started on the fifth try, and they roared back out through the gates and Teddy saw them a minute later, racing up the incline behind the hospital toward Ward C.

Cawley walked into the compound, paused to pick up a piece of his roof and stare at it before dropping it back to the watery ground. His gaze swept past Teddy and Chuck twice before he recognized them in their white orderly clothing and their black slickers and black ranger's hats. He gave them an ironic smile and seemed about to approach them when a doctor with a stethoscope around his neck jogged out of the hospital and ran up to him.

"Number two's gone. We can't get it back up. We've got those two criticals. They'll die, John."

"Where's Harry?"

"Harry's working on it, but he can't get a charge. What good's a backup if it doesn't back anything up?"

"All right. Let's get in there."

They strode off into the hospital, and Teddy said, "Their backup generator failed?"

Chuck said, "These things will happen in a hurricane apparently."

"You see any lights?"

Chuck looked around at the windows. "Nope."

"You think the whole electrical system is fried?"

Chuck said, "Good possibility."

"That would mean fences."

Chuck picked up an apple as it floated onto his foot. He went into a windup and kicked his leg and fired it into the wall. "Stee-rike one!" He turned to Teddy. "That would mean fences, yes."

"Probably all electronic security. Gates. Doors."

Chuck said, "Oh, dear God, help us." He picked up another apple, tossed it above his head, and caught it behind his back. "You want to go into that fort, don't you?"

Teddy tilted his face into the soft rain. "Perfect day for it."

The warden made an appearance, driving into the compound with three guards in a jeep, the water churning out from the tires. The warden noticed Chuck and Teddy standing idly in the yard, and it seemed to annoy him. He was taking them for orderlies, Teddy realized, just as Cawley had, and it pissed him off that they didn't have rakes or water pumps in their hands. He drove past, though, his head snapping forward, on to more important things. Teddy realized he had yet to hear the man's voice, and he wondered if it was as black as his hair or as pale as his skin.

"Probably should get going, then," Chuck said. "This won't hold forever."

Teddy started walking toward the gate.

Chuck caught up with him. "I'd whistle, but my mouth's too dry."

"Scared?" Teddy said lightly.

"I believe the term is shit-scared, boss." He rifled the apple into another section of wall.

They approached the gate and the guard there had a little boy's face and cruel eyes. He said, "All orderlies are to report to Mr. Willis in the admin office. You guys are on cleanup detail."

Chuck and Teddy looked at each other's white shirts and pants.

Chuck said, "Eggs Benedict."

Teddy nodded. "Thanks. I was wondering. Lunch?"

"A thinly sliced Reuben."

Teddy turned to the guard, flashed his badge. "Our clothes are still in the laundry."

The guard glanced at Teddy's badge, then looked at Chuck, waiting.

Chuck sighed and removed his wallet, flipped it open under the guard's nose.

The guard said, "What's your business outside the wall? The missing patient was found."

Any explanation, Teddy decided, would make them look weak and place the balance of power firmly in this little shit's hand. Teddy had had a dozen little shits like this in his company during the war. Most of them didn't come home, and Teddy had often wondered if anyone really minded. You couldn't reach this type of asshole, couldn't teach him anything. But you could back him off if you understood that the only thing he respected was power.

Teddy stepped up to the guy, searched his face, a small smile tugging the corner of his lips, waiting until the guy met his eyes and held them.

"We're going on a stroll," Teddy said.

"You don't have authorization."

"Yes, we do." Teddy stepped closer so the boy had to tilt his eyes up. He could smell his breath. "We're federal marshals on a federal facility. That's the authorization of God himself. We don't answer to you. We don't explain to you. We can choose to shoot you in the dick, boy, and there's not a court in the country that would even hear the case." Teddy leaned in another half inch. "So open the fucking gate."

The kid tried to hold Teddy's stare. He swallowed. He tried to harden his eyes.

Teddy said, "I repeat: Open that—"

"Okay."

"I didn't hear you," Teddy said.

"Yes, sir."

Teddy kept the evil eye in the kid's face for another second, exhaled audibly through his nostrils.

"Good enough, son. Hoo-ah."

"Hoo-ah," the kid said reflexively, his Adam's apple bulging.

He turned his key in the lock and swung back the gate, and Teddy walked through without a look back.

They turned right and walked along the outside of the wall for a bit before Chuck said, "Nice touch with the 'hoo-ah.' "

Teddy looked over at him. "I liked that one, myself."

"You were a ballbuster overseas, weren't you?"

"I was a battalion sergeant with a bunch of kids under my command. Half of 'em died without ever getting laid. You don't 'nice' your way to respect, you fucking scare it into 'em."

"Yes, Sergeant. Damn straight." Chuck snapped a salute at him. "Even with the power out, you recall that this is a fort we're trying to infiltrate, don't you?"

"It did not slip my mind, no."

"Any ideas?"

"Nope."

"You think they have a moat? That'd be something."

"Maybe some vats of hot oil up on the battlements."

"Archers," Chuck said. "If they have archers, Teddy . . ."

"And us without our chain mail."

They stepped over a fallen tree, the ground soggy and slick with wet leaves. Through the shredded vegetation ahead of them, they could see the fort, its great gray walls, see the tracks from the jeeps that had been going back and forth all morning.

"That guard had a point," Chuck said.

"How so?"

"Now that Rachel's been found, our authority here—such as it was—is pretty much nonexistent. We get caught, boss, there's no way we'll be able to come up with a logical explanation."

Teddy felt the riot of discarded, shredded green in the back of his eyes. He felt exhausted, a bit hazy. Four hours of drug-induced, nightmare-ridden sleep last night was all he'd had. The drizzle pattered the top of his hat, collected in the brim. His brain buzzed, almost imperceptibly, but constantly. If the ferry came today—and he doubted it would—one part of him wanted to just hop on it and go. Get the fuck off this rock. But without something to show for this trip, whether that was evidence for Senator Hurly or Laeddis's death certificate, he'd be returning a failure. Still borderline-suicidal, but with the added weight to his conscience that he'd done nothing to effect change.

He flipped open his notebook. "Those rock piles Rachel left us yesterday. This is the broken code." He handed the notebook to Chuck.

Chuck cupped a hand around it, kept it close to his chest. "So, he's here."

"He's here."

"Patient sixty-seven, you think?"

"Be my guess."

Teddy stopped by an outcropping in the middle of a muddy slope. "You can go back, Chuck. You don't have to be involved in this."

Chuck looked up at him and flapped the notebook against his hand. "We're marshals, Teddy. What do marshals always do?"

Teddy smiled. "We go through the doors."

"First," Chuck said. "We go through the doors first. We don't wait for some city doughnut cops to back us up if time's a-wasting. We go through that fucking door."

"Yes, we do."

"Well, all right, then," Chuck said and handed the notebook back to him and they continued toward the fort.

. . .

ONE LOOK AT it from up close, nothing separating them but a stand of trees and a short field, and Chuck said what Teddy was thinking:

"We're fucked."

The Cyclone fence that normally surrounded it had been blown out of the ground in sections. Parts of it lay flat on the ground, others had been flung to the far tree line, and the rest sagged in various states of uselessness.

Armed guards roamed the perimeter, though. Several of them did steady circuits in jeeps. A contingent of orderlies picked up the debris around the exterior and another group of them set to work on a thick tree that had downed itself against the wall. There was no moat, but there was only one door, a small red one of dimpled iron set in the center of the wall. Guards stood sentry up on the battlements, rifles held to their shoulders and chests. The few small window squares cut into the stone were barred. There were no patients outside the door, manacled or not. Just guards and orderlies in equal measure.

Teddy saw two of the roof guards step to the side, saw several orderlies step up to the edge of the battlements and call out to those on the ground to stand clear. They wrestled half a tree to the edge of the roof and then pushed and pulled it until it teetered there. Then they disappeared, getting behind it and pushing, and the half-tree rammed forward another couple of feet and then tipped and men shouted as it sped down the wall and then crashed to the ground. The orderlies came back up to the edge of the battlements and looked down at their handiwork and shook hands and clapped shoulders.

"There's got to be a duct of some sort, right?" Chuck said. "Maybe to dump water or waste out into the sea? We could go in that way."

Teddy shook his head. "Why bother? We're just going to walk right in."

"Oh, like Rachel walked out of Ward B? I get it. Take some of that invisible powder she had. Good idea."

Chuck frowned at him and Teddy touched the collar of his rain slicker. "We're not dressed like marshals, Chuck. Know what I mean?"

Chuck looked back at the orderlies working the perimeter and watched one come out through the iron door with a cup of coffee in his hand, the steam rising through the drizzle in small snakes of smoke.

"Amen," he said. "Amen, brother."

THEY SMOKED CIGARETTES and talked gibberish to each other as they walked down the road toward the fort.

Halfway across the field, they were met by a guard, his rifle hanging lazily under his arm and pointed at the ground.

Teddy said, "They sent us over. Something about a tree on the roof?"

The guard looked back over his shoulder. "Nah. They took care of that."

"Oh, great," Chuck said, and they started to turn away.

"Whoa, Trigger," the guard said. "There's still plenty of work to be done."

They turned back.

Teddy said, "You got thirty guys working that wall."

"Yeah, well, the inside's a fucking mess. A storm ain't gonna knock a place like this down, but it's still gonna get inside. You know?"

"Oh, sure," Teddy said.

"WHERE'S THE MOP detail?" Chuck said to the guard lounging against the wall by the door.

He jerked his thumb and opened the door and they passed through into the receiving hall.

"I don't want to appear ungrateful," Chuck said, "but that was too easy."

Teddy said, "Don't overthink it. Sometimes you get lucky."

The door closed behind them.

"Luck," Chuck said, a small vibration in his voice. "That's what we're calling it?"

"That's what we're calling it."

The first thing that hit Teddy was the smells. An aroma of industrial-strength disinfectant doing its level best to disguise the reek of vomit, feces, sweat, and most of all, urine.

Then the noise billowed out from the rear of the building and down from the upper floors: the rumble of running feet, shouts that bounced and echoed off the thick walls and dank air, sudden high-pitched yelps that seized the ear and then died, the pervasive yammering of several different voices all talking at once.

Someone shouted, "You can't! You fucking can't do that! You hear me? You can't. Get away . . . ," and the words trailed off.

Somewhere above them, around the curve of a stone staircase, a man sang "A Hundred Bottles of Beer on the Wall." He'd finished the seventy-seventh bottle and started on the seventy-sixth.

Two canisters of coffee sat up on a card table along with stacks of paper cups and a few bottles of milk. A guard sat at another card table at the base of the staircase, looking at them, smiling.

"First time, huh?"

Teddy looked over at him even as the old sounds were replaced by new ones, the whole place a kind of sonic orgy, yanking the ears in every direction.

"Yeah. Heard stories, but . . ."

"You get used to it," the guard said. "You get used to anything."

"Ain't that the truth."

He said, "If you guys aren't working the roof, you can hang your coats and hats in the room behind me."

"They told us we're on the roof," Teddy said.

"Who'd you piss off?" The guard pointed. "Just follow those stairs. We got most of the bugsies locked down to their beds now, but a few are running free. You see one, you shout, all right? Whatever you do, don't try to restrain him yourself. This ain't Ward A. You know? These fuckers'll kill you. Clear?"

"Clear."

They started up the steps and the guard said, "Wait a minute."

They stopped, looked back down at him.

He was smiling, pointing a finger at them.

They waited.

"I know you guys." His voice had a singsong lilt to it.

Teddy didn't speak. Chuck didn't speak.

"I *know* you guys," the guard repeated.

Teddy managed a "Yeah?"

"Yeah. You're the guys who got stuck with roof detail. In the fucking rain." He laughed and extended the finger and slapped the card table with his other hand.

"That's us," Chuck said. "Ha ha."

"Ha *fucking* ha," the guard said.

Teddy pointed back at him and said, "You got us, pal," and turned up the stairs. "You really got our number."

The idiot's laughter trailed them up the stairs.

At the first landing, they paused. They faced a great hall with an arched ceiling of hammered copper, a dark floor polished to mirror gloss. Teddy knew he could throw a baseball or one of Chuck's apples from the landing and not reach the other side of the room. It was empty and the gate facing them was ajar, and Teddy felt mice scurry along his ribs as he stepped into the room because it reminded him of the room in his dream, the one where Laeddis had offered him a drink and Rachel had slaughtered her children. It was hardly the same room—the one in his dream had had high windows with thick curtains and streams of light and a parquet floor and heavy chandeliers—but it was close enough.

Chuck clapped a hand on his shoulder, and Teddy felt beads of sweat pop out along the side of his neck.

"I repeat," Chuck whispered with a weak smile, "this is too easy. Where's the guard on that gate? Why isn't it locked?"

Teddy could see Rachel, wild-haired and shrieking, as she ran through the room with a cleaver.

"I don't know."

Chuck leaned in and hissed in his ear. "This is a setup, boss."

Teddy began to cross the room. His head hurt from the lack of sleep. From the rain. From the muffled shouting and running feet above him. The two boys and the little girl had held hands, looking over their shoulders. Trembled.

Teddy could hear the singing patient again: ". . . you take one down, pass it around, fifty-four bottles of beer on the wall."

They flashed before his eyes, the two boys and that girl, swimming through the swimming air, and Teddy saw those yellow pills Cawley had placed in his hand last night, felt a slick of nausea eddy in his stomach.

"Fifty-four bottles of beer on the wall, fifty-four bottles of beer . . ."

"We need to go right back out, Teddy. We need to leave. This is bad. You can feel it, I can feel it."

At the other end of the hall, a man jumped into the doorway.

He was barefoot and bare-chested, wearing only a pair of white pajama bottoms. His head was shaved, but the rest of his features were impossible to see in the dim light.

He said, "Hi!"

Teddy walked faster.

The man said, "Tag! You're it!" and bolted from the doorway.

Chuck caught up with Teddy. "Boss, for Christ's sake."

He was in here. Laeddis. Somewhere. Teddy could feel him.

They reached the end of the hall and were met with a wide stone landing and a stairwell that curved down steeply into darkness, another that rose toward the shouting and the chattering, all of it louder now, and Teddy could hear snaps of metal and chains. Heard someone shout, "Billings! All right now, boy! Just calm down! Nowhere to run. Hear?"

Teddy heard someone breathing beside him. He turned his head to the left, and the shaven head was an inch from his own.

"You're it," the guy said and tapped Teddy's arm with his index finger.

Teddy looked into the guy's gleaming face.

"I'm it," Teddy said.

"'Course, I'm so close," the guy said, "you could just flick your wrist and I'd be it again and then I could flick mine and you'd be it and we could go on like that for hours, all day even, we could just stand here turning each other into it, over and over, not even break for lunch, not even break for dinner, we could just go on and on."

"What fun would that be?" Teddy said.

"You know what's out there?" The guy gestured with his head in the direction of the stairs. "In the sea?"

"Fish," Teddy said.

"Fish." The guy nodded. "Very good. Fish, yes. Lots of fish. But, yes, fish, very good, fish, yes, but also, also? Subs. Yeah. That's right. Soviet submarines. Two hundred, three hundred miles off our coast. We hear that, right? We're told. Sure. And we get used to the idea. We forget, really. I mean, 'Okay, there are subs. Thanks for the info.' They become part of our daily existence. We know they're there, but we stop thinking about it. Okay? But there they are and they're armed with rockets. They're pointing them at New York and Washington. At Boston. And they're out there. Just sitting. Does that ever bother you?"

Teddy could hear Chuck beside him taking slow breaths, waiting for his cue.

Teddy said, "Like you said, I choose not to think about it too much."

"Mmm." The guy nodded. He stroked the stubble on his chin. "We hear things in here. You wouldn't think so, right? But we do. A new guy comes in, he tells us things. The guards talk. You orderlies, you talk. We know, we know. About the outside world. About the H-bomb tests, the atolls. You know how a hydrogen bomb works?"

"With hydrogen?" Teddy said.

"Very good. Very clever. Yes, yes." The guy nodded several times. "With hydrogen, yes. But, also, also, not like any other bombs. You drop a bomb, even an atom bomb, it explodes. Right? Right you are. But a hydrogen bomb, it implodes. It falls in on itself and goes through a series of internal breakdowns, collapsing and collapsing. But all that collapsing? It creates mass and density. See, the fury of its own self-destruction creates an entirely new monster. You get it? Do you? The bigger the breakdown, then the bigger the destruction of self, then the more potent it becomes. And then, okay, okay? Fucking *blammo*! Just . . . bang, boom, whoosh. In its absence of self, it spreads. Creates an *ex*plosion off of its *im*plosion that is a hundred times, a thousand times, a million times more devastating than any bomb in history. That's our legacy. And don't you forget it." He tapped Teddy's arm several times, light taps, as if playing a drumbeat with his fingers. "You're it! To the tenth degree. Hee!"

He leapt down the dark stairwell and they heard him shouting "Blammo" all the way down.

". . . forty-nine bottles of beer! You take one down . . ."

Teddy looked over at Chuck. His face was damp, and he exhaled carefully through his mouth.

"You're right," Teddy said. "Let's get out of here."

"Now you're talking."

It came from the top of the stairwell:

"Somebody give me a fucking hand here! Jesus!"

Teddy and Chuck looked up and saw two men coming down the stairs in a ball. One wore guard blues, the other patient whites, and they slammed to a stop at the curve in the staircase on the widest stair. The patient got a hand free and dug it into the guard's face just below his left eye and pulled a flap of skin free, and the guard screamed and wrenched his head back.

Teddy and Chuck ran up the steps. The patient's hand plunged down again, but Chuck grabbed it at the wrist.

The guard wiped at his eye and smeared blood down to his chin. Teddy could hear all four of them take breaths, hear the distant beer-bottle song, that patient on forty-two now, rounding the corner for forty-one, and then he saw the guy below him rear up with his mouth wide open, and he said, "Chuck, watch it," and slammed the heel of his hand into the patient's forehead before he could take a bite out of Chuck's wrist.

"You got to get off him," he said to the guard. "Come on. Get off."

The guard freed himself of the patient's legs and scrambled back up two steps. Teddy came over the patient's body and clamped down hard on his shoulder, pinning it to the stone, and he looked back over his shoulder at Chuck, and the baton sliced between them, cut the air with a hiss and a whistle, and broke the patient's nose.

Teddy felt the body underneath him go slack and Chuck said, "Jesus Christ!"

The guard swung again and Teddy turned on the patient's body and blocked the arm with his elbow.

He looked into his bloody face. "Hey! Hey! He's out cold. Hey!"

The guard could smell his own blood, though. He cocked the baton.

Chuck said, "Look at me! Look at me!"

The guard's eyes jerked to Chuck's face.

"You stand the fuck down. You hear me? You stand *down*. This patient is subdued." Chuck let go of the patient's wrist and his arm flopped to his chest. Chuck sat back against the wall, kept his stare locked on the guard. "Do you hear me?" he said softly.

The guard dropped his eyes and lowered the baton. He touched the wound on his cheekbone with his shirt, looked at the blood on the fabric. "He tore my face open."

Teddy leaned in, took a look at the wound. He'd seen a lot worse; the kid wouldn't die from it or anything. But it was ugly. No doctor would ever be able to sew it back clean.

He said, "You'll be fine. Couple of stitches."

Above them they could hear the crash of several bodies and some furniture.

"You got a riot on your hands?" Chuck said.

The guard chugged air in and out of his mouth until the color returned to his face. "Close to."

"Inmates taken over the asylum?" Chuck said lightly.

The kid looked at Teddy carefully, then over at Chuck. "Not yet."

Chuck pulled a handkerchief from his pocket, handed it to the kid.

The kid nodded his thanks and pressed it to his face.

Chuck lifted the patient's wrist again, and Teddy watched him feel for a pulse. He dropped the wrist and pushed back one of the man's eyelids. He looked at Teddy. "He'll live."

"Let's get him up," Teddy said.

They slung the patient's arms around their shoulders and followed the guard up the steps. He didn't weigh much, but it was a long staircase, and the tops of his feet kept hugging the edges of the risers. When they reached the top, the guard turned, and he looked older, maybe a bit more intelligent.

"You're the marshals," he said.

"What's that?"

He nodded. "You are. I saw you when you arrived." He gave Chuck a small smile. "That scar on your face, you know?"

Chuck sighed.

"What are you doing in here?" the kid said.

"Saving your face," Teddy said.

The kid took the handkerchief from his wound, looked at it, and pressed it back there again.

"Guy you're holding there?" he said. "Paul Vingis. West Virginia. Killed his brother's wife and two daughters while the brother was serving in Korea. Kept them in a basement, you know, pleasuring himself, while they were rotting."

Teddy resisted the urge to step out from under Vingis's arm, let him drop back down the stairs.

"Truth is," the kid said and cleared his throat. "Truth is, he had me." He met their eyes and his own were red.

"What's your name?"

"Baker. Fred Baker."

Teddy shook his hand. "Look, Fred? Hey, we're glad we could help."

The kid looked down at his shoes, the spots of blood there. "Again: what are you doing here?"

"Taking a look around," Teddy said. "A couple of minutes, and we'll be gone."

The kid took some time considering that, and Teddy could feel the previous two years of his life—losing Dolores, honing in on Laeddis, finding out about this place, stumbling across George Noyce and his stories of drug and lobotomy experiments, making contact with Senator Hurly, waiting for the right moment to cross the harbor like they'd waited to cross the English Channel to Normandy—all of it hanging in the balance of this kid's pause.

"You know," the kid said, "I've worked a few rough places. Jails, a max prison, another place was also a hospital for the criminally insane . . ." He looked at the door and his eyes widened as if with a yawn except that his mouth didn't open. "Yeah. Worked some places. But this place?" He gave each of them a long, level gaze. "They wrote their own playbook here."

He stared at Teddy and Teddy tried to read the answer in the kid's eyes, but the stare was of the thousand-yards variety, flat, ancient.

"A couple of minutes?" The kid nodded to himself. "All right. No one'll notice in all this fucking mayhem. You take your couple minutes and then get out, okay?"

"Sure," Chuck said.

"And, hey." The kid gave them a small smile as he reached for the door. "Try not to die in those few minutes, okay? I'd appreciate that."

15

THEY WENT THROUGH the door and entered a cell block of granite walls and granite floors that ran the length of the fort under archways ten feet wide and fourteen feet tall. Tall windows at either end of the floor provided the only light, and the ceiling dripped water and the floors were filled with puddles. The cells stood off to their right and left, buried in the dark.

Baker said, "Our main generator blew at around four this morning. The locks on the cells are controlled electronically. That's one of our more recent innovations. Great fucking idea, huh? So all the cells opened at four. Luckily we can still work those locks manually, so we got most of the patients back inside and locked them in, but some prick has a key. He keeps sneaking in and getting to at least one cell before he takes off again."

Teddy said, "Bald guy, maybe?"

Baker looked over at him. "Bald guy? Yeah. He's one we can't account for. Figured it might be him. His name's Litchfield."

"He's playing tag in that stairwell we just came up. The lower half."

Baker led them to the third cell on the right and opened it. "Toss him in there."

It took them a few seconds to find the bed in the dark and then Baker clicked on a flashlight and shone the beam inside and they lay Vingis on the bed and he moaned and the blood bubbled in his nostrils.

"I need to get some backup and go after Litchfield," Baker said. "The basement's where we keep the guys we don't even feed unless there's six guards in the room. If they get out, it'll be the fucking Alamo in here."

"You get medical assistance first," Chuck said.

Baker found an unstained section of handkerchief and pressed it back over his wound. "Don't got time."

"For *him*," Chuck said.

Baker looked in through the bars at them. "Yeah. All right. I'll find a doctor. And you two? In and out in record time, right?"

"Right. Get the guy a doctor," Chuck said as they left the cell.

Baker locked the cell door. "I'm on it."

He jogged down the cell block, sidestepping three guards dragging a bearded giant toward his cell, kept running.

"What do you think?" Teddy said. Through the archways he could see a man by the far window, hanging up on the bars, some guards dragging in a hose. His eyes were beginning to adjust to what there was of the pewter light in the main corridor, but the cells remained black.

"There has to be a set of files in here somewhere," Chuck said. "If only for basic medical and reference purposes. You look for Laeddis, I look for files?"

"Where do you figure those files are?"

Chuck looked back at the door. "By the sounds of it, it gets less dangerous the higher you go in here. I figure their admin' has gotta be up."

"Okay. Where and when do we meet?"

"Fifteen minutes?"

The guards had gotten the hose working and fired a blast, blew the guy off the bars, pushed him across the floor.

Some men clapped in their cells, others moaned, moans so deep and abandoned they could have come from a battlefield.

"Fifteen sounds right. Meet back in that big hall?"

"Sure."

They shook hands and Chuck's was damp, his upper lip slick.

"You watch your ass, Teddy."

A patient banged through the door behind them and ran past them into the ward. His feet were bare and grimy and he ran like he was training for a prizefight—fluid strides working in tandem with shadow-boxing arms.

"See what I can do." Teddy gave Chuck a smile.

"All right, then."

"All right."

Chuck walked to the door. He paused to look back. Teddy nodded.

Chuck opened the door as two orderlies came through from the stairs. Chuck turned the corner and disappeared, and one of the orderlies said to Teddy, "You see the Great White Hope come through here?"

Teddy looked back through the archway, saw the patient dancing in place on his heels, punching the air with combinations.

Teddy pointed and the three of them fell into step.

"He was a boxer?" Teddy said.

The guy on his left, a tall, older black guy, said, "Oh, you come up from the beach, huh? The vacation wards. Uh-huh. Yeah, well, Willy there, he think he training for a bout at Madison Square with Joe Louis. Thing is, he ain't half bad."

They were nearing the guy, and Teddy watched his fists shred the air.

"It's going to take more than three of us."

The older orderly chuckled. "Won't take but one. I'm his manager. You didn't know?" He called out, "Yo, Willy. Gotta get you a massage, my man. Ain't but an hour till the fight."

"Don't want no massage." Willy started tapping the air with quick jabs.

"Can't have my meal ticket cramping up on me," the orderly said. "Hear?"

"Only cramped-up that time I fought Jersey Joe."

"And look how that turned out."

Willy's arms snapped to his sides. "You got a point."

"Training room, right over here." The orderly swept his arm out to the left with a flourish.

"Just don't touch me. I don't like to be touched before a fight. You know that."

"Oh, I know, killer." He opened up the cell. "Come on now."

Willy walked toward the cell. "You can really hear 'em, you know? The crowd."

"SRO, my man. SRO."

Teddy and the other orderly kept walking, the orderly holding out a brown hand. "I'm Al."

Teddy shook the hand. "Teddy, Al. Nice to meet you."

"Why you all got up for the outside, Teddy?"

Teddy looked at his slicker. "Roof detail. Saw a patient on the stairs, though, chased him in here. Figured you guys could use an extra hand."

A wad of feces hit the floor by Teddy's foot and someone cackled from the dark of a cell and Teddy kept his eyes straight ahead and didn't break stride.

Al said, "You want to stay as close to the middle as possible. Even so, you get hit with just about everything 'least once a week. You see your man?"

Teddy shook his head. "No, I—"

"Aww, shit," Al said.

"What?"

"I see mine."

He was coming right at them, soaking wet, and Teddy saw the guards dropping the hose and giving chase. A small guy with red hair, a face like a swarm of bees, covered in blackheads, red eyes that matched his hair. He broke right at the last second, hitting a hole only he saw as Al's arms swept over his head and the little guy slid on his knees, rolled, and then scrambled up.

Al broke into a run after him and then the guards rushed past Teddy, batons held over their heads, as wet as the man they chased.

Teddy had started to step into the chase, if from nothing else but instinct, when he heard the whisper:

"Laeddis."

He stood in the center of the room, waiting to hear it again. Nothing. The collective moaning, momentarily stopped by the pursuit of the little redhead, began to well up again, starting as a buzz amid the stray rattlings of bedpans.

Teddy thought about those yellow pills again. If Cawley suspected, *really* suspected, that he and Chuck were—

"Laed. Dis."

He turned and faced the three cells to his right. All dark. Teddy waited, knowing the speaker could see him, wondering if it could be Laeddis himself.

"You were supposed to save me."

It came from either the one in the center or the one to the left of it. Not Laeddis's voice. Definitely not. But one that seemed familiar just the same.

Teddy approached the bars in the center. He fished in his pockets. He found a box of matches, pulled it out. He struck the match against the flint strip and it flared and he saw a small sink and a man with sunken ribs kneeling on the bed, writing on the wall. He looked back over his shoulder at Teddy. Not Laeddis. Not anyone he knew.

"Do you mind? I prefer to work in the dark. Thank you oh so much."

Teddy backed away from the bars, turning to his left and noticing that the entire left wall of the man's cell was covered in script, not an inch to spare, thousands of cramped, precise lines of it, the words so small they were unreadable unless you pressed your eyes to the wall.

He crossed to the next cell and the match went out and the voice, close now, said, "You failed me."

Teddy's hand shook as he struck the next match and the wood snapped and broke away against the flint strip.

"You told me I'd be free of this place. You promised."

Teddy struck another match and it flew off into the cell, unlit.

"You lied."

The third match left the flint with a sizzle and the flame flared high over his finger and he held it to the bars and stared in. The man sitting on the bed in the left corner had his head down, his face pressed between his knees, his arms wrapped around his calves. He was bald up the middle, salt-and-pepper on the sides. He was naked except for a pair of white boxer shorts. His bones shook against his flesh.

Teddy licked his lips and the roof of his mouth. He stared over the match and said, "Hello?"

"They took me back. They say I'm theirs."

"I can't see your face."

"They say I'm home now."

"Could you raise your head?"

"They say this is home. I'll never leave."

"Let me see your face."

"Why?"

"Let me see your face."

"You don't recognize my voice? All the conversations we had?"

"Lift your head."

"I used to like to think it became more than strictly professional. That we became friends of a sort. That match is going to go out soon, by the way."

Teddy stared at the swath of bald skin, the trembling limbs.

"I'm telling you, buddy—"

"Telling me what? Telling me what? What can you tell me? More lies, that's what."

"I don't—"

"You are a liar."

"No, I'm not. Raise your—"

The flame burned the tip of his index finger and the side of his thumb and he dropped the match.

The cell vanished. He could hear the bedsprings wheeze, a coarse whisper of fabric against stone, a creaking of bones.

Teddy heard the name again:

"Laeddis."

It came from the right side of the cell this time.

"This was never about the truth."

He pulled two matches free, pressed them together.

"Never."

He struck the match. The bed was empty. He moved his hand to the right and saw the man standing in the corner, his back to him.

"Was it?"

"What?" Teddy said.

"About the truth."

"Yes."

"No."

"This is about the truth. Exposing the—"

"This is about you. And Laeddis. This is all it's ever been about. I was incidental. I was a way in."

The man spun. Walked toward him. His face was pulverized. A swollen mess of purple and black and cherry red. The nose broken and covered in an X of white tape.

"Jesus," Teddy said.

"You like it?"

"Who did this?"

"You did this."

"How the hell could I have—"

George Noyce stepped up to the bars, his lips as thick as bicycle tires and black with sutures. "All your talk. All your fucking talk and I'm back in here. Because of you."

Teddy remembered the last time he'd seen him in the visiting room at the prison. Even with the jailhouse tan, he'd looked healthy, vibrant, most of his dark clouds lifted. He'd told a joke, something about an Italian and a German walking into a bar in El Paso.

"You look at me," George Noyce said. "Don't look away. You never wanted to expose this place."

"George," Teddy said, keeping his voice low, calm, "that's not true."

"It is."

"No. What do you think I've spent the last year of my life planning for? This. Now. Right here."

"Fuck you!"

Teddy could feel the scream hit his face.

"Fuck you!" George yelled again. "You spent the last year of your life planning? Planning to kill. That's all. Kill Laeddis. That's your fucking game. And look where it got *me*. Here. Back here. I can't take here. I can't take this fucking horror house. Do you hear me? Not again, not again, not again."

"George, listen. How did they get to you? There have to be transfer orders. There have to be psychiatric consultations. Files, George. Paperwork."

George laughed. He pressed his face between the bars and jerked his eyebrows up and down. "You want to hear a secret?"

Teddy took a step closer.

George said, "This is good . . ."

"Tell me," Teddy said.

And George spit in his face.

Teddy stepped back and dropped the matches and wiped the phlegm off his forehead with his sleeve.

In the dark, George said, "You know what dear Dr. Cawley's specialty is?"

Teddy ran a palm over his forehead and the bridge of his nose, found it dry. "Survivor guilt, grief trauma."

"Noooo." The word left George's mouth in a dry chuckle. "Violence. In the male of the species, specifically. He's doing a study."

"No. That's Naehring."

"Cawley," George said. "All Cawley. He gets the most violent patients and felons shipped in from all over the country. Why do you think the patient base here is so small? And do you think, do you honestly think that anyone is going to look closely at the transfer paperwork of someone with a history of violence and a history of psychological issues? Do you honestly fucking think that?"

Teddy fired up another two matches.

"I'm never getting out now," Noyce said. "I got away once. Not twice. Never twice."

Teddy said, "Calm down, calm down. How did they get to you?"

"They *knew.* Don't you get it? Everything you were up to. Your whole plan. This is a game. A handsomely mounted stage play. All this"—his arm swept the air above him—"is for you."

Teddy smiled. "They threw in a hurricane just for me, huh? Neat trick."

Noyce was silent.

"Explain that," Teddy said.

"I can't."

"Didn't think so. Let's relax with the paranoia. Okay?"

"Been alone much?" Noyce said, staring through the bars at him.

"What?"

"Alone. Have you ever been alone since this whole thing started?"

Teddy said, "All the time."

George cocked one eyebrow. "*Completely* alone?"

"Well, with my partner."

"And who's your partner?"

Teddy jerked a thumb back up the cell block. "His name's Chuck. He's—"

"Let me guess," Noyce said. "You've never worked with him before, have you?"

Teddy felt the cell block around him. The bones in his upper arms were cold. For a moment he was unable to speak, as if his brain had forgotten how to connect with his tongue.

Then he said, "He's a U.S. marshal from the Seattle—"

"You've *never worked with him before,* have you?"

Teddy said, "That's irrelevant. I know men. I know this guy. I trust him."

"Based on what?"

There was no simple answer for that. How did anyone know where faith developed? One moment, it wasn't there, the next it was. Teddy had known men in war whom he'd trust with his life on a battlefield and yet never with his wallet once they were off it. He'd known men he'd trust with his wallet *and* his wife but never to watch his back in a fight or go through a door with him.

Chuck could have refused to accompany him, could have chosen to stay back in the men's dormitory, sleeping off the storm cleanup, waiting for word of the ferry. Their job was done—Rachel Solando had been found. Chuck had no cause, no vested interest, in following Teddy on his search for Laeddis, his quest to prove Ashecliffe was a mockery of the Hippocratic oath. And yet he was here.

"I trust him," Teddy repeated. "That's the only way I know how to put it."

Noyce looked at him sadly through the steel tubing. "Then they've already won."

Teddy shook the matches out and dropped them. He pushed open the cardboard box and found the last match. He heard Noyce, still at the bars, sniffing the air.

"Please," he whispered, and Teddy knew he was weeping. "Please."

"What?"

"Please don't let me die here."

"You won't die here."

"They're going to take me to the lighthouse. You know that."

"The lighthouse?"

"They're going to cut out my brain."

Teddy lit the match, saw in the sudden flare that Noyce gripped the bars and shook, the tears falling from his swollen eyes and down his swollen face.

"They're not going to—"

"You go there. You see that place. And if you come back alive, you tell me what they do there. See it for yourself."

"I'll go, George. I'll do it. I'm going to get you out of here."

Noyce lowered his head and pressed his bare scalp to the bars and wept silently, and Teddy remembered that last time they'd met in the visitors' room and George had said, "If I ever had to go back to that place, I'd kill myself," and Teddy had said, "That's not going to happen."

A lie apparently.

Because here Noyce was. Beaten, broken, shaking with fear.

"George, look at me."

Noyce raised his head.

"I'm going to get you out of here. You hold on. Don't do anything you can't come back from. You hear me? You hold on. I will come back for you."

George Noyce smiled through the stream of tears and shook his head very slowly. "You can't kill Laeddis and expose the truth at the same time. You have to make a choice. You understand that, don't you?"

"Where is he?"

"Tell me you understand."

"I understand. Where is he?"

"You have to choose."

"I won't kill anyone. George? I won't."

And looking through the bars at Noyce, he felt this to be true. If that's what it took to get this poor wreck, this terrible victim, home, then Teddy would bury his vendetta. Not extinguish it. Save it for another time. And hope Dolores understood.

"I won't kill anyone," he repeated.

"Liar."

"No."

"She's dead. Let her go."

He pressed his smiling, weeping face between the bars and held Teddy with his soft swollen eyes.

Teddy felt her in him, pressed at the base of his throat. He could see her sitting in the early July haze, in that dark orange light a city gets on summer nights just after sundown, looking up as he pulled to the curb and the kids returned to their stickball game in the middle of the street, and the laundry flapped overhead, and she watched him approach with her chin propped on the heel of her hand and the cigarette held up by her ear, and he'd brought flowers for once, and she was so simply his love, his girl, watching him approach as if she were memorizing him and his walk and those flowers and this moment, and he wanted to ask her what sound a heart made when it broke from pleasure, when just the sight of someone filled you the way food, blood, and air never could, when you felt as if you'd been born for only one moment, and this, for whatever reason, was it.

Let her go, Noyce had said.

"I can't," Teddy said, and the words came out cracked and too high and he could feel screams welling in the center of his chest.

Noyce leaned back as far as he could and still maintain his grip on the bars and he cocked his head so that the ear rested on his shoulder.

"Then you'll never leave this island."

Teddy said nothing.

And Noyce sighed as if what he was about to say bored him to the point of falling asleep on his feet. "He was transferred out of Ward C. If he's not in Ward A, there's only one place he can be."

He waited until Teddy got it.

"The lighthouse," Teddy said.

Noyce nodded, and the final match went out.

For a full minute Teddy stood there, staring into the dark, and then he heard the bedsprings again as Noyce lay down.

He turned to go.

"Hey."

He stopped, his back to the bars, and waited.

"God help you."

16

TURNING TO WALK back through the cell block, he found Al waiting for him. He stood in the center of the granite corridor and fixed
Teddy in a lazy gaze and Teddy said, "You get your guy?"

Al fell into step beside him. "Sure did. Slippery bastard, but in
here there's only so far you can go before you run out of room."

They walked up the cell block, keeping to the center, and Teddy
could hear Noyce asking if he'd ever been alone here. How long, he
wondered, had Al been watching him? He thought back through his
three days here, tried to find a single instance in which he'd been
entirely alone. Even using the bathroom, he was using staff facilities, a
man at the next stall or waiting just outside the door.

But, no, he and Chuck had gone out on the island alone several
times . . .

He and Chuck.

What exactly did he know about Chuck? He pictured his face for a
moment, could see him on the ferry, looking off at the ocean . . .

Great guy, instantly likeable, had a natural ease with people, the kind of guy you wanted to be around. From Seattle. Recently transferred. Hell of a poker player. Hated his father—the one thing that didn't seem to jibe with the rest of him. There was something else off too, something buried in the back of Teddy's brain, something . . . What was it?

Awkward. That was the word. But, no, there was nothing awkward about Chuck. He was smooth incarnate. Slick as shit through a goose, to use an expression Teddy's father had been fond of. No, there was nothing remotely awkward about the man. But wasn't there? Hadn't there been one blip in time when Chuck had been clumsy in his movements? Yes. Teddy was sure the moment had happened. But he couldn't remember the specifics. Not right now. Not here.

And, anyway, the whole idea was ridiculous. He trusted Chuck. Chuck had broken into Cawley's desk, after all.

Did you see him do it?

Chuck, right now, was risking his career to get to Laeddis's file.

How do you know?

They'd reached the door and Al said, "Just go back to the stairwell and follow those steps up. You'll find the roof easy enough."

"Thanks."

Teddy waited, not opening the door just yet, wanting to see how long Al would hang around.

But Al just nodded and walked back into the cell block and Teddy felt vindicated. Of course they weren't watching him. As far as Al knew, Teddy was just another orderly. Noyce was paranoid. Understandably so—who wouldn't be in Noyce's shoes?—but paranoid, just the same.

Al kept walking and Teddy turned the knob of the door and opened it, and there were no orderlies or guards waiting on the landing. He was alone. Completely alone. Unwatched. And he let the door close behind him and turned to go down the stairs and saw Chuck standing at the curve where they'd run into Baker and Vingis. He pinched his cigarette and took hard, quick hits off it and looked up at Teddy as he came down the steps, and turned and started moving fast.

"I thought we were meeting in the hall."

"They're here," Chuck said as Teddy caught up to him and they turned into the vast hall.

"Who?"

"The warden and Cawley. Just keep moving. We gotta fly."

"They see you?"

"I don't know. I was coming out of the records room two floors up. I see them down the other end of the hall. Cawley's head turns and I go right through the exit door into the stairwell."

"So, they probably didn't give it a second thought."

Chuck was practically jogging. "An orderly in a rain slicker and a ranger's hat coming out of the records room on the admin' floor? Oh, I'm sure we're fine."

The lights went on above them in a series of liquid cracks that sounded like bones breaking underwater. Electric charges hummed in the air and were followed by an explosion of yells and catcalls and wailing. The building seemed to rise up around them for a moment and then settle back down again. Alarm bells pealed throughout the stone floors and walls.

"Power's back. How nice," Chuck said and turned into the stairwell.

They went down the stairs as four guards came running up, and they shouldered the wall to let them pass.

The guard at the card table was still there, on the phone, looking up with slightly glazed eyes as they descended, and then his eyes cleared and he said "Wait a sec" into the phone, and then to them as they cleared the last step, "Hey, you two, hold on a minute."

A crowd was milling around in the foyer—orderlies, guards, two manacled patients splattered in mud—and Teddy and Chuck moved right into them, sidestepped a guy backing up from the coffee table, swinging his cup carelessly toward Chuck's chest.

And the guard said, "Hey! You two! Hey!"

They didn't break stride and Teddy saw faces looking around, just now hearing the guard's voice, wondering who he was calling to.

Another second or two, those same faces would hone in on him and Chuck.

"I said, 'Hold up!' "

Teddy hit the door chest high with his hand.

It didn't budge.

"Hey!"

He noticed the brass knob, another pineapple like the one in Cawley's house, and he gripped it, found it slick with rain.

"I need to talk to you!"

Teddy turned the knob and pushed the door open and two guards were coming up the steps. Teddy pivoted and held the door open as Chuck passed through and the guard on the left gave him a nod of thanks. He and his partner passed through and Teddy let go of the door and they walked down the steps.

He saw a group of identically dressed men to their left, standing around smoking cigarettes and drinking coffee in the faint drizzle, a few of them leaning back against the wall, everyone joking, blowing smoke hard into the air, and he and Chuck crossed the distance to them, never looking back, waiting for the sound of the door opening behind them, a fresh round of calls.

"You find Laeddis?" Chuck said.

"Nope. Found Noyce, though."

"What?"

"You heard me."

They nodded at the group as they reached them. Smiles and waves and Teddy got a light off one of the guys and then they kept walking down the wall, kept walking as the wall seemed to stretch a quarter mile, kept walking as what could have been shouts in their direction hit the air, kept walking seeing the rifle shafts peeking over the battlements fifty feet above them.

They reached the end of the wall and turned left into a soggy green field and saw that sections of the fence had been replaced there, groups of men filling the post holes with liquid cement, and they could see it stretching all the way around back, and they knew there was no way out there.

They turned back and came out past the wall, into the open, and Teddy knew the only way was straight ahead. Too many eyes would notice if they went in any other direction but past the guards.

"We're going to gut it out, aren't we, boss?"

"Damn straight."

Teddy removed his hat and Chuck followed suit and then their slickers came off and they draped them over their arms and walked in the specks of rain. The same guard was waiting for them, and Teddy said to Chuck, "Let's not even slow down."

"Deal."

Teddy tried to read the guy's face. It was dead flat and he wondered whether it was impassive from boredom or because he was steeling himself for conflict.

Teddy waved as he passed, and the guard said, "They got trucks now."

They kept going, Teddy turning and walking backward as he said, "Trucks?"

"Yeah, to take you guys back. You want to wait, one just left about five minutes ago. Should be back anytime."

"Nah. Need the exercise."

For a moment, something flickered in the guard's face. Maybe it was just Teddy's imagination or maybe the guard knew a whiff of bullshit when he smelled it.

"Take care now." Teddy turned his back, and he and Chuck walked toward the trees and he could feel the guard watching, could feel the whole fort watching. Maybe Cawley and the warden were on the front steps right now or up on the roof. Watching.

They reached the trees and no one shouted, no one fired a warning shot, and then they went deeper and vanished in the stand of thick trunks and disrupted leaves.

"Jesus," Chuck said. "Jesus, Jesus, Jesus."

Teddy sat down on a boulder and felt the sweat saturating his body, soaking his white shirt and pants, and he felt exhilarated. His heart still thumped, and his eyes itched, and the back of his shoulders and neck tingled, and he knew this was, outside of love, the greatest feeling in the world.

To have escaped.

He looked at Chuck and held his eyes until they both started laughing.

"I turned that corner and saw that fence back in place," Chuck said, "and oh *shit,* Teddy, I thought that was it."

Teddy lay back against the rock, feeling free in a way he'd only felt as a child. He watched the sky begin to appear behind smoky clouds and he felt the air on his skin. He could smell wet leaves and wet soil and wet bark and hear the last faint ticking of the rain. He wanted to close his eyes and wake back up on the other side of the harbor, in Boston, in his bed.

He almost nodded off, and that reminded him of how tired he was, and he sat up and fished a cigarette from his shirt pocket and bummed a light off Chuck. He leaned forward on his knees and said, "We have to assume, from this point, that they'll find out we were inside. That's if they don't know already."

Chuck nodded. "Baker, for sure, will fold under questioning."

"That guard by the stairs, he was tipped to us, I think."

"Or he just wanted us to sign out."

"Either way, we'll be remembered."

The foghorn of Boston Light moaned across the harbor, a sound Teddy had heard every night of his childhood in Hull. The loneliest sound he knew. Made you want to hold something, a person, a pillow, yourself.

"Noyce," Chuck said.

"Yeah."

"He's really here."

"In the flesh."

Chuck said, "For Christ's sake, Teddy, how?"

And Teddy told him about Noyce, about the beating he'd taken, about his animosity toward Teddy, his fear, his shaking limbs, his weeping. He told Chuck everything except what Noyce had suggested about Chuck. And Chuck listened, nodding occasionally, watching Teddy the way a child watches a camp counselor around the fire as the late-night boogeyman story unfolds.

And what was all this, Teddy was beginning to wonder, if not that?

When he was done, Chuck said, "You believe him?"

"I believe he's here. No doubt about that."

"He could have had a psychological break, though. I mean, an actual one. He does have the history. This could all be legitimate. He cracks up in prison and they say, 'Hey, this guy was once a patient at Ashecliffe. Let's send him back.' "

"It's possible," Teddy said. "But the last time I saw him, he looked pretty damn sane to me."

"When was that?"

"A month ago."

"Lot can change in a month."

"True."

"And what about the lighthouse?" Chuck said. "You believe there's a bunch of mad scientists in there, implanting antennas into Laeddis's skull as we speak?"

"I don't think they fence off a septic processing plant."

"I'll grant you," Chuck said. "But it's all a bit Grand Guignol, don't you think?"

Teddy frowned. "I don't know what the fuck that means."

"Horrific," Chuck said. "In a fairy-tale, *boo-ga-boo-ga-boo-ga* kind of way."

"I understand that," Teddy said. "What was the gran-gweeg-what?"

"Grand Guignol," Chuck said. "It's French. Forgive me."

Teddy watched Chuck trying to smile his way through it, probably thinking of a way to change the subject.

Teddy said, "You study a lot of French growing up in Portland?"

"Seattle."

"Right." Teddy placed a palm to his chest. "Forgive *me*."

"I like the theater, okay?" Chuck said. "It's a theatrical term."

"You know, I knew a guy worked the Seattle office," Teddy said.

"Really?" Chuck patted his pockets, distracted.

"Yeah. You probably knew him too."

"Probably," Chuck said. "You want to see what I got from the Laeddis file?"

"His name was Joe. Joe . . ." Teddy snapped his fingers, looked at Chuck. "Help me out here. It's on the tip of my tongue. Joe, um, Joe . . ."

"There's a lot of Joes," Chuck said, reaching around to his back pocket.

"I thought it was a small office."

"Here it is." Chuck's hand jerked up from his back pocket and his hand was empty.

Teddy could see the folded square of paper that had slipped from his grasp still sticking out of the pocket.

"Joe Fairfield," Teddy said, back at the way Chuck's hand had jerked out of that pocket. Awkwardly. "You know him?"

Chuck reached back again. "No."

"I'm sure he transferred there."

Chuck shrugged. "Name doesn't ring a bell."

"Oh, maybe it was Portland. I get them mixed up."

"Yeah, I've noticed."

Chuck pulled the paper free and Teddy could see him the day of their arrival handing over his gun to the guard in a fumble of motion, having trouble with the holster snap. Not something your average marshal had trouble with. Kind of thing, in point of fact, that got you killed on the job.

Chuck held out the piece of paper. "It's his intake form. Laeddis's. That and his medical records were all I could find. No incident reports, no session notes, no picture. It was weird."

"Weird," Teddy said. "Sure."

Chuck's hand was still extended, the piece of folded paper drooping off his fingers.

"Take it," Chuck said.

"Nah," Teddy said. "You hold on to it."

"You don't want to see it?"

Teddy said, "I'll look at it later."

He looked at his partner. He let the silence grow.

"What?" Chuck said finally. "I don't know who Joe Whoever-the-Fuck is, so now you're looking at me funny?"

"I'm not looking at you funny, Chuck. Like I said, I get Portland and Seattle mixed up a lot."

"Right. So then—"

"Let's keep walking," Teddy said.

Teddy stood. Chuck sat there for a few seconds, looking at the piece of paper still dangling from his hand. He looked at the trees around them. He looked up at Teddy. He looked off toward the shore.

The foghorn sounded again.

Chuck stood and returned the piece of paper to his back pocket.

He said, "Okay." He said, "Fine." He said, "By all means, lead the way."

Teddy started walking east through the woods.

"Where you going?" Chuck said. "Ashecliffe's the other way."

Teddy looked back at him. "I'm not going to Ashecliffe."

Chuck looked annoyed, maybe even frightened. "Then where the fuck are we going, Teddy?"

Teddy smiled.

"The lighthouse, Chuck."

"WHERE ARE WE?" Chuck said.

"Lost."

They'd come out of the woods and instead of facing the fence around the lighthouse, they'd somehow managed to move well north of it. The woods had been turned into a bayou by the storm, and they'd been forced off a straight path by a number of downed or leaning trees. Teddy had known they'd be off course by a bit, but judging by his latest calculations, they'd meandered their way almost as far as the cemetery.

He could see the lighthouse just fine. Its upper third peeked out from behind a long rise and another notch of trees and a brown and green swath of vegetation. Directly beyond the patch of field where they stood was a long tidal marsh, and beyond that, jagged black rocks formed a natural barrier to the slope, and Teddy knew that the one approach left them was to go back through the woods and hope to find the place where they'd taken the wrong turn without having to return all the way to their point of origin.

He said as much to Chuck.

Chuck used a stick to swipe at his pant legs, free them of burrs. "Or we could loop around, come at it from the east. Remember with McPherson last night? That driver was using a *semblance* of an access road. That's got to be the cemetery over that hill there. We work our way around?"

"Better than what we just came through."

"Oh, you didn't like that?" Chuck ran a palm across the back of his neck. "Me, I love mosquitoes. Fact, I think I have one or two spots left on my face that they didn't get to."

It was the first conversation they'd had in over an hour, and Teddy could feel both of them trying to reach past the bubble of tension that had grown between them.

But the moment passed when Teddy remained silent too long and Chuck set off along the edge of the field, moving more or less northwest, the island at all times pushing them toward its shores.

Teddy watched Chuck's back as they walked and climbed and walked some more. His partner, he'd told Noyce. He trusted him, he said. But why? Because he'd had to. Because no man could be expected to go up against this alone.

If he disappeared, if he never returned from this island, Senator Hurly was a good friend to have. No question. His inquiries would be noted. They'd be heard. But in the current political climate, would the voice of a relatively unknown Democrat from a small New England state be loud enough?

The marshals took care of their own. They'd certainly send men. But the question was one of time—Would they get there before Ashecliffe and its doctors had altered Teddy irreparably, turned him into Noyce? Or worse, the guy who played tag?

Teddy hoped so, because the more he found himself looking at Chuck's back, the more certain he grew that he was now alone on this. Completely alone.

"MORE ROCKS," Chuck said. "Jesus, boss."

They were on a narrow promontory with the sea a straight drop down on their right and an acre of scrub plain below them to the left, the wind picking up as the sky turned red brown and the air tasted of salt.

The rock piles were spaced out in the scrub plain. Nine of them in three rows, protected on all sides by slopes that cupped the plain in a bowl.

Teddy said, "What, we ignore it?"

Chuck raised a hand to the sky. "We're going to lose the sun in a couple hours. We're not at the lighthouse, in case you haven't noticed. We're not even at the cemetery. We're not even sure we can get there from here. And you want to climb all the way down there and look at rocks."

"Hey, if it's code . . ."

"What does it matter by this point? We have proof that Laeddis is here. You saw Noyce. All we have to do is head back home with that information, that proof. And we've done your job."

He was right. Teddy knew that.

Right, however, only if they were still working on the same side.

If they weren't, and this was a code Chuck didn't want him to see . . .

"Ten minutes down, ten minutes to get back up," Teddy said.

Chuck sat down wearily on the dark rockface, pulled a cigarette from his jacket. "Fine. But I'm sitting this one out."

"Suit yourself."

Chuck cupped his hands around the cigarette as he got it going. "That's the plan."

Teddy watched the smoke flow out through his curved fingers and drift out over the sea.

"See you," Teddy said.

Chuck's back was to him. "Try not to break your neck."

Teddy made it down in seven minutes, three less than his estimate, because the ground was loose and sandy and he'd slid several times. He wished he'd had more than coffee this morning because his stomach was yowling from its own emptiness, and the lack of sugar in his blood combined with lack of sleep had produced eddies in his head, stray, floating specks in front of his eyes.

He counted the rocks in each pile and wrote them in his notebook with their alphabetical assignations beside them:

13(M)-21(U)-25(Y)-18(R)-1(A)-5(E)-8(H)-15(O)-9(I)

He closed the notebook, placed it in his front pocket, and began the climb back up the sandy slope, clawing his way through the steepest part, taking whole clumps of sea grass with him when he slipped and slid. It took him twenty-five minutes to get back up and the sky had turned a dark bronze and he knew that Chuck had been right, whatever side he was on: they were losing the day fast and this had been a waste of time, whatever the code turned out to be.

They probably couldn't reach the lighthouse now, and if they could, what then? If Chuck was working with them, then Teddy going with him to the lighthouse was like a bird flying toward a mirror.

Teddy saw the top of the hill and the jutting edge of the promontory and the bronze sky arched above it all and he thought, This may have to be it, Dolores. This may be the best I can offer for now. Laeddis will live. Ashecliffe will go on. But we'll content ourselves knowing we've begun a process, a process that could, ultimately, bring the whole thing tumbling down.

He found a cut at the top of the hill, a narrow opening where it met the promontory and enough erosion had occurred for Teddy to stand in the cut with his back against the sandy wall and get both hands on the flat rock above and push himself up just enough so that he could flop his chest onto the promontory and swing his legs over after him.

He lay on his side, looking out at the sea. So blue at this time of day, so vibrant as the afternoon died around it. He lay there feeling the breeze on his face and the sea spreading out forever under the darkening sky and he felt so small, so utterly human, but it wasn't a debilitating feeling. It was an oddly proud one. To be a part of this. A speck, yes. But part of it, one with it. Breathing.

He looked across the dark flat stone, one cheek pressed to it, and only then did it occur to him that Chuck wasn't up there with him.

17

CHUCK'S BODY LAY at the bottom of the cliff, the water lapping over him.

Teddy slid over the lip of the promontory legs first, searched the black rocks with the soles of his shoes until he was almost sure they'd take his weight. He let out a breath he hadn't even known he'd been holding and slid his elbows off the lip and felt his feet sink into the rocks, felt one shift and his right ankle bend to the left with it, and he slapped at the cliff face and leaned the weight of his upper body back against it, and the rocks beneath his feet held.

He turned his body around and lowered himself until he was pressed like a crab to the rocks, and he began to climb down. There was no fast way to do it. Some rocks were wedged hard into the cliff, as secure as bolts in a battleship hull. Others weren't held there by anything but the ones below them, and you couldn't tell which were which until you placed your weight on one.

After about ten minutes, he saw one of Chuck's Luckies, half smoked, the coal gone black and pointed like the tip of a carpenter's pencil.

What had caused the fall? The breeze had picked up, but it wasn't strong enough to knock a man off a flat ledge.

Teddy thought of Chuck, up there, alone, smoking his cigarette in the last minute of his life, and he thought of all the others he'd cared for who had died while he was asked to soldier on. Dolores, of course. And his father, somewhere on the floor of this same sea. His mother, when he was sixteen. Tootie Vicelli, shot through the teeth in Sicily, smiling curiously at Teddy as if he'd swallowed something whose taste surprised him, the blood trickling out of the corners of his mouth. Martin Phelan, Jason Hill, that big Polish machine gunner from Pittsburgh—what was his name?—Yardak. That was it. Yardak Gilibiowski. The blond kid who'd made them laugh in Belgium. Shot in the leg, seemed like nothing until it wouldn't stop bleeding. And Frankie Gordon, of course, who he'd left in the Cocoanut Grove that night. Two years later, Teddy'd flicked a cigarette off Frankie's helmet and called him a shitbird Iowan asshole and Frankie said, "You curse better than any man I've—" and stepped on a mine. Teddy still had a piece of the shrapnel in his left calf.

And now Chuck.

Would Teddy ever know if he should have trusted him? If he should've given him that last benefit of the doubt? Chuck, who'd made him laugh and made the whole cranial assault of the last three days so much easier to bear. Chuck, who just this morning had said they'd be serving eggs Benedict for breakfast and a thinly sliced Reuben for lunch.

Teddy looked back up at the promontory lip. By his estimation, he was now about halfway down and the sky was the dark blue of the sea and getting darker every second.

What could have pitched Chuck off that ledge?

Nothing natural.

Unless he'd dropped something. Unless he'd followed something down. Unless, like Teddy now, he'd tried to work his way down the cliff, grasping and toeing stones that might not hold.

Teddy paused for breath, the sweat dripping off his face. He removed one hand gingerly from the cliff and wiped it on his pants until it was dry. He returned it, got a grip, and did the same thing with the other hand, and as he placed that hand back over a pointed shard of rock, he saw the piece of paper beside him.

It was wedged between a rock and a brown tendril of roots and it flapped lightly in the sea air. Teddy took his hand from the black shard and pinched it between his fingers and he didn't have to unfold it to know what it was.

Laeddis's intake form.

He slid it into his back pocket, remembering the way it had nestled unsteadily in Chuck's back pocket, and he knew now why Chuck had come down here.

For this piece of paper.

For Teddy.

THE LAST TWENTY feet of cliff face was comprised of boulders, giant black eggs covered in kelp, and Teddy turned when he reached them, turned so that his arms were behind him and the heels of his hands supported his weight, and worked his way across to them and down them and saw rats hiding in their crevices.

When he reached the last of them, he was at the shore, and he spied Chuck's body and walked over to it and realized it wasn't a body at all. Just another rock, bleached white by the sun, and covered in thick black ropes of seaweed.

Thank . . . something. Chuck was not dead. He was not this long narrow rock covered in seaweed.

Teddy cupped his hands around his mouth and called Chuck's name back up the cliff. Called and called it and heard it ride out to sea and bounce off the rocks and carry on the breeze, and he waited to see Chuck's head peek over the promontory.

Maybe he'd been preparing to come down to look for Teddy. Maybe he was up there right now, getting ready.

Teddy shouted his name until his throat scratched with it.

Then he stopped and waited to hear Chuck call back to him. It was growing too dark to see up to the top of that cliff. Teddy heard the breeze. He heard the rats in the crevices of the boulders. He heard a gull caw. The ocean lap. A few minutes later, he heard the foghorn from Boston Light again.

His vision adjusted to the dark and he saw eyes watching him. Dozens of them. The rats lounged on the boulders and stared at him, unafraid. This was their beach at night, not his.

Teddy was afraid of water, though. Not rats. Fuck the little slimy bastards. He could shoot them. See how many of them hung tough once a few of their friends exploded.

Except that he didn't have a gun and they'd doubled in number while he watched. Long tails sweeping back and forth over the stone. Teddy felt the water against his heels and he felt all those eyes on his body and, fear or no fear, he was starting to feel a tingling in his spine, an itching sensation in his ankles.

He started walking slowly along the shore and he saw that there were hundreds of them, taking to the rocks in the moonlight like seals to the sun. He watched as they plopped off the boulders onto the sand where he'd been standing only moments before, and he turned his head, looked at what was left of his stretch of beachfront.

Not much. Another cliff jutted out into the water about thirty yards ahead, effectively cutting off the shore, and to the right of it, out in the ocean, Teddy saw an island he hadn't even known was there. It lay under the moonlight like a bar of brown soap, and its grip on the sea seemed tenuous. He'd been up on those cliffs that first day with McPherson. There'd been no island out there. He was sure of it.

So where the hell did it come from?

He could hear them now, a few of them fighting, but mostly they clicked their nails over the rocks and squeaked at one another, and Teddy felt the itch in his ankles spread to his knees and inner thighs.

He looked back down the beach and the sand had disappeared under them.

He looked up the cliff, thankful for the moon, which was near full, and the stars, which were bright and countless. And then he saw a color that didn't make any more sense than the island that hadn't been there two days ago.

It was orange. Midway up the larger cliff. Orange. In a black cliff face. At dusk.

Teddy stared at it and watched as it flickered, as it subsided and then flared and subsided and flared. Pulsed, really.

Like flame.

A cave, he realized. Or at least a sizeable crevice. And someone was in there. Chuck. It had to be. Maybe he had chased that paper down off the promontory. Maybe he'd gotten hurt and had ended up working his way across instead of down.

Teddy took off his ranger cap and approached the nearest boulder. A half-dozen pairs of eyes considered him and Teddy whacked at them with the hat and they jerked and twisted and flung their nasty bodies off the boulder and Teddy stepped up there fast and kicked at a few on the next boulder and they went over the side and he ran up the boulders then, jumping from one to the next, a few less rats every time, until there were none waiting for him on the last few black eggs, and then he was climbing the cliff face, his hands still bleeding from the descent.

This was the easier climb, though. It was higher and far wider than the first, but it had noticeable grades to it and more outcroppings.

It took him an hour and a half in the moonlight, and he climbed with the stars studying him much the way the rats had, and he lost Dolores as he climbed, couldn't picture her, couldn't see her face or her hands or her too-wide lips. He felt her gone from him as he'd never felt since she died, and he knew it was all the physical exertion and lack of sleep and lack of food, but she was gone. Gone as he climbed under the moon.

But he could hear her. Even as he couldn't picture her, he could hear her in his brain and she was saying, Go on, Teddy. Go on. You can live again.

Was that all there was to it? After these two years of walking underwater, of staring at his gun on the end table in the living room as he sat in the dark listening to Tommy Dorsey and Duke Ellington, of being certain that he couldn't possibly take one more step into this fucking shithole of a life, of missing her so completely he'd once snapped off the end of an incisor gritting his teeth against the need for her—after all that, could this honestly be the moment when he put her away?

I didn't dream you, Dolores. I know that. But, at this moment, it feels like I did.

And it should, Teddy. It should. Let me go.

Yeah?

Yeah, baby.

I'll try. Okay?

Okay.

Teddy could see the orange light flickering above him. He could feel the heat, just barely, but unmistakably. He placed his hand on the ledge above him, and saw the orange reflect off his wrist and he pulled himself up and onto the ledge and pulled himself forward on his elbows and saw the light reflecting off the craggy walls. He stood. The roof of the cave was just an inch above his head and he saw that the opening curved to the right and he followed it around and saw that the light came from a pile of wood in a small hole dug into the cave floor and a woman stood on the other side of the fire with her hands behind her back and said, "Who are you?"

"Teddy Daniels."

The woman had long hair and wore a patient's light pink shirt and drawstring pants and slippers.

"That's your name," she said. "But what do you do?"

"I'm a cop."

She tilted her head, her hair just beginning to streak with gray. "You're the marshal."

Teddy nodded. "Could you take your hands from behind your back?"

"Why?" she said.

"Because I'd like to know what you're holding."

"Why?"

"Because I'd like to know if it could hurt me."

She gave that a small smile. "I suppose that's fair."

"I'm glad you do."

She removed her hands from behind her back, and she was holding a long, thin surgical scalpel. "I'll hold on to it, if you don't mind."

Teddy held up his hands. "Fine with me."

"Do you know who I am?"

Teddy said, "A patient from Ashecliffe."

She gave him another head tilt and touched her smock. "My. What gave me away?"

"Okay, okay. Good point."

"Are all U.S. marshals so astute?"

Teddy said, "I haven't eaten in a while. I'm a little slower than usual."

"Slept much?"

"What's that?"

"Since you've been on-island. Have you slept much?"

"Not well if that means anything."

"Oh, it does." She hiked up her pants at the knees and sat on the floor, beckoned him to do the same.

Teddy sat and stared at her over the fire.

"You're Rachel Solando," he said. "The real one."

She shrugged.

"You kill your children?" he said.

She poked a log with the scalpel. "I never had children."

"No?"

"No. I was never married. I was, you'll be surprised to realize, more than just a patient here."

"How can you be more than just a patient?"

She poked another log and it settled with a crunch, and sparks rose above the fire and died before hitting the roof.

"I was staff," she said. "Since just after the war."

"You were a nurse?"

She looked over the fire at him. "I was a doctor, Marshal. The first female doctor on staff at Drummond Hospital in Delaware. The first on staff here at Ashecliffe. You, sir, are looking at a genuine pioneer."

Or a delusional mental patient, Teddy thought.

He looked up and found her eyes on him, and hers were kind and wary and knowing. She said, "You think I'm crazy."

"No."

"What else would you think, a woman who hides in a cave?"

"I've considered that there might be a reason."

She smiled darkly and shook her head. "I'm not crazy. I'm not. Of course what else would a crazy person claim? That's the Kafkaesque genius of it all. If you're not crazy but people have told the world you are, then all your protests to the contrary just underscore their point. Do you see what I'm saying?"

"Sort of," Teddy said.

"Look at it as a syllogism. Let's say the syllogism begins with this principle: 'Insane men deny that they are insane.' You follow?"

"Sure," Teddy said.

"Okay, part two: 'Bob denies he is insane.' Part three, the 'ergo' part. 'Ergo—Bob is insane.' " She placed the scalpel on the ground by her knee and stoked the fire with a stick. "If you are deemed insane, then all actions that would otherwise prove you are not do, in actuality, fall into the framework of an insane person's actions. Your sound protests constitute *denial.* Your valid fears are deemed *paranoia.* Your survival instincts are labeled *defense mechanisms.* It's a no-win situation. It's a death penalty really. Once you're here, you're not getting out. No one leaves Ward C. No one. Well, a few have, okay, I'll grant you, a few have gotten out. But they've had surgery. In the brain. Squish—right through the eye. It's a barbaric medical practice, unconscionable, and I told them that. I fought them. I wrote letters. And they could've removed me, you know? They could've fired me or dismissed me, let me take a teaching post or even practice out of state, but that wasn't good enough. They couldn't let me leave, just couldn't do that. No, no, no."

She'd grown more and more agitated as she spoke, stabbing the fire with her stick, talking more to her knees than to Teddy.

"You really were a doctor?" Teddy said.

"Oh, yes. I was a doctor." She looked up from her knees and her stick. "I still am, actually. But, yes, I was on staff here. I began to ask about large shipments of Sodium Amytal and opium-based hallucinogens. I began to wonder—aloud unfortunately—about surgical procedures that seemed highly experimental, to put it mildly."

"What are they up to here?" Teddy said.

She gave him a grin that was both pursed and lopsided. "You have no idea?"

"I know they're flouting the Nuremberg Code."

"Flouting it? They've obliterated it."

"I know they're performing radical treatments."

"Radical, yes. Treatments, no. There is no treating going on here, Marshal. You know where the funding for this hospital comes from?"

Teddy nodded. "HUAC."

"Not to mention slush funds," she said. "Money flows into here. Now ask yourself, how does pain enter the body?"

"Depends upon where you're hurt."

"No." She shook her head emphatically. "It has nothing to do with the flesh. The brain sends neural transmitters down through the nervous system. The brain controls pain," she said. "It controls fear. Sleep. Empathy. Hunger. Everything we associate with the heart or the soul or the nervous system is actually controlled by the brain. Everything."

"Okay . . ."

Her eyes shone in the firelight. "What if you could control it?"

"The brain?"

She nodded. "Re-create a man so that he doesn't need sleep, doesn't feel pain. Or love. Or sympathy. A man who can't be interrogated because his memory banks are wiped clean." She stoked the fire and looked up at him. "They're creating ghosts here, Marshal. Ghosts to go out into the world and do ghostly work."

"But that kind of ability, that kind of knowledge is—"

"Years off," she agreed. "Oh, yes. This is a decades-long process, Marshal. Where they've begun is much the same place the Soviets have—brainwashing. Deprivation experiments. Much like the Nazis experimented on Jews to see the effect of hot and cold extremes and apply those results to help the soldiers of the Reich. But, don't you see, Marshal? A half century from now, people in the know will look back and say this"—she struck the dirt floor with her index finger—"this is where it all began. The Nazis used Jews. The Soviets used prisoners in their own gulags. Here, in America, we tested patients on Shutter Island."

Teddy said nothing. No words occurred to him.

She looked back at the fire. "They can't let you leave. You know that, don't you?"

"I'm a federal marshal," Teddy said. "How are they going to stop me?"

That elicited a gleeful grin and a clap of her hands. "I was an esteemed psychiatrist from a respected family. I once thought that would be enough. I hate to inform you of this, but it wasn't. Let me ask you—any past traumas in your life?"

"Who doesn't have those?"

"Ah, yes. But we're not taking about generalities, other people. We're talking about particulars. You. Do you have psychological weaknesses that they could exploit? Is there an event or events in your past that could be considered predicating factors to your losing your sanity? So that when they commit you here, and they will, your friends and colleagues will say, 'Of course. He cracked. Finally. And who wouldn't? It was the war that did it to him. And losing his mother—or what have you—like that.' Hmm?"

Teddy said, "That could be said about anyone."

"Well, that's the point. Don't you see? Yes, it could be said about anyone, but they're going to say it about you. How's your head?"

"My head?"

She chewed on her lower lip and nodded several times. "The block atop your neck, yes. How is it? Any funny dreams lately?"

"Sure."

"Headaches?"

"I'm prone to migraines."

"Jesus. You're not."

"I am."

"Have you taken pills since you've come here, even aspirin?"

"Yes."

"Feeling just a bit off, maybe? Not a hundred percent yourself? Oh, it's no big deal, you say, you just feel a little punkish. Maybe your brain isn't making connections *quite* as fast as normal. But you haven't been sleeping well, you say. A strange bed, a strange place, a storm. You say these things to yourself. Yes?"

Teddy nodded.

"And you've eaten in the cafeteria, I assume. Drank the coffee they've given you. Tell me, at least, that you've been smoking your own cigarettes."

"My partner's," Teddy admitted.

"Never took one from a doctor or an orderly?"

Teddy could feel the cigarettes he'd won in poker that night nestled in his shirt pocket. He remembered smoking one of Cawley's the day they'd arrived, how it had tasted sweeter than other tobaccos he'd had in his life.

She could see the answer in his face.

"It takes an average of three to four days for neuroleptic narcotics to reach workable levels in the bloodstream. During that time, you'd barely notice their effects. Sometimes, patients have seizures. Seizures can often be dismissed as migraines, particularly if the patient has a migraine history. These seizures are rare, in any event. Usually, the only noticeable effects are that the patient—"

"Stop calling me a patient."

"—dreams with an increased vividness and for longer sections of time, the dreams often stringing together and piggybacking off one another until they come to resemble a novel written by Picasso. The other noticeable effect is that the patient feels just a bit, oh, foggy. His thoughts are a wee bit less accessible. But he hasn't been sleeping well, all those dreams you know, and so he can be forgiven for feeling a bit sluggish. And no, Marshal, I wasn't calling you a 'patient.' Not yet. I was speaking rhetorically."

"If I avoid all food, cigarettes, coffee, pills, how much damage could already be done?"

She pulled her hair back off her face and twisted it into a knot behind her head. "A lot, I'm afraid."

"Let's say I can't get off this island until tomorrow. Let's say the drugs have begun to take effect. How will I know?"

"The most obvious indicators will be a dry mouth coupled paradoxically with a drool impulse and, oh yes, palsy. You'll notice small tremors. They begin where your wrist meets your thumb and they usually ride along that thumb for a while before they own your hands."

Own.

Teddy said, "What else?"

"Sensitivity to light, left-brain headaches, words begin to stick. You'll stutter more."

Teddy could hear the ocean outside, the tide coming in, smashing against the rocks.

"What goes on in the lighthouse?" he said.

She hugged herself and leaned toward the fire. "Surgery."

"Surgery? They can do surgery in the hospital."

"Brain surgery."

Teddy said, "They can do that there too."

She stared into the flames. "Exploratory surgery. Not the 'Let's-open-the-skull-and-fix-that' kind. No. The 'Let's-open-the-skull-and-see-what-happens-if-we-pull-on-this' kind. The illegal kind, Marshal. Learned-it-from-the-Nazis kind." She smiled at him. "That's where they try to build their ghosts."

"Who knows about this? On the island, I mean?"

"About the lighthouse?"

"Yes, the lighthouse."

"Everyone."

"Come on. The orderlies, the nurses?"

She held Teddy's eyes through the flame, and hers were steady and clear.

"Everyone," she repeated.

HE DIDN'T REMEMBER falling asleep, but he must have, because she was shaking him.

She said, "You have to go. They think I'm dead. They think I drowned. If they come looking for you, they could find me. I'm sorry. But you have to go."

He stood and rubbed his cheeks just below his eyes.

"There's a road," she said. "Just east of the top of this cliff. Follow it and it winds down to the west. It'll take you out behind the old commander's mansion after about an hour's walk."

"Are you Rachel Solando?" he said. "I know the one I met was a fake."

"How do you know?"

Teddy thought back to his thumbs the night before. He'd been staring at them as they put him to bed. When he woke, they'd been cleaned. Shoe polish, he'd thought, but then he remembered touching her face . . .

"Her hair was dyed. Recently," he said.

"You need to go." She turned his shoulder gently toward the opening.

"If I need to come back," he said.

"I won't be here. I move during the day. New places every night."

"But I could come get you, take you off here."

She gave him a sad smile and brushed the hair back along his temples. "You haven't heard a word I've said, have you?"

"I have."

"You'll never get off here. You're one of us now." She pressed her fingers to his shoulder, nudged him toward the opening.

Teddy stopped at the ledge, looked back at her. "I had a friend. He was with me tonight and we got separated. Have you seen him?"

She gave him the same sad smile.

"Marshal," she said, "you have no friends."

18

BY THE TIME he reached the back of Cawley's house, he could barely walk.

He made his way out from behind the house and started up the road to the main gate, feeling as if the distance had quadrupled since this morning, and a man came out of the dark on the road beside him and slid his arm under Teddy's and said, "We've been wondering when you'd show up."

The warden.

His skin was the white of candle wax, as smooth as if it were lacquered, and vaguely translucent. His nails, Teddy noticed, were as long and white as his skin, their points stopping just short of hooking and meticulously filed. But his eyes were the most disruptive thing about him. A silken blue, filled with a strange wonderment. The eyes of a baby.

"Nice to finally meet you, Warden. How are you?"

"Oh," the man said, "I'm tip-top. Yourself?"

"Never better."

The warden squeezed his arm. "Good to hear. Taking a leisurely stroll, were we?"

"Well, now that the patient's been found, I thought I'd tour the island."

"Enjoyed yourself, I trust."

"Completely."

"Wonderful. Did you come across our natives?"

It took Teddy a minute. His head was buzzing constantly now. His legs were barely holding him up.

"Oh, the rats," he said.

The warden clapped his back. "The rats, yes! There's something strangely regal about them, don't you think?"

Teddy looked into the man's eyes and said, "They're rats."

"Vermin, yes. I understand. But the way they sit on their haunches and stare at you if they believe they're at a safe distance, and how swiftly they move, in and out of a hole before you can blink . . ." He looked up at the stars. "Well, maybe *regal* is the wrong word. How about *utile*? They're exceptionally utile creatures."

They'd reached the main gate and the warden kept his grip on Teddy's arm and turned in place until they were looking back at Cawley's house and the sea beyond.

"Did you enjoy God's latest gift?" the warden said.

Teddy looked at the man and sensed disease in those perfect eyes. "I'm sorry?"

"God's gift," the warden said, and his arm swept the torn grounds. "His violence. When I first came downstairs in my home and saw the tree in my living room, it reached toward me like a divine hand. Not literally, of course. But figuratively, it stretched. God loves violence. You understand that, don't you?"

"No," Teddy said, "I don't."

The warden walked a few steps forward and turned to face Teddy. "Why else would there be so much of it? It's in us. It comes out of us. It is what we do more naturally than we breathe. We wage war. We burn sacrifices. We pillage and tear at the flesh of our brothers. We fill great fields with our stinking dead. And why? To show Him that we've learned from His example."

Teddy watched the man's hand stroking the binding of the small book he pressed to his abdomen.

He smiled and his teeth were yellow.

"God gives us earthquakes, hurricanes, tornadoes. He gives us mountains that spew fire onto our heads. Oceans that swallow ships. He gives us nature, and nature is a smiling killer. He gives us disease so that in our death we believe He gave us orifices only so that we could feel our life bleed out of them. He gave us lust and fury and greed and our filthy hearts. So that we could wage violence in His honor. There is no moral order as pure as this storm we've just seen. There is no moral order at all. There is only this—can my violence conquer yours?"

Teddy said, "I'm not sure I—"

"Can it?" The warden stepped in close, and Teddy could smell his stale breath.

"Can what?" Teddy asked.

"Can my violence conquer yours?"

"I'm not violent," Teddy said.

The warden spit on the ground near their feet. "You're as violent as they come. I know, because I'm as violent as they come. Don't embarrass yourself by denying your own blood lust, son. Don't embarrass me. If the constraints of society were removed, and I was all that stood between you and a meal, you'd crack my skull with a rock and eat my meaty parts." He leaned in. "If my teeth sank into your eye right now, could you stop me before I blinded you?"

Teddy saw glee in his baby eyes. He pictured the man's heart, black and beating, behind the wall of his chest.

"Give it a try," he said.

"That's the spirit," the warden whispered.

Teddy set his feet, could feel the blood rushing through his arms.

"Yes, yes," the warden whispered. " 'My very chains and I grew friends.' "

"What?" Teddy found himself whispering, his body vibrating with a strange tingling.

"That's Byron," the warden said. "You'll remember that line, won't you?"

Teddy smiled as the man took a step back. "They really broke the mold with you, didn't they, Warden?"

A thin smile to match Teddy's own.

"He thinks it's okay."

"What's okay?"

"You. Your little endgame. He thinks it's relatively harmless. But I don't."

"No, huh?"

"No." The warden dropped his arm and took a few steps forward. He crossed his hands behind his back so that his book was pressed against the base of his spine and then turned and set his feet apart in the military fashion and stared at Teddy. "You say you were out for a stroll, but I know better. I know you, son."

"We just met," Teddy said.

The warden shook his head. "Our kind have known each other for centuries. I know you to your core. And I think you're sad. I really do." He pursed his lips and considered his shoes. "Sad is fine. Pathetic in a man, but fine because it has no effect on me. But I also think you're dangerous."

"Every man has a right to his opinion," Teddy said.

The warden's face darkened. "No, he doesn't. Men are foolish. They eat and drink and pass gas and fornicate and procreate, and this last is particularly unfortunate, because the world would be a much better place with far fewer of us in it. Retards and mud children and lunatics and people of low moral character—that's what we produce. That's what we spoil this earth with. In the South now, they're trying to keep their niggers in line. But I'll tell you something, I've spent time in the South, and they're all niggers down there, son. White niggers, black niggers, women niggers. Got niggers everywhere and they're no more use than two-legged dogs. Least the dog can still sniff out a scent from time to time. You're a nigger, son. You're of low fiber. I can smell it in you."

His voice was surprisingly light, almost feminine.

"Well," Teddy said, "you won't have to worry about me after the morning, will you, Warden?"

The warden smiled. "No, I won't, son."

"I'll be out of your hair and off your island."

The warden took two steps toward him, his smile dissolving. He cocked his head at Teddy and held him in his fetal gaze.

"You're not going anywhere, son."

"I beg to differ."

"Beg all you want." The warden leaned in and sniffed the air to the left of Teddy's face, then moved his head, sniffed the air to the right of it.

Teddy said, "Smell something?"

"Mmm-hmm." The warden leaned back. "Smells like fear to me, son."

"You probably want to take a shower, then," Teddy said. "Wash that shit off yourself."

Neither of them spoke for a bit, and then the warden said, "Remember those chains, nigger. They're your friends. And know that I'm very much looking forward to our final dance. Ah," he said, "what carnage we'll achieve."

And he turned and walked up the road toward his house.

THE MEN'S DORMITORY was abandoned. Not a soul inside the place. Teddy went up to his room and hung his slicker in the closet and looked for any evidence that Chuck had returned there, but there was none.

He thought of sitting on the bed, but he knew if he did, he'd pass out and probably not wake until morning, so he went down to the bathroom and splashed cold water on his face and slicked back his crew cut with a wet comb. His bones felt scraped and his blood seemed thick as a malted, and his eyes were sunken and ringed red and his skin was gray. He splashed a few more handfuls of cold water up into his face and then dried off and went outside into the main compound.

No one.

The air was actually warming up, growing humid and sticky, and crickets and cicadas had begun to find their voices. Teddy walked the grounds, hoping that somehow Chuck had arrived ahead of him and was maybe doing the same thing, wandering around until he bumped into Teddy.

There was the guard on the gate, and Teddy could see lights in the rooms, but otherwise, the place was empty. He made his way over to the hospital and went up the steps and pulled on the door only to find it locked. He heard a squeak of hinges and looked out to see that the guard had opened the gate and gone out to join his comrade on the other side, and when the gate swung closed again, Teddy could hear his shoes scrape on the concrete landing as he stepped back from the door.

He sat on the steps for a minute. So much for Noyce's theory. Teddy was now, beyond any doubt, completely alone. Locked in, yes. But unwatched as far as he could tell.

He walked around to the back of the hospital and his chest filled when he saw an orderly sitting on the back landing, smoking a cigarette.

Teddy approached, and the kid, a slim, rangy black kid, looked up at him. Teddy pulled a cigarette from his pocket and said, "Got a light?"

"Sure do."

Teddy leaned in as the kid lit his cigarette, smiled his thanks as he leaned back and remembered what the woman had told him about smoking their cigarettes, and he let the smoke flow slowly out of his mouth without inhaling.

"How you doing tonight?" he said.

"All right, sir. You?"

"I'm okay. Where is everyone?"

The kid jerked his thumb behind him. "In there. Some big meeting. Don't know about what."

"All the doctors and nurses?"

The kid nodded. "Some of the patients too. Most of us orderlies. I got stuck with this here door 'cause the latch don't work real good. Otherwise, though, yeah. Everyone in there."

Teddy took another cigar puff off his cigarette, hoped the kid didn't notice. He wondered if he should just bluff his way up the stairs, hope the kid took him for another orderly, one from Ward C maybe.

Then he saw through the window behind the kid that the hallway was filling and people were heading for the front door.

He thanked the kid for the light and walked around out front, was met with a crowd of people milling there, talking, lighting cigarettes. He saw Nurse Marino say something to Trey Washington, put her hand on his shoulder as she did, and Trey threw back his head and laughed.

Teddy started to walk over to them when Cawley called to him from the stairs. "Marshal!"

Teddy turned and Cawley came down the stairs toward him, touched Teddy's elbow, and began walking toward the wall.

"Where've you been?" Cawley said.

"Wandering. Looking at your island."

"Really?"

"Really."

"Find anything amusing?"

"Rats."

"Well, sure, we have plenty of those."

"How's the roof repair coming?" Teddy said.

Cawley sighed. "I have buckets all over my house catching water. The attic is done, wrecked. So's the floor in the guest bedroom. My wife's going to be beside herself. Her wedding gown was in that attic."

"Where is your wife?" Teddy said.

"Boston," Cawley said. "We keep an apartment there. She and the kids needed a break from this place, so they took a week's vacation. It gets to you sometimes."

"I've been here three days, Doctor, and it gets to me."

Cawley nodded with a soft smile. "But you'll be going."

"Going?"

"Home, Marshal. Now that Rachel's been found. The ferry usually gets here around eleven in the morning. Have you back in Boston by noon, I'd expect."

"Won't that be nice."

"Yes, won't it?" Cawley ran a hand over his head. "I don't mind telling you, Marshal, and meaning no offense—"

"Oh, here we go again."

Cawley held up a hand. "No, no. No personal opinions regarding your emotional state. No, I was about to say that your presence here has had an agitating effect on a lot of the patients. You know—Johnny Law's in town. That made several of them a bit tense."

"Sorry about that."

"Not your fault. It was what you represent, not you personally."

"Oh, well, that makes it all okay, then."

Cawley leaned against the wall, propped a foot there, looking as tired as Teddy felt in his wrinkled lab coat and loosened tie.

"There was a rumor going around Ward C this afternoon that an unidentified man in orderly's clothes was on the main floor."

"Really?"

Cawley looked at him. "Really."

"How about that."

Cawley picked at some lint on his tie, flicked it off his fingers. "Said stranger apparently had some experience subduing dangerous men."

"You don't say."

"Oh, I do. I do."

"What else did Said Stranger get up to?"

"Well." Cawley stretched his shoulders back and removed his lab coat, draped it over his arm, "I'm glad you're interested."

"Hey, nothing like a little rumor, a little gossip."

"I agree. Said Stranger allegedly—and I can't confirm this, mind you—had a long conversation with a known paranoid schizophrenic named George Noyce."

"Hmm," Teddy said.

"Indeed."

"So this, um . . ."

"Noyce," Cawley said.

"Noyce," Teddy repeated. "Yeah, that guy—he's delusional, huh?"

"To the extreme," Cawley said. "He spins his yarns and his tall tales and he gets everyone agitated—"

"There's that word again."

"I'm sorry. Yes, well, he gets people in a disagreeable mood. Two weeks ago, in fact, he got people so cross that a patient beat him up."

"Imagine that."

Cawley shrugged. "It happens."

"So, what kind of yarns?" Teddy asked. "What kind of tales?"

Cawley waved at the air. "The usual paranoid delusions. The whole world being out to get him and such." He looked up at Teddy as he lit a cigarette, his eyes brightening with the flame. "So, you'll be leaving."

"I guess so."

"The first ferry."

Teddy gave him a frosty smile. "As long as someone wakes us up."

Cawley returned the smile. "I think we can handle that."

"Great."

"Great." Cawley said, "Cigarette?"

Teddy held up a hand to the proffered pack. "No, thanks."

"Trying to quit?"

"Trying to cut down."

"Probably a good thing. I've been reading in journals how tobacco might be linked to a host of terrible things."

"Really?"

He nodded. "Cancer, I've heard, for one."

"So many ways to die these days."

"Agreed. More and more ways to cure, though."

"You think so?"

"I wouldn't be in this profession otherwise." Cawley blew the smoke in a stream above his head.

Teddy said, "Ever have a patient here named Andrew Laeddis?"

Cawley dropped his chin back toward his chest. "Doesn't ring a bell."

"No?"

Cawley shrugged. "Should it?"

Teddy shook his head. "He was a guy I knew. He—"

"How?"

"What's that?"

"How did you know him?"

"In the war," Teddy said.

"Oh."

"Anyway, I'd heard he went a little bugs, got sent here."

Cawley took a slow drag off his cigarette. "You heard wrong."

"Apparently."

Cawley said, "Hey, it happens. I thought you said 'us' a minute ago."

"What?"

" 'Us,' " Cawley said. "As in first-person plural."

Teddy put a hand to his chest. "Referring to myself?"

Cawley nodded. "I thought you said, 'As long as someone wakes us up.' *Us* up."

"Well, I did. Of course. Have you seen him by the way?"

Cawley raised his eyebrows at him.

Teddy said, "Come on. Is he here?"

Cawley laughed, looked at him.

"What?" Teddy said.

Cawley shrugged. "I'm just confused."

"Confused by what?"

"You, Marshal. Is this some weird joke of yours?"

"What joke?" Teddy said. "I just want to know if he's here."

"Who?" Cawley said, a hint of exasperation in his voice.

"Chuck."

"Chuck?" Cawley said slowly.

"My partner," Teddy said. "Chuck."

Cawley came off the wall, the cigarette dangling from his fingers. "You don't have a partner, Marshal. You came here alone."

19

TEDDY SAID, "Wait a minute . . ."

Found Cawley, closer now, peering up at him.

Teddy closed his mouth, felt the summer night find his eyelids.

Cawley said, "Tell me again. About your partner."

Cawley's curious gaze was the coldest thing Teddy had ever seen. Probing and intelligent and fiercely bland. It was the gaze of a straight man in a vaudeville revue, pretending not to know where the punch line would come from.

And Teddy was Ollie to his Stan. A buffoon with loose suspenders and a wooden barrel for pants. The last one in on the joke.

"Marshal?" Cawley taking another small step forward, a man stalking a butterfly.

If Teddy protested, if he demanded to know where Chuck was, if he even argued that there *was* a Chuck, he played into their hands.

Teddy met Cawley's eyes and he saw the laughter in them.

"Insane men deny they're insane," Teddy said.

Another step. "Excuse me?"

"Bob denies he's insane."

Cawley crossed his arms over his chest.

"Ergo," Teddy said, "Bob is insane."

Cawley leaned back on his heels, and now the smile found his face. Teddy met it with one of his own.

They stood there like that for some time, the night breeze moving through the trees above the wall with a soft flutter.

"You know," Cawley said, toeing the grass at his feet, head down, "I've built something valuable here. But valuable things also have a way of being misunderstood in their own time. Everyone wants a quick fix. We're tired of being afraid, tired of being sad, tired of feeling overwhelmed, tired of feeling tired. We want the old days back, and we don't even remember them, and we want to push into the future, paradoxically, at top speed. Patience and forbearance become the first casualties of progress. This is not news. Not news at all. It's always been so." Cawley raised his head. "So as many powerful friends as I have, I have just as many powerful enemies. People who would wrest what I've built from my control. I can't allow that without a fight. You understand?"

Teddy said, "Oh, I understand, Doctor."

"Good." Cawley unfolded his arms. "And this partner of yours?"

Teddy said, "What partner?"

TREY WASHINGTON WAS in the room when Teddy got back, lying on the bed reading an old issue of *Life*.

Teddy looked at Chuck's bunk. The bed had been remade and the sheet and blanket were tucked tight and you'd never know someone had slept there two nights before.

Teddy's suit jacket, shirt, tie, and pants had been returned from the laundry and hung in the closet under plastic wrap and he changed out of his orderly clothes and put them on as Trey flipped the glossy pages of the magazine.

"How you doing tonight, Marshal?"

"Doing okay."

"That's good, that's good."

He noticed that Trey wouldn't look at him, kept his eyes on that magazine, turning the same pages over and over.

Teddy transferred the contents of his pockets, placing Laeddis's intake form in his inside coat pocket along with his notebook. He sat on Chuck's bunk across from Trey and tied his tie, tied his shoes, and then sat there quietly.

Trey turned another page of the magazine. "Going to be hot tomorrow."

"Really?"

"Hot as a motherfucker. Patients don't like the heat."

"No?"

He shook his head, turned another page. "No, sir. Make 'em all itchy and whatnot. Got us a full moon too coming tomorrow night. Just make things a whole lot worse. All we need."

"Why is that?"

"What's that, Marshal?"

"The full moon. You think it makes people crazy?"

"I know it does." Found a wrinkle in one of the pages and used his index finger to smooth it out.

"How come?"

"Well, you think about it—the moon affects the tide, right?"

"Sure."

"Has some sort of magnet effect or something on water."

"I'll buy that."

"Human brain," Trey said, "is over fifty percent water."

"No kidding?"

"No kidding. You figure ol' Mr. Moon can jerk the ocean around, think what it can do to the head."

"How long you been here, Mr. Washington?"

He finished smoothing out the wrinkle, turned the page. "Oh, long time now. Since I got out of the army in 'forty-six."

"You were in the army?"

"Yes, I was. Came there for a gun, they gave me a pot. Fought the Germans with bad cooking, sir."

"That was bullshit," Teddy said.

"That was some bullshit, yes, Marshal. They let us into the war, it would have been over by 'forty-four."

"You'll get no argument from me."

"You was in all sorts of places, huh?"

"Yeah, I was. Saw the world."

"What'd you think of it?"

"Different languages, same shit."

"Yeah, that's the truth, huh?"

"You know what the warden called me tonight, Mr. Washington?"

"What's that, Marshal?"

"A nigger."

Trey looked up from the magazine. "He what?"

Teddy nodded. "Said there were too many people in this world who were of low fiber. Mud races. Niggers. Retards. Said I was just a nigger to him."

"You didn't like that, did you?" Trey chuckled, and the sound died as soon as it left his mouth. "You don't know what it is to be a nigger, though."

"I'm aware of that, Trey. This man is your boss, though."

"Ain't my boss. I work for the hospital end of things. The White Devil? He on the prison side."

"Still your boss."

"No, he ain't." Trey rose up on his elbow. "You hear? I mean, are we definitely clear on that one, Marshal?"

Teddy shrugged.

Trey swung his legs over the bed and sat up. "You trying to make me mad, sir?"

Teddy shook his head.

"So then why don't you agree with me when I tell you I don't work for that white son of a bitch?"

Teddy gave him another shrug. "In a pinch, if it came down to it and he started giving orders? You'd hop to."

"I'd what?"

"Hop to. Like a bunny."

Trey ran a hand along his jaw, considered Teddy with a hard grin of disbelief.

"I don't mean any offense," Teddy said.

"Oh, no, no."

"It's just I've noticed that people on this island have a way of creating their own truth. Figure they say it's so enough times, then it must be so."

"I don't work for that man."

Teddy pointed at him. "Yeah, that's the island truth I know and love."

Trey looked ready to hit him.

"See," Teddy said, "they held a meeting tonight. And afterward, Dr. Cawley comes up and tells me I never had a partner. And if I ask you, you'll say the same thing. You'll deny that you sat with the man and played poker with the man and laughed with the man. You'll deny he ever said the way you should have dealt with your mean old aunt was to run faster. You'll deny he ever slept right here in this bed. Won't you, Mr. Washington?"

Trey looked down at the floor. "Don't know what you're talking about, Marshal."

"Oh, I know, I know. I never had a partner. That's the truth now. It has been decided. I never had a partner and he's not somewhere out on this island hurt. Or dead. Or locked up in Ward C or the lighthouse. I never had a partner. You want to repeat that after me, just so we're clear? I never had a partner. Come on. Try it."

Trey looked up. "You never had a partner."

Teddy said, "And you don't work for the warden."

Trey clasped his hands on his knees. He looked at Teddy and Teddy could see that this was eating him. His eyes grew moist and the flesh along his chin trembled.

"You need to get out of here," he whispered.

"I'm aware of that."

"No." Trey shook his head several times. "You don't have any idea what's really going on here. Forget what you heard. Forget what you think you know. They going to get to you. And there ain't no coming back from what they going to do to you. No coming back no how."

"Tell me," Teddy said, but Trey was shaking his head again. "Tell me what's going on here."

"I can't do that. I can't. Look at me." Trey's eyebrows rose and his eyes widened. "I. Cannot. Do. That. You on your own. And I wouldn't be waiting on no ferry."

Teddy chuckled. "I can't even get out of this compound, never mind off this island. And even if I could, my partner is—"

"Forget your partner," Trey hissed. "He gone. You got it? He ain't coming back, man. You gotta git. You gotta watch out for yourself and only yourself."

"Trey," Teddy said, "I'm locked in."

Trey stood and went to the window, looked out into the dark or at his own reflection, Teddy couldn't tell which.

"You can't ever come back. You can't ever tell no one I told you anything."

Teddy waited.

Trey looked back over his shoulder at him. "We agreed?"

"Agreed," Teddy said.

"Ferry be here tomorrow at ten. Leave for Boston at eleven sharp. A man was to stow away on that boat, he might just make it across the harbor. Otherwise, a man would have to wait two or three more days and a fishing trawler, name of *Betsy Ross,* she pull up real close to the southern coast, drop a few things off the side." He looked back at Teddy. "Kinda things men ain't supposed to have on this island. Now she don't come all the way in. No, sir. So a man'd have to swim his way out to her."

"I can't do three fucking days on this island," Teddy said. "I don't know the terrain. The warden and his men damn sure do, though. They'll find me."

Trey didn't say anything for a while.

"Then it's the ferry," he said eventually.

"It's the ferry. But how do I get out of the compound?"

"Shit," Trey said. "You might not buy this, but it *is* your lucky day. Storm fucked up everything, particularly the electrical systems. Now we repaired most of the wires on the wall. Most of them."

Teddy said, "Which sections didn't you get to?"

"The southwest corner. Those two are dead, right where the wall meets in a ninety-degree angle. The rest of them will fry you like chicken, so don't slip and reach out and grab one. Hear?"

"I hear."

Trey nodded to his reflection. "I'd suggest you git. Time's wasting."

Teddy stood. "Chuck," he said.

Trey scowled. "There is no Chuck. All right? Never was. You get back to the world, you talk about Chuck all you like. But here? The man never happened."

IT OCCURRED TO Teddy as he faced the southwest corner of the wall that Trey could be lying. If Teddy put a hand to those wires, got a good grip, and they were live, they'd find his body in the morning at the foot of the wall, as black as last month's steak. Problem solved. Trey gets employee of the year, maybe a nice gold watch.

He searched around until he found a long twig, and then he turned to a section of wire to the right of the corner. He took a running jump at the wall, got his foot on it, and leapt up. He slapped the twig down on the wire and the wire spit out a burst of flame and the twig caught fire. Teddy came back to earth and looked at the wood in his hand. The flame went out, but the wood smoldered.

He tried it again, this time on the wire over the right side of the corner. Nothing.

He stood down below again, taking a breath, and then he jumped up the left wall, hit the wire again. And again, nothing.

There was a metal post atop the section where the wall met, and Teddy took three runs at the wall before he got a grip. He held tight and climbed up to the top of the wall and his shoulders hit the wire and his knees hit the wire and his forearms hit the wire, and each time, he thought he was dead.

He wasn't. And once he'd reached the top, there wasn't much to do but lower himself down to the other side.

He stood in the leaves and looked back at Ashecliffe.

He'd come here for the truth, and didn't find it. He'd come here for Laeddis, and didn't find him either. Along the way, he'd lost Chuck.

He'd have time to regret all that back in Boston. Time to feel guilt and shame then. Time to consider his options and consult with Senator Hurly and come up with a plan of attack. He'd come back. Fast. There couldn't be any question of that. And hopefully he'd be armed with subpoenas and federal search warrants. And they'd have their own goddamned ferry. Then he'd be angry. Then he'd be righteous in his fury.

Now, though, he was just relieved to be alive and on the other side of this wall.

Relieved. And scared.

IT TOOK HIM an hour and a half to get back to the cave, but the woman had left. Her fire had burned down to a few embers, and Teddy sat by it even though the air outside was unseasonably warm and growing clammier by the hour.

Teddy waited for her, hoping she'd just gone out for more wood, but he knew, in his heart, that she wasn't going to return. Maybe she believed he'd already been caught and was, at this moment, telling the warden and Cawley about her hiding place. Maybe—and this was too much to hope for, but Teddy allowed himself the indulgence—Chuck had found her and they'd gone to a location she believed was safer.

When the fire went out, Teddy took off his suit jacket and draped it over his chest and shoulders and placed his head back against the wall. Just as he had the night before, the last thing he noticed before he passed out were his thumbs.

They'd begun to twitch.

DAY FOUR

The Bad Sailor

20

ALL THE DEAD and maybe-dead were getting their coats.

They were in a kitchen and the coats were on hooks and Teddy's father took his old pea coat and shrugged his arms into it and then helped Dolores with hers and he said to Teddy, "You know what I'd like for Christmas?"

"No, Dad."

"Bagpipes."

And Teddy understood that he meant golf clubs and a golf bag.

"Just like Ike," he said.

"Exactly," his father said and handed Chuck his topcoat.

Chuck put it on. It was a nice coat. Prewar cashmere. Chuck's scar was gone, but he still had those delicate, borrowed hands, and he held them in front of Teddy and wiggled the fingers.

"Did you go with that woman doctor?" Teddy said.

Chuck shook his head. "I'm far too overeducated. I went to the track."

"Win?"

"Lost big."

"Sorry."

Chuck said, "Kiss your wife good-bye. On the cheek."

Teddy leaned in past his mother and Tootie Vicelli smiling at him with a bloody mouth, and he kissed Dolores's cheek and he said, "Baby, why you all wet?"

"I'm dry as a bone," she said to Teddy's father.

"If I was half my age," Teddy's father said, "I'd marry you, girl."

They were all soaking wet, even his mother, even Chuck. Their coats dripped all over the floor.

Chuck handed him three logs and said, "For the fire."

"Thanks." Teddy took the logs and then forgot where he'd put them.

Dolores scratched her stomach and said, "Fucking rabbits. What good are they?"

Laeddis and Rachel Solando walked into the room. They weren't wearing coats. They weren't wearing anything at all, and Laeddis passed a bottle of rye over Teddy's mother's head and then took Dolores in his arms and Teddy would have been jealous, but Rachel dropped to her knees in front of him and unzipped Teddy's trousers and took him in her mouth, and Chuck and his father and Tootie Vicelli and his mother all gave him a wave as they took their leave and Laeddis and Dolores stumbled back together into the bedroom and Teddy could hear them in there on the bed, fumbling with their clothes, breathing hoarsely, and it all seemed kind of perfect, kind of wonderful, as he lifted Dolores off her knees and could hear Rachel and Laeddis in there fucking like mad, and he kissed his wife, and placed a hand over the hole in her belly, and she said, "Thank you," and he slid into her from behind, pushing the logs off the kitchen counter, and the warden and his men helped themselves to the rye

Laeddis had brought and the warden winked his approval of Teddy's fucking technique and raised his glass to him and said to his men:

"That's one well-hung white nigger. You see him, you shoot first. You hear me? You don't give it a second thought. This man gets off the island, we are all summarily fucked, gentlemen."

Teddy threw his coat off his chest and crawled to the edge of the cave.

The warden and his men were up on the ridge above him. The sun was up. Seagulls shrieked.

Teddy looked at his watch: 8 A.M.

"You do not take chances," the warden said. "This man is combat-trained, combat-tested, and combat-hardened. He has the Purple Heart and the Oak Leaf with Clusters. He killed two men in Sicily with his bare hands."

That information was in his personnel file, Teddy knew. But how the fuck did they get his personnel file?

"He is adept with the knife and very adept at hand-to-hand combat. Do not get in close with this man. You get the chance, you put him down like a two-legged dog."

Teddy found himself smiling in spite of his situation. How many other times had the warden's men been subjected to two-legged-dog comparisons?

Three guards came down the side of the smaller cliff face on ropes and Teddy moved away from the ledge and watched them work their way down to the beach. A few minutes later, they climbed back up and Teddy heard one of them say, "He's not down there, sir."

He listened for a while as they searched up near the promontory and the road and then they moved off and Teddy waited a full hour before he left the cave, waiting to hear if anyone was taking up the rear, and giving the search party enough time so that he wouldn't bump into them.

It was twenty past nine by the time he reached the road and he followed it back toward the west, trying to maintain a fast pace but still listen for men moving either ahead or behind him.

Trey had been right in his weather prediction. It was hot as hell and Teddy removed his jacket and folded it over his arm. He loosened his tie enough to pull it over his head and placed it in his pocket. His mouth was as dry as rock salt, and his eyes itched from the sweat.

He saw Chuck again in his dream, putting on his coat, and the image stabbed him deeper than the one of Laeddis fondling Dolores. Until Rachel and Laeddis had shown up, everyone in that dream was dead. Except for Chuck. But he'd taken his coat from the same set of hooks and followed them out the door. Teddy hated what that symbolized. If they'd gotten to Chuck on the promontory, they'd probably been dragging him away while Teddy climbed his way back out of the field. And whoever had sneaked up on him must have been very good at his job because Chuck hadn't even gotten off a scream.

How powerful did you have to be to make not one but two U.S. marshals vanish?

Supremely powerful.

And if the plan was for Teddy to be driven insane, then it couldn't have been the same for Chuck. Nobody would believe two marshals had lost their minds in the same four-day span. So Chuck would have had to meet with an accident. In the hurricane probably. In fact, if they were really smart—and it seemed they were—then maybe Chuck's death would be represented as the event that had tipped Teddy past the point of no return.

There was an undeniable symmetry to the idea.

But if Teddy didn't make it off this island, the Field Office would never accept the story, no matter how logical, without sending other marshals out here to see for themselves.

And what would they find?

Teddy looked down at the tremors in his wrists and thumbs. They were getting worse. And his brain felt no fresher for a night's sleep. He felt foggy, thick-tongued. If by the time the field office got men out here, the drugs had taken over, they'd probably find Teddy drooling into his bathrobe, defecating where he sat. And the Ashecliffe version of the truth would be validated.

He heard the ferry blow its horn and came up on a rise in time to see it finish its turn in the harbor and begin to steam backward toward the dock. He picked up his pace, and ten minutes later he could see the back of Cawley's Tudor through the woods.

He turned off the road into the woods, and he heard men unloading the ferry, the thump of boxes tossed to the dock, the clang of metal dollies, footfalls on wooden planks. He reached the final stand of trees and saw several orderlies down on the dock, and the two ferry pilots leaning back against the stern, and he saw guards, lots of guards, rifle butts resting on hips, bodies turned toward the woods, eyes scanning the trees and the grounds that led up to Ashecliffe.

When the orderlies had finished unloading the cargo, they pulled their dollies with them back up the dock, but the guards remained, and Teddy knew that their only job this morning was to make damn sure he didn't reach that boat.

He crept back through the woods and came out by Cawley's house. He could hear men upstairs in the house, saw one out on the roof where it pitched, his back to Teddy. He found the car in the carport on the western side of the house. A '47 Buick Roadmaster. Maroon with white leather interior. Waxed and shiny the day after a hurricane. A beloved vehicle.

Teddy opened the driver's door and he could smell the leather, as if it were a day old. He opened the glove compartment and found several packs of matches, and he took them all.

He pulled his tie from his pocket, found a small stone on the ground, and knotted the narrow end of the tie around it. He lifted the license plate and unscrewed the gas tank cap, and then he threaded the tie and the stone down the pipe and into the tank until all that hung out of the pipe was the fat, floral front of the tie, as if it hung from a man's neck.

Teddy remembered Dolores giving him this tie, draping it across his eyes, sitting in his lap.

"I'm sorry, honey," he whispered. "I love it because you gave it to me. But truth is, it is one ugly fucking tie."

And he smiled up at the sky in apology to her and used one match to light the entire book and then used the book to light the tie.

And then he ran like hell.

He was halfway through the woods when the car exploded. He heard men yell and he looked back, and through the trees he could see the flames vaulting upward in balls, and then there was a set of smaller explosions, like firecrackers, as the windows blew out.

He reached the edge of the woods and he balled up his suit coat and placed it under a few rocks. He saw the guards and the ferrymen running up the path toward Cawley's house, and he knew if he was going to do this, he had to do it right now, no time to second-guess the idea, and that was good because if he gave any thought at all to what he was about to do, he'd never do it.

He came out of the woods and ran along the shore, and just before he reached the dock and would've left himself exposed to anyone running back to the ferry, he cut hard to his left and ran into the water.

Jesus, it was ice. Teddy had hoped the heat of the day might have warmed it up a bit, but the cold tore up through his body like electric current and punched the air out of his chest. But Teddy kept plowing forward, trying not to think about what was in that water with him— eels and jellyfish and crabs and sharks too, maybe. Seemed ridiculous but Teddy knew that sharks attacked humans, on average, in three feet of water, and that's about where he was now, the water at his waist and getting higher, and Teddy heard shouts coming from up by Cawley's house, and he ignored the sledgehammer strokes of his heart and dove under the water.

He saw the girl from his dreams, floating just below him, her eyes open and resigned.

He shook his head and she vanished and he could see the keel ahead of him, a thick black stripe that undulated in the green water, and he swam to it and got his hands on it. He moved along it to the front and came around the other side, and forced himself to come up out of the water slowly, just his head. He felt the sun on his face as he exhaled and then sucked in oxygen and tried to ignore a vision of his legs dangling down there in the depths, some creature swimming along and seeing them, wondering what they were, coming close for a sniff . . .

The ladder was where he remembered it. Right in front of him, and he got a hand on the third rung and hung there. He could hear the men running back to the dock now, hear their heavy footsteps on the planks, and then he heard the warden:

"Search that boat."

"Sir, we were only gone—"

"You left your post, and now you wish to argue?"

"No, sir. Sorry, sir."

The ladder dipped in his hand as several men placed their weight on the ferry, and Teddy heard them going through the boat, heard doors opening and furniture shifting.

Something slid between his thighs like a hand, and Teddy gritted his teeth and tightened his grip on the ladder and forced his mind to go completely blank because he did not want to imagine what it looked like. Whatever it was kept moving, and Teddy let out a breath.

"My car. He blew up my fucking car." Cawley, sounding ragged and out of breath.

The warden said, "This has gone far enough, Doctor."

"We agreed that it's my decision to make."

"If this man gets off the island—"

"He's not going to get off the island."

"I'm sure you didn't think he was going to turn your buggy into an inferno, either. We have to break this operation down now and cut our losses."

"I've worked too hard to throw in the towel."

The warden's voice rose. "If that man gets off this island, we'll be destroyed."

Cawley's voice rose to match the warden's. "He's not going to get off the fucking island!"

Neither spoke for a full minute. Teddy could hear their weight shifting on the dock.

"Fine, Doctor. But that ferry stays. It does not leave this dock until that man is found."

Teddy hung there, the cold finding his feet and burning them.

Cawley said, "They'll want answers for that in Boston."

Teddy closed his mouth before his teeth could chatter.

"Then give them answers. But that ferry stays."

Something nudged the back of Teddy's left leg.

"All right, Warden."

Another nudge against his leg, and Teddy kicked back, heard the splash he made hit the air like a gunshot.

Footsteps on the stern.

"He's not in there, sir. We checked everywhere."

"So where did he go?" the warden said. "Anyone?"

"Shit!"

"Yes, Doctor?"

"He's headed for the lighthouse."

"That thought did occur to me."

"I'll handle it."

"Take some men."

"I said I'll handle it. We've got men there."

"Not enough."

"I'll handle it, I said."

Teddy heard Cawley's shoes bang their way back up the dock and get softer as they hit the sand.

"Lighthouse or no lighthouse," the warden said to his men, "this boat goes nowhere. Get the engine keys from the pilot and bring them to me."

HE SWAM MOST of the way there.

Dropped away from the ferry and swam toward shore until he was close enough to the sandy bottom to use it, clawing along until he'd gone far enough to raise his head from the water and risk a glance back. He'd covered a few hundred yards and he could see the guards forming a ring around the dock.

He slipped back under the water and continued clawing, unable to risk the splashing that freestyle or even doggie-paddling would cause, and after a while, he came to the bend in the shoreline and made his way around it and walked up onto the sand and sat in the sun and shook from the cold. He walked as much of the shore as he could before he ran into a set of outcroppings that pushed him back into the water and he tied his shoes together and hung them around his neck and went for another swim and envisioned his father's bones some-where on this same ocean floor and envisioned sharks and their fins and their great snapping tails and barracuda with rows of white teeth and he knew he was getting through this because he had to and the water had numbed him and he had no choice now *but* to do this and he might have to do it again in a couple of days when the *Betsy Ross* dropped its booty off the island's southern tip, and he knew that the only way to conquer fear was to face it, he'd learned that in the war enough, but even so, if he could manage it, he would never, ever, get in the ocean again. He could feel it watching him and touching him. He could feel the age of it, more ancient than gods and prouder of its body count.

He saw the lighthouse at about one o'clock. He couldn't be sure because his watch was back in his suit jacket, but the sun was in roughly the right place. He came ashore just below the bluff on which it stood and he lay against a rock and took the sun on his body until the shakes stopped and his skin grew less blue.

If Chuck was up there, no matter his condition, Teddy was bringing him out. Dead or alive, he wouldn't leave him behind.

You'll die then.

It was Dolores's voice, and he knew she was right. If he had to wait two days for the arrival of the *Betsy Ross,* and he had anything but a fully alert, fully functional Chuck with him, they'd never make it. They'd be hunted down . . .

Teddy smiled.

. . . like two-legged dogs.

I can't leave him, he told Dolores. Can't do it. If I can't find him, that's one thing. But he's my partner.

You only just met him.

Still my partner. If he's in there, if they're hurting him, holding him against his will, I have to bring him out.

Even if you die?

Even if I die.

Then I hope he's not in there.

He came down off the rock and followed a path of sand and shells that curled around the sea grass, and it occurred to him that what Cawley had thought suicidal in him was not quite that. It was more a death wish. For years he couldn't think of a good reason to live, true. But he also couldn't think of a good reason to die, either. By his own hand? Even in his most desolate nights, that had seemed such a pathetic option. Embarrassing. Puny.

But to—

The guard was suddenly standing there, as surprised by Teddy's appearance as Teddy was by his, the guard's fly still open, the rifle slung behind his back. He started to reach for his fly first, then changed his mind, but by then Teddy had driven the heel of his hand into his Adam's apple. He grabbed his throat, and Teddy dropped to a crouch and swung his leg into the back of the guard's and the guard flipped over on his back and Teddy straightened up and kicked him hard in the right ear and the guard's eyes rolled back in his head and his mouth flopped open.

Teddy bent down by him and slid the rifle strap off his shoulder and pulled the rifle out from under him. He could hear the guy breathing. So he hadn't killed him.

And now he had a gun.

HE USED IT on the next guard, the one in front of the fence. He disarmed him, a kid, a baby, really, and the guard said, "You going to kill me?"

"Jesus, kid, no," Teddy said and snapped the butt of the rifle into the kid's temple.

THERE WAS A small bunkhouse inside the fence perimeter, and Teddy checked that first, found a few cots and girlie magazines, a pot of old coffee, a couple of guard uniforms hanging from a hook on the door.

He went back out and crossed to the lighthouse and used the rifle to push open the door and found nothing on the first floor but a dank cement room, empty of anything but mold on the walls, and a spiral staircase made from the same stone as the walls.

He followed that up to a second room, as empty as the first, and he knew there had to be a basement here, something large, maybe connected to the rest of the hospital by those corridors, because so far, this was nothing but, well, a lighthouse.

He heard a scraping sound above him and he went back out to the stairs and followed them up another flight and came to a heavy iron door, and he pressed the tip of the rifle barrel to it and felt it give a bit.

He heard that scraping sound again and he could smell cigarette smoke and hear the ocean and feel the wind up here, and he knew that if the warden had been smart enough to place guards on the other side of this door, then Teddy was dead as soon as he pushed it open.

Run, baby.

Can't.

Why not?

Because it all comes to this.

What does?

All of it. Everything.

I don't see how it—

You. Me. Laeddis. Chuck. Noyce, that poor fucking kid. It all comes to this. Either it stops now. Or I stop now.

It was his hands. Chuck's hands. Don't you see?

No. What?

His hands, Teddy. They didn't fit him.

Teddy knew what she meant. He knew something about Chuck's hands was important, but not so important he could waste any more time in this stairwell thinking about it.

I've got to go through this door now, honey.

Okay. Be careful.

Teddy crouched to the left of the door. He held the rifle butt against his left rib cage and placed his right hand on the floor for balance and then he kicked out with his left foot and the door swung wide and he dropped to his knee in the swinging of it and placed the rifle to his shoulder and sighted down the barrel.

At Cawley.

Sitting behind a table, his back to a small window square, the ocean spread blue and silver behind him, the smell of it filling the room, the breeze fingering the hair on the sides of his head.

Cawley didn't look startled. He didn't look scared. He tapped his cigarette against the side of the ashtray in front of him and said to Teddy:

"Why you all wet, baby?"

21

THE WALLS BEHIND Cawley were covered in pink bedsheets, their corners fastened by wrinkled strips of tape. On the table in front of him were several folders, a military-issue field radio, Teddy's notebook, Laeddis's intake form, and Teddy's suit jacket. Propped on the seat of a chair in the corner was a reel-to-reel tape recorder, the reels moving, a small microphone sitting on top and pointing out at the room. Directly in front of Cawley was a black, leather-bound notebook. He scribbled something in it and said, "Take a seat."

"What did you say?"

"I said take a seat."

"Before that?"

"You know exactly what I said."

Teddy brought the rifle down from his shoulder but kept it pointed at Cawley and entered the room.

Cawley went back to scribbling. "It's empty."

"What?"

"The rifle. It doesn't have any bullets in it. Given all your experi-ence with firearms, how could you fail to notice that?"

Teddy pulled back the breech and checked the chamber. It was empty. Just to be sure, he pointed at the wall to his left and fired, but got nothing for his effort but the dry click of the hammer.

"Just put it in the corner," Cawley said.

Teddy lay the rifle on the floor and pulled the chair out from the table but didn't sit in it.

"What's under the sheets?"

"We'll get to that. Sit down. Take a load off. Here." Cawley reached down to the floor, came back up with a heavy towel and tossed it across the table to Teddy. "Dry yourself off a bit. You'll catch cold."

Teddy dried his hair and then stripped off his shirt. He balled it up and tossed it in the corner and dried his upper body. When he fin-ished, he took his jacket from the table.

"You mind?"

Cawley looked up. "No, no. Help yourself."

Teddy put the jacket on and sat in the chair.

Cawley wrote a bit more, the pen scratching the paper. "How badly did you hurt the guards?"

"Not too," Teddy said.

Cawley nodded and dropped his pen to the notebook and took the field radio and worked the crank to give it juice. He lifted the phone receiver out of its pouch and flicked the transmit switch and spoke into the phone. "Yeah, he's here. Have Dr. Sheehan take a look at your men before you send him up."

He hung up the phone.

"The elusive Dr. Sheehan," Teddy said.

Cawley moved his eyebrows up and down.

"Let me guess—he arrived on the morning ferry."

Cawley shook his head. "He's been on the island the whole time."

"Hiding in plain sight," Teddy said.

Cawley held out his hands and gave a small shrug. "He's a brilliant psychiatrist. Young, but full of promise. This was our plan, his and mine."

Teddy felt a throb in his neck just below his left ear. "How's it working out for you so far?"

Cawley lifted a page of his notebook, glanced at the one underneath, then let it drop from his fingers. "Not so well. I'd had higher hopes."

He looked across at Teddy and Teddy could see in his face what he'd seen in the stairwell the second morning and in the staff meeting just before the storm, and it didn't fit with the rest of the man's profile, didn't fit with this island, this lighthouse, this terrible game they were playing.

Compassion.

If Teddy didn't know any better, he'd swear that's what it was.

Teddy looked away from Cawley's face, looked around at the small room, those sheets on the walls. "So this is it?"

"This is it," Cawley agreed. "This is the lighthouse. The Holy Grail. The great truth you've been seeking. Is it everything you hoped for and more?"

"I haven't seen the basement."

"There is no basement. It's a lighthouse."

Teddy looked at his notebook lying on the table between them.

Cawley said, "Your case notes, yes. We found them with your jacket in the woods near my house. You blew up my car."

Teddy shrugged. "Sorry."

"I loved that car."

"I did get that feeling, yeah."

"I stood in that showroom in the spring of 'forty-seven and I remember thinking as I picked it out, Well, John, that box is checked

off. You won't have to shop for another car for fifteen years at least."
He sighed. "I so enjoyed checking off that box."

Teddy held up his hands. "Again, my apologies."

Cawley shook his head. "Did you think for one second that we'd
let you get to that ferry? Even if you'd blown up the whole island as a
diversion, what did you think would happen?"

Teddy shrugged.

"You're one man," Cawley said, "and the only job *anyone* had this
morning was to keep you off that ferry. I just don't understand your
logic there."

Teddy said, "It was the only way off. I had to try."

Cawley stared at him in confusion and then muttered, "Christ, I
loved that car," and looked down at his own lap.

Teddy said, "You got any water?"

Cawley considered the request for a while and then turned his
chair to reveal a pitcher and two glasses on the windowsill behind him.
He poured each of them a glass and handed Teddy's across the table.

Teddy drained the entire glass in one long swallow.

"Dry mouth, huh?" Cawley said. "Settled in your tongue like an itch
you can't scratch no matter how much you drink?" He slid the pitcher
across the table and watched as Teddy refilled his glass. "Tremors in your
hands. Those are getting pretty bad. How's your headache?"

And as he said it, Teddy felt a hot wire of pain behind his left eye
that extended out to his temple and then went north over his scalp and
south down his jaw.

"Not bad," he said.

"It'll get worse."

Teddy drank some more water. "I'm sure. That woman doctor told
me as much."

Cawley sat back with a smile and tapped his pen on his notebook.
"Who's this now?"

"Didn't get her name," Teddy said, "but she used to work with you."

"Oh. And she told you what exactly?"

"She told me the neuroleptics took four days to build up workable levels in the bloodstream. She predicted the dry mouth, the headaches, the shakes."

"Smart woman."

"Yup."

"It's not from neuroleptics."

"No?"

"No."

"What's it from, then?"

"Withdrawal," Cawley said.

"Withdrawal from what?"

Another smile and then Cawley's gaze grew distant, and he flipped open Teddy's notebook to the last page he'd written, pushed it across the table to him.

"That's your handwriting, correct?"

Teddy glanced down at it. "Yeah."

"The final code?"

"Well, it's code."

"But you didn't break it."

"I didn't have the chance. Things got a bit hectic in case you didn't notice."

"Sure, sure." Cawley tapped the page. "Care to break it now?"

Teddy looked down at the nine numbers and letters:

13(M)-21(U)-25(Y)-18(R)-1(A)-5(E)-8(H)-15(O)-9(I)

He could feel the wire poking the back of his eye.

"I'm not really feeling my best at the moment."

"But it's simple," Cawley said. "Nine letters."

"Let's give my head a chance to stop throbbing."

"Fine."

"Withdrawal from what?" Teddy said. "What did you give me?"

Cawley cracked his knuckles and leaned back into his chair with a shuddering yawn. "Chlorpromazine. It has its downsides. Many, I'm afraid. I'm not too fond of it. I'd hoped to start you on imipramine before this latest series of incidents, but I don't think that will happen now." He leaned forward. "Normally, I'm not a big fan of pharmacology, but in your case, I definitely see the need for it."

"Imipramine?"

"Some people call it Tofranil."

Teddy smiled. "And chlorpro . . ."

". . . mazine." Cawley nodded. "Chlorpromazine. That's what you're on now. What you're withdrawing from. The same thing we've been giving you for the last two years."

Teddy said, "The last what?"

"Two years."

Teddy chuckled. "Look, I know you guys are powerful. You don't have to oversell your case, though."

"I'm not overselling anything."

"You've been drugging me for two years?"

"I prefer the term 'medicating.' "

"And, what, you had a guy working in the U.S. marshals' office? Guy's job was to spike my joe every morning? Or maybe, wait, he worked for the newsstand where I *buy* my cup of coffee on the way in. That would be better. So for two years, you've had someone in Boston, slipping me drugs."

"Not Boston," Cawley said quietly. "Here."

"Here?"

He nodded. "Here. You've been here for two years. A patient of this institution."

Teddy could hear the tide coming in now, angry, hurling itself against the base of the bluff. He clasped his hands together to quiet the tremors and tried to ignore the pulsing behind his eye, growing hotter and more insistent.

"I'm a U.S. marshal," Teddy said.

"*Were* a U.S. marshal," Cawley said.

"Am," Teddy said. "I am a federal marshal with the United States government. I left Boston on Monday morning, September the twenty-second, 1954."

"Really?" Cawley said. "Tell me how you got to the ferry. Did you drive? Where did you park?"

"I took the subway."

"The subway doesn't go out that far."

"Transferred to a bus."

"Why didn't you drive?"

"Car's in the shop."

"Oh. And Sunday, what is your recollection of Sunday? Can you tell me what you did? Can you honestly tell me anything about your day before you woke up in the bathroom of the ferry?"

Teddy could. Well, he would have been able to, but the fucking wire in his head was digging through the back of his eye and into his sinus passages.

All right. Remember. Tell him what you did Sunday. You came home from work. You went to your apartment on Buttonwood. No, no. Not Buttonwood. Buttonwood burned to the ground when Laeddis lit it on fire. No, no. Where do you live? Jesus. He could see the place. Right, right. The place on . . . the place on . . . Castlemont. That's it. Castlemont Avenue. By the water.

Okay, okay. Relax. You came back to the place on Castlemont and you ate dinner and drank some milk and went to bed. Right? Right.

Cawley said, "What about this? Did you get a chance to look at this?"

He pushed Laeddis's intake form across the table.

"No."

"No?" He whistled. "You came here for it. If you got that piece of paper back to Senator Hurly—proof of a sixty-seventh patient we claim to have no record of—you could have blown the lid off this place."

"True."

"Hell yes, true. And you couldn't find time in the last twenty-four hours to give it a glance?"

"Again, things were a bit—"

"Hectic, yes. I understand. Well, take a look at it now."

Teddy glanced down at it, saw the pertinent name, age, date of intake info for Laeddis. In the comments section, he read:

Patient is highly intelligent and highly delusional. Known proclivity for violence. Extremely agitated. Shows no remorse for his crime because his denial is such that no crime ever took place. Patient has erected a series of highly developed and highly fantastical narratives which preclude, at this time, his facing the truth of his actions.

The signature below read *Dr. L. Sheehan.*

Teddy said, "Sounds about right."

"About right?"

Teddy nodded.

"In regards to whom?"

"Laeddis."

Cawley stood. He walked over to the wall and pulled down one of the sheets.

Four names were written there in block letters six inches high:

EDWARD DANIELS—ANDREW LAEDDIS
RACHEL SOLANDO—DOLORES CHANAL

Teddy waited, but Cawley seemed to be waiting too, neither of them saying a word for a full minute.

Eventually Teddy said, "You have a point, I'm guessing."

"Look at the names."

"I see them."

"Your name, Patient Sixty-seven's name, the missing patient's name, and your wife's name."

"Uh-huh. I'm not blind."

"There's your rule of four," Cawley said.

"How so?" Teddy rubbed his temple hard, trying to massage that wire out of there.

"Well, you're the genius with code. You tell me."

"Tell you what?"

"What do the names Edward Daniels and Andrew Laeddis have in common?"

Teddy looked at his own name and Laeddis's for a moment. "They both have thirteen letters."

"Yes, they do," Cawley said. "Yes, they do. Anything else?"

Teddy stared and stared. "Nope."

"Oh, come on." Cawley removed his lab coat, placed it over the back of a chair.

Teddy tried to concentrate, already tiring of this parlor game.

"Take your time."

Teddy stared at the letters until their edges grew soft.

"Anything?" Cawley said.

"No. I can't see anything. Just thirteen letters."

Cawley whacked the names with the back of his hand. "Come on!"

Teddy shook his head and felt nauseated. The letters jumped.

"Concentrate."

"I am concentrating."

"What do these letters have in common?" Cawley said.

"I don't . . . There are thirteen of them. Thirteen."

"What else?"

Teddy peered at the letters until they blurred. "Nothing."

"Nothing?"

"Nothing," Teddy said. "What do you want me to say? I can't tell you what I don't know. I can't—"

Cawley shouted it: "They're the same letters!"

Teddy hunched forward, tried to get the letters to stop quivering. "What?"

"They're the same letters."

"No."

"The names are anagrams for each other."

Teddy said it again: "No."

"No?" Cawley frowned and moved his hand across the line. "Those are the exact same letters. Look at them. Edward Daniels. Andrew Laeddis. Same letters. You're gifted with code, even flirted with becoming a code breaker in the war, isn't that right? Tell me that you don't see the same thirteen letters when you look up at these two names."

"No!" Teddy rammed the heels of his hands against his eyes, trying to clear them or blot out the light, he wasn't sure.

" 'No,' as in they're not the same letters? Or 'no,' as in you don't *want* them to be the same letters."

"They can't be."

"They are. Open your eyes. Look at them."

Teddy opened his eyes but continued to shake his head and the quivering letters canted from side to side.

Cawley slapped the next line with the back of his hand. "Try this, then. 'Dolores Chanal and Rachel Solando.' Both thirteen letters. You want to tell me what *they* have in common?"

Teddy knew what he was seeing, but he also knew it wasn't possible.

"No? Can't grasp that one either?"

"It can't be."

"It is," Cawley said. "The same letters again. Anagrams for each other. You came here for the truth? Here's your truth, Andrew."

"Teddy," Teddy said.

Cawley stared down at him, his face once again filling with lies of empathy.

"Your name is Andrew Laeddis," Cawley said. "The sixty-seventh patient at Ashecliffe Hospital? He's you, Andrew."

22

"BULLSHIT!"

Teddy screamed it and the scream rocketed through his head.

"Your name is Andrew Laeddis," Cawley repeated. "You were committed here by court order twenty-two months ago."

Teddy threw his hand at that. "This is below even you guys."

"Look at the evidence. Please, Andrew. You—"

"Don't call me that."

"—came here two years ago because you committed a terrible crime. One that society can't forgive, but I can. Andrew, look at me."

Teddy's eyes rose from the hand Cawley had extended, up the arm and across the chest and into Cawley's face, the man's eyes brimming now with that false compassion, that imitation of decency.

"My name is Edward Daniels."

"No." Cawley shook his head with an air of weary defeat. "Your name is Andrew Laeddis. You did a terrible thing, and you can't forgive yourself, no matter what, so you playact. You've created a dense, complex narrative structure in which you are the hero, Andrew. You convince yourself you're still a U.S. marshal and you're here on a case. And you've uncovered a conspiracy, which means that anything we tell you to the contrary plays into your fantasy that we're conspiring against you. And maybe we could let that go, let you live in your fantasy world. I'd like that. If you were harmless, I'd like that a lot. But you're violent, you're very violent. And because of your military and law enforcement training, you're too good at it. You're the most dangerous patient we have here. We can't contain you. It's been decided—look at me."

Teddy looked up, saw Cawley half stretching across the table, his eyes pleading.

"It's been decided that if we can't bring you back to sanity—now, right now—permanent measures will be taken to ensure you never hurt anyone again. Do you understand what I'm saying to you?"

For a moment—not even a full moment, a tenth of a moment—Teddy almost believed him.

Then Teddy smiled.

"It's a nice act you've got going, Doc. Who's the bad cop—Sheehan?" He glanced back at the door. "He's about due, I'd say."

"Look at me," Cawley said. "Look into my eyes."

Teddy did. They were red and swimming from lack of sleep. And more. What was it? Teddy held Cawley's gaze, studied those eyes. And then it came to him—if he didn't know otherwise, he'd swear Cawley was suffering from a broken heart.

"Listen," Cawley said, "I'm all you've got. I'm all you've ever had. I've been hearing this fantasy for two years now. I know every detail, every wrinkle—the codes, the missing partner, the storm, the woman in the cave, the evil experiments in the lighthouse. I know about Noyce and the fictitious Senator Hurly. I know you dream of Dolores all the time and her belly leaks and she's soaking with water. I know about the logs."

"You're full of shit," Teddy said.

"How would I know?"

Teddy ticked off the evidence on his trembling fingers:

"I've been eating your food, drinking your coffee, smoking your cigarettes. Hell, I took three 'aspirin' from you the morning I arrived. Then you drugged me the other night. You were sitting there when I woke up. I haven't been the same since. That's where all this started. That night, after my migraine. What'd you give me?"

Cawley leaned back. He grimaced as if he were swallowing acid and looked off at the window.

"I'm running out of time," he whispered.

"What's that?"

"Time," he said softly. "I was given four days. I'm almost out."

"So let me go. I'll go back to Boston, file a complaint with the marshals' office, but don't worry—with all your powerful friends I'm sure it won't amount to much."

Cawley said, "No, Andrew. I'm almost out of friends. I've been fighting a battle here for eight years and the scales have tipped in the other side's favor. I'm going to lose. Lose my position, lose my funding. I swore before the entire board of overseers that I could construct the most extravagant role-playing experiment psychiatry has ever seen and it would save you. It would bring you back. But if I was wrong?" His eyes widened and he pushed his hand up into his chin, as if he were trying to pop his jaw back into place. He dropped the hand, looked across the table at Teddy. "Don't you understand, Andrew? If you fail, I fail. If I fail, it's all over."

"Gee," Teddy said, "that's too bad."

Outside, some gulls cawed. Teddy could smell the salt and the sun and the damp, briny sand.

Cawley said, "Let's try this another way—do you think it's a coincidence that Rachel Solando, a figment of your own imagination by the way, would have the same letters in her name as your dead wife and the same history of killing her children?"

Teddy stood and the shakes rocked his arms from the shoulders on down. "My wife did not kill her kids. We never had kids."

"You never had kids?" Cawley walked over to the wall.

"We never had kids, you stupid fuck."

"Oh, okay." Cawley pulled down another sheet.

On the wall behind it—a crime-scene diagram, photographs of a lake, photographs of three dead children. And then the names, written in the same tall block letters:

EDWARD LAEDDIS

DANIEL LAEDDIS

RACHEL LAEDDIS

Teddy dropped his eyes and stared at his hands; they jumped as if they were no longer attached to him. If he could step on them, he would.

"Your children, Andrew. Are you going to stand there and deny they ever lived? Are you?"

Teddy pointed across the room at him with his jerking hand. "Those are Rachel Solando's children. That is the crime-scene diagram of Rachel Solando's lake house."

"That's your house. You went there because the doctors suggested it for your wife. You remember? After she *accidentally* set your previous apartment on fire? Get her out of the city, they said, give her a more bucolic setting. Maybe she'd get better."

"She wasn't ill."

"She was insane, Andrew."

"Stop fucking calling me that. She was not insane."

"Your wife was clinically depressed. She was diagnosed as manic-depressive. She was—"

"She was not," Teddy said.

"She was suicidal. She hurt the children. You refused to see it. You thought she was weak. You told yourself sanity was a choice, and all she had to do was remember her *responsibilities*. To you. To the children. You drank, and your drinking got worse. You floated into your own shell. You stayed away from home. You ignored all the signs. You ignored what the teachers told you, the parish priest, her own family."

"My wife was not insane!"

"And why? Because you were *embarrassed*."

"My wife was not—"

"The only reason she ever saw a psychiatrist was because she tried to commit suicide and ended up in the hospital. Even you couldn't control that. And they told you she was a danger to herself. They told you—"

"We never saw any psychiatrists!"

"—she was a danger to the children. You were warned time and time again."

"We never had children. We talked about it, but she couldn't get pregnant."

Christ! His head felt like someone was beating glass into it with a rolling pin.

"Come over here," Cawley said. "Really. Come up close and look at the names on these crime-scene photos. You'll be interested to know—"

"You can fake those. You can make up your own."

"You dream. You dream all the time. You can't stop dreaming, Andrew. You've told me about them. Have you had any lately with the two boys and the little girl? Huh? Has the little girl taken you to your headstone? You're 'a bad sailor,' Andrew. You know what that means? It means you're a bad father. You didn't navigate for them, Andrew. You didn't save them. You want to talk about the logs? Huh? Come over here and look at them. Tell me they're not the children from your dreams."

"Bullshit."

"Then look. Come here and *look.*"

"You drug me, you kill my partner, you say he never existed. You're going to lock me up here because I know what you're doing. I know about the experiments. I know what you're giving schizophrenics, your liberal use of lobotomies, your utter disregard for the Nuremberg Code. I am fucking *onto you,* Doctor."

"You are?" Cawley leaned against the wall and folded his arms. "Please, educate me. You've had the run of the place the last four days. You've gained access to every corner of this facility. Where are the Nazi doctors? Where are the satanic ORs?"

He walked back over to the table and consulted his notes for a moment:

"Do you still believe we're brainwashing patients, Andrew? Implementing some decades-long experiment to create—what did you call them once? Oh, here it is—ghost soldiers? Assassins?" He chuckled. "I mean, I have to give you credit, Andrew—even in these days of rampant paranoia, your fantasies take the cake."

Teddy pointed a quaking finger at him. "You are an experimental hospital with radical approaches—"

"Yes, we are."

"You take only the most violent patients."

"Correct again. With a caveat—the most violent *and* the most delusional."

"And you . . ."

"We what?"

"You experiment."

"Yes!" Cawley clapped his hands and took a quick bow. "Guilty as charged."

"Surgically."

Cawley held up a finger. "Ah, no. Sorry. We do not experiment with surgery. It is used as a last resort, and that last resort is employed always over my most vocal protests. I'm one man, however, and even I can't change decades of accepted practices overnight."

"You're lying."

Cawley sighed. "Show me one piece of evidence that your theory can hold water. Just one."

Teddy said nothing.

"And to all the evidence that *I've* presented, you have refused to respond."

"That's because it's not evidence at all. It's fabricated."

Cawley pressed his hands together and raised them to his lips as if in prayer.

"Let me off this island," Teddy said. "As a federally appointed officer of the law, I demand that you let me leave."

Cawley closed his eyes for a moment. When he opened them, they were clearer and harder. "Okay, okay. You got me, Marshal. Here, I'll make it easy on you."

He pulled a soft leather briefcase off the floor and undid the buckles and opened it and tossed Teddy's gun onto the table.

"That's your gun, right?"

Teddy stared at it.

"Those are your initials engraved on the handle, correct?"

Teddy peered at it, sweat in his eyes.

"Yes or no, *Marshal*? Is that your gun?"

He could see the dent in the barrel from the day when Phillip Stacks took a shot at him and hit the gun instead and Stacks ended up shot from the ricochet of his own bullet. He could see the initials E.D. engraved on the handle, a gift from the field office after he ended up shooting it out with Breck in Maine. And there, on the underside of the trigger guard, the metal was scraped and worn away a bit from when he'd dropped the gun during a foot chase in St. Louis in the winter of '49.

"Is that your gun?"

"Yeah."

"Pick it up, Marshal. Make sure it's loaded."

Teddy looked at the gun, looked back at Cawley.

"Go ahead, Marshal. Pick it up."

Teddy lifted the gun off the table and it shook in his hand.

"Is it loaded?" Cawley asked.

"Yes."

"You're sure?"

"I can feel the weight."

Cawley nodded. "Then blast away. Because that's the only way you're ever getting off this island."

Teddy tried to steady his arm with his other hand, but that was shaking too. He took several breaths, exhaling them slowly, sighting down the barrel through the sweat in his eyes and the tremors in his body, and he could see Cawley at the other end of the gun sights, two feet away at most, but he was listing up and down and side to side as if they both stood on a boat in the high seas.

"You have five seconds, Marshal."

Cawley lifted the phone out of the radio pack and cranked the handle, and Teddy watched him place the phone to his mouth.

"Three seconds now. Pull that trigger or you spend your dying days on this island."

Teddy could feel the weight of the gun. Even with the shakes, he had a chance if he took it now. Killed Cawley, killed whoever was waiting outside.

Cawley said, "Warden, you can send him up."

And Teddy's vision cleared and his shakes reduced themselves to small vibrations and he looked down the barrel as Cawley put the phone back in the pack.

Cawley got a curious look on his face, as if only now did it occur to him that Teddy might have the faculties left to pull this off.

And Cawley held up a hand.

He said, "Okay, okay."

And Teddy shot him dead center in the chest.

Then he raised his hands a half an inch and shot Cawley in the face. With water.

Cawley frowned. Then he blinked several times. He took a hand-kerchief from his pocket.

The door opened behind Teddy, and he spun in his chair and took aim as a man entered the room.

"Don't shoot," Chuck said. "I forgot to wear my raincoat."

23

CAWLEY WIPED HIS face with the handkerchief and took his seat
again and Chuck came around the table to Cawley's side and Teddy
turned the gun in his palm and stared down at it.

He looked across the table as Chuck took his seat, and Teddy
noticed he was wearing a lab coat.

"I thought you were dead," Teddy said.

"Nope," Chuck said.

It was suddenly hard to get words out. He felt the inclination to
stutter, just as the woman doctor had predicted. "I . . . I . . . was . . . I
was willing to die to bring you out of here. I . . ." He dropped the gun
to the table, and he felt all strength drain from his body. He fell into
his chair, unable to go on.

"I'm genuinely sorry about that," Chuck said. "Dr. Cawley and I
agonized over that for weeks before we put this into play. I never
wanted to leave you feeling betrayed or cause you undue anguish. You
have to believe me. But we were certain we had no alternative."

"There's a bit of a clock ticking on this one," Cawley said. "This was our last-ditch effort to bring you back, Andrew. A radical idea, even for this place, but I'd hoped it would work."

Teddy wiped at the sweat in his eyes, ended up smearing it there. He looked through the blur at Chuck.

"Who are you?" he said.

Chuck stretched a hand across the table. "Dr. Lester Sheehan," he said.

Teddy left the hand hanging in the air and Sheehan eventually withdrew it.

"So," Teddy said and sucked wet air through his nostrils, "you let me go on about how we needed to find Sheehan when you . . . you were Sheehan."

Sheehan nodded.

"Called me 'boss.' Told me jokes. Kept me entertained. Kept a watch on me at all times, is that right, Lester?"

He looked across the table at him, and Sheehan tried to hold his eyes, but he failed and dropped his gaze to his tie and flapped it against his chest. "I had to keep an eye on you, make sure you were safe."

"Safe," Teddy said. "So that made everything okay. Moral."

Sheehan dropped his tie. "We've known each other for two years, Andrew."

"That's not my name."

"Two years. I've been your primary psychiatrist. Two years. Look at me. Don't you even recognize me?"

Teddy used the cuff of his suit jacket to wipe the sweat from his eyes, and this time they cleared, and he looked across the table at Chuck. Good ol' Chuck with his awkwardness around firearms and those hands that didn't fit his job description because they weren't the hands of a cop. They were the hands of a doctor.

"You were my friend," Teddy said. "I trusted you. I told you about my wife. I talked to you about my father. I climbed down a fucking cliff looking for you. Were you watching me then? Keeping me safe then? You were my friend, Chuck. Oh, I'm sorry. Lester."

Lester lit a cigarette and Teddy was pleased to see that his hands shook too. Not much. Not nearly as bad as Teddy's and the tremors stopped as soon as he got the cigarette lit and tossed the match in an ashtray. But still . . .

I hope you've got it too, Teddy thought. Whatever this is.

"Yeah," Sheehan said (and Teddy had to remind himself not to think of him as Chuck), "I was keeping you safe. My disappearance was, yes, part of your fantasy. But you were supposed to see Laeddis's intake form on the road, not down the cliff. I dropped it off the promontory by mistake. Just pulling it out of my back pocket, and it blew away. I went down after it, because I knew if I didn't, *you* would. And I froze. Right under the lip. Twenty minutes later, you drop down right in front of me. I mean, a foot away. I almost reached out and grabbed you."

Cawley cleared his throat. "We almost called it off when we saw you were going to go down that cliff. Maybe we should have."

"Called it off." Teddy suppressed a giggle into his fist.

"Yes," Cawley said. "Called it off. This was a pageant, Andrew. A—"

"My name's Teddy."

"—play. You wrote it. We helped you stage it. But the play wouldn't work without an ending, and the ending was always your reaching this lighthouse."

"Convenient," Teddy said and looked around at the walls.

"You've been telling this story to us for almost two years now. How you came here to find a missing patient and stumbled onto our Third Reich–inspired surgical experiments, Soviet-inspired brainwashing. How the patient Rachel Solando had killed her children in much the same way your wife killed yours. How just when you got close, your partner—and don't you love the name you gave him? Chuck Aule. I mean, Jesus, say it a couple of times fast. It's just another of your jokes, Andrew—your partner was taken and you were left to fend for yourself, but we got to you. We drugged you. And you were committed before you could get the story back to your imaginary Senator Hurly. You want the names of the current senators from the state of New Hampshire, Andrew? I have them here."

"You faked all this?" Teddy said.

"Yes."

Teddy laughed. He laughed as hard as he'd laughed since before Dolores had died. He laughed and heard the boom of it, and the echoes of it curled back into themselves and joined the stream still coming from his mouth, and it roiled above him and soaped the walls and mushroomed out into the surf.

"How do you fake a hurricane?" he said and slapped the table. "Tell me that, Doctor."

"You can't fake a hurricane," Cawley said.

"No," Teddy said, "you can't." And he slapped the table again.

Cawley looked at his hand, then up into his eyes. "But you can predict one from time to time, Andrew. Particularly on an island."

Teddy shook his head, felt a grin still plastered to his face, even as the warmth of it died, even as it probably appeared silly and weak. "You guys never give up."

"A storm was essential to your fantasy," Cawley said. "We waited for one."

Teddy said, "Lies."

"Lies? Explain the anagrams. Explain how the children in those pictures—children you've never seen if they belonged to Rachel

Solando—are the same children in your dreams. Explain, Andrew, how I knew to say to you when you walked through this door, 'Why you all wet, baby?' Do you think I'm a mind reader?"

"No," Teddy said. "I think I was wet."

For a moment, Cawley looked like his head was going to shoot off his neck. He took a long breath, folded his hands together, and leaned into the table. "Your gun was filled with water. Your codes? They're showing, Andrew. You're playing jokes on yourself. Look at the one in your notebook. The last one. Look at it. Nine letters. Three lines. Should be a piece of cake to break. Look at it."

Teddy looked down at the page:

$$13(M)-21(U)-25(Y)-18(R)-1(A)-5(E)-8(H)-15(O)-9(I)$$

"We're running out of time," Lester Sheehan said. "Please understand, it's all changing. Psychiatry. It's had its own war going on for some time, and we're losing."

$$M-U-Y-R-A-E-H-O-I$$

"Yeah?" Teddy said absently. "And who's 'we'?"

Cawley said, "Men who believe that the way to the mind is not by way of ice picks through the brain or large dosages of dangerous medicine but through an honest reckoning of the self."

"An honest reckoning of the self," Teddy repeated. "Gee, that's good."

Three lines, Cawley had said. Three letters per line probably.

"Listen to me," Sheehan said. "If we fail here, we've lost. Not just with you. Right now, the balance of power is in the hands of the surgeons, but that's going to change fast. The pharmacists will take over, and it won't be any less barbaric. It'll just seem so. The same zombiefication and warehousing that are going on now will continue under a more publicly palatable veneer. Here, in this place, it comes down to you, Andrew."

"My name is Teddy. Teddy Daniels."

Teddy guessed the first line was probably "you."

"Naehring's got an OR reserved in your name, Andrew."

Teddy looked up from the page.

Cawley nodded. "We had four days on this. If we fail, you go into surgery."

"Surgery for what?"

Cawley looked at Sheehan. Sheehan studied his cigarette.

"Surgery for what?" Teddy repeated.

Cawley opened his mouth to speak, but Sheehan cut him off, his voice worn:

"A transorbital lobotomy."

Teddy blinked at that and looked back at his page, found the second word: "are."

"Just like Noyce," he said. "I suppose you'll tell me he's not here, either."

"He's here," Cawley said. "And a lot of the story you told Dr. Sheehan about him is true, Andrew. But he never came back to Boston. You never met him in a jail. He's been here since August of 'fifty. He did get to the point where he transferred out of Ward C and was trusted enough to live in Ward A. But then you assaulted him."

Teddy looked up from the final three letters. "I what?"

"You assaulted him. Two weeks ago. Damn near killed him."

"Why would I do that?"

Cawley looked over at Sheehan.

"Because he called you Laeddis," Sheehan said.

"No, he didn't. I saw him yesterday and he—"

"He what?"

"He didn't call me Laeddis, that's for damn sure."

"No?" Cawley flipped open his notebook. "I have the transcript of your conversation. I have the tapes back in my office, but for now let's go with the transcripts. Tell me if this sounds familiar." He adjusted his glasses, head bent to the page. "I'm quoting here—'This is about you. And, Laeddis, this is all it's ever been about. I was incidental. I was a way in.' "

Teddy shook his head. "He's not calling me Laeddis. You switched the emphasis. He was saying this is about you—meaning me—*and* Laeddis."

Cawley chuckled. "You really are something."

Teddy smiled. "I was thinking the same thing about you."

Cawley looked down at the transcript. "How about this— Do you remember asking Noyce what happened to his face?"

"Sure. I asked him who was responsible."

"Your exact words were 'Who did this?' That sound right?"

Teddy nodded.

"And Noyce replied—again I'm quoting here—'You did this.' "

Teddy said, "Right, but . . ."

Cawley considered him as if he were considering an insect under glass. "Yes?"

"He was speaking like . . ."

"I'm listening."

Teddy was having trouble getting words to connect into strings, to follow in line like boxcars.

"He was saying"—he spoke slowly, deliberately—"that my failure to keep him from getting transported back here led, in an indirect way, to his getting beaten up. He wasn't saying I beat him."

"He said, *You did this.*"

Teddy shrugged. "He did, but we differ on the interpretation of what that means."

Cawley turned a page. "How about this, then? Noyce speaking again—'They *knew*. Don't you get it? Everything you were up to. Your whole plan. This is a game. A handsomely mounted stage play. All this is for you.' "

Teddy sat back. "All these patients, all these people I've supposedly known for two years, and none of them said a word to me while I was performing my, um, masquerade the last four days?"

Cawley closed the notebook. "They're used to it. You've been flashing that plastic badge for a year now. At first I thought it was a worthy test—give it to you and see how you'd react. But you ran with it in a way I never could have calculated. Go on. Open your wallet. Tell me if it's plastic or not, Andrew."

"Let me finish the code."

"You're almost done. Three letters to go. Want help, Andrew?"

"Teddy."

Cawley shook his head. "Andrew. Andrew Laeddis."

"Teddy."

Cawley watched him arrange the letters on the page.

"What's it say?"

Teddy laughed.

"Tell us."

Teddy shook his head.

"No, please, share it with us."

Teddy said, "You did this. You left those codes. You created the name Rachel Solando using my wife's name. This is all you."

Cawley spoke slowly, precisely. "What does the last code say?"

Teddy turned the notebook so they could see it:

you

are

him

"Satisfied?" Teddy said.

Cawley stood. He looked exhausted. Stretched to the end of his rope. He spoke with an air of desolation Teddy hadn't heard before.

"We hoped. We hoped we could save you. We stuck our reputations on the line. And now word will get out that we allowed a patient to play act his grandest delusion and all we got for it were a few injured guards and a burned car. I have no problem with the professional humiliation." He stared out the small window square. "Maybe I've outgrown this place. Or it's outgrown me. But someday, Marshal, and it's not far off, we'll medicate human experience right out of the human experience. Do you understand that?"

Teddy gave him nothing. "Not really."

"I expect you wouldn't." Cawley nodded and folded his arms across his chest, and the room was silent for a few moments except for the breeze and the ocean's crash. "You're a decorated soldier with extreme hand-to-hand combat training. Since you've been here, you've injured eight guards, not including the two today, four patients, and five orderlies. Dr. Sheehan and I have fought for you as long and as hard as we've been able. But most of the clinical staff and the entire penal staff is demanding we show results or else we incapacitate you."

He came off the window ledge and leaned across the table and fixed Teddy in his sad, dark gaze. "This was our last gasp, Andrew. If you don't accept who you are and what you did, if you don't make an effort to swim toward sanity, we can't save you."

He held out his hand to Teddy.

"Take it," he said, and his voice was hoarse. "Please. Andrew? Help me save you."

Teddy shook the hand. He shook it firmly. He gave Cawley his most forthright grip, his most forthright gaze. He smiled.

He said, "Stop calling me Andrew."

24

THEY LED HIM to Ward C in shackles.

Once inside, they took him down into the basement where the men yelled to him from their cells. They promised to hurt him. They promised to rape him. One swore he'd truss him up like a sow and eat his toes one by one.

While he remained manacled, a guard stood on either side of him while a nurse entered the cell and injected something into his arm.

She had strawberry hair and smelled of soap and Teddy caught a whiff of her breath as she leaned in to deliver the shot, and he knew her.

"You pretended to be Rachel," he said.

She said, "Hold him."

The guards gripped his shoulders, straightened his arms.

"It was you. With dye in your hair. You're Rachel."

She said, "Don't flinch," and sank the needle into his arm.

He caught her eye. "You're an excellent actress. I mean, you really had me, all that stuff about your dear, dead Jim. Very convincing, Rachel."

She dropped her eyes from his.

"I'm Emily," she said and pulled the needle out. "You sleep now."

"Please," Teddy said.

She paused at the cell door and looked back at him.

"It was you," he said.

The nod didn't come from her chin. It came from her eyes, a tiny, downward flick of them, and then she gave him a smile so bereft he wanted to kiss her hair.

"Good night," she said.

He never felt the guards remove the manacles, never heard them leave. The sounds from the other cells died and the air closest to his face turned amber and he felt as if he were lying on his back in the center of a wet cloud and his feet and hands had turned to sponge.

And he dreamed.

And in his dreams he and Dolores lived in a house by a lake.

Because they'd had to leave the city.

Because the city was mean and violent.

Because she'd lit their apartment on Buttonwood on fire.

Trying to rid it of ghosts.

He dreamed of their love as steel, impervious to fire or rain or the beating of hammers.

He dreamed that Dolores was insane.

And his Rachel said to him one night when he was drunk, but not so drunk that he hadn't managed to read her a bedtime story, his Rachel said, "Daddy?"

He said, "What, sweetie?"

"Mommy looks at me funny sometimes."

"Funny how?"

"Just funny."

"It makes you laugh?"

She shook her head.

"No?"

"No," she said.

"Well, how's she look at you, then?"

"Like I make her really sad."

And he tucked her in and kissed her good night and nuzzled her neck with his nose and told her she didn't make anyone sad. Wouldn't, couldn't. Ever.

ANOTHER NIGHT, HE came to bed and Dolores was rubbing the scars on her wrists and looking at him from the bed and she said, "When you go to the other place, part of you doesn't come back."

"What other place, honey?" He placed his watch on the bedstand.

"And that part of you that does?" She bit her lip and looked like she was about to punch herself in the face with both fists. "Shouldn't."

SHE THOUGHT THE butcher on the corner was a spy. She said he smiled at her while blood dripped off his cleaver, and she was sure he knew Russian.

She said that sometimes she could feel that cleaver in her breasts.

LITTLE TEDDY SAID to him once when they were at Fenway Park, watching the ball game, "We could live here."

"We do live here."

"In the park, I mean."

"What's wrong with where we live?"

"Too much water."

Teddy took a hit off his flask. He considered his son. He was a tall boy and strong, but he cried too quickly for a boy his age and he was easily spooked. That was the way kids were growing up these days, overprivileged and soft in a booming economy. Teddy wished that his mother were still alive so she could teach her grandkids you had to get hard, strong. The world didn't give a shit. It didn't bestow. It took.

Those lessons could come from a man, of course, but it was a woman who instilled them with permanence.

Dolores, though, filled their heads with dreams, fantasies, took them to the movies too much, the circus and carnivals.

He took another hit off his flask and said to his son, "Too much water. Anything else?"

"No, sir."

HE WOULD SAY to her: "What's wrong? What don't I do? What don't I give you? How can I make you happy?"

And she'd say, "I'm happy."

"No, you're not. Tell me what I need to do. I'll do it."

"I'm fine."

"You get so angry. And if you're not angry, you're too happy, bouncing off the walls."

"Which is it?"

"It scares the kids, scares me. You're not fine."

"I am."

"You're sad all the time."

"No," she'd say. "That's you."

HE TALKED TO the priest and the priest made a visit or two. He talked to her sisters, and the older one, Delilah, came up from Virginia for a week once, and that seemed to help for a while.

They both avoided any suggestion of doctors. Doctors were for crazy people. Dolores wasn't crazy. She was just tense.

Tense and sad.

TEDDY DREAMED SHE woke him up one night and told him to get his gun. The butcher was in their house, she said. Downstairs in the kitchen. Talking on their phone in Russian.

THAT NIGHT ON the sidewalk in front of the Cocoanut Grove, leaning into the taxi, his face an inch from hers . . .

He'd looked in and he thought:

I know you. I've known you my whole life. I've been waiting. Waiting for you to make an appearance. Waiting all these years.

I knew you in the womb.

It was simply that.

He didn't feel the GI's desperation to have sex with her before he shipped out because he knew, at that moment, that he'd be coming back from the war. He'd be coming back because the gods didn't align the stars so you could meet the other half of your soul and then take her away from you.

He leaned into the car and told her this.

And he said, "Don't worry. I'm coming back home."

She touched his face with her finger. "Do that, won't you?"

HE DREAMED HE came home to the house by the lake.

He'd been in Oklahoma. Spent two weeks chasing a guy from the South Boston docks to Tulsa with about ten stops in between, Teddy always half a step behind until he literally bumped into the guy as he was coming out of a gas station men's room.

He walked back in the house at eleven in the morning, grateful that it was a weekday and the boys were in school, and he could feel the road in his bones and a crushing desire for his own pillow. He walked into the house and called out to Dolores as he poured himself a double scotch and she came in from the backyard and said, "There wasn't enough."

He turned with his drink in hand and said, "What's that, hon?" and noticed that she was wet, as if she'd just stepped from the shower, except she wore an old dark dress with a faded floral print. She was barefoot and the water dripped off her hair and dripped off her dress.

"Baby," he said, "why you all wet?"

She said, "There wasn't enough," and placed a bottle down on the counter. "I'm still awake."

And she walked back outside.

Teddy saw her walk toward the gazebo, taking long, meandering steps, swaying. And he put his drink down on the counter and picked up the bottle and saw that it was the laudanum the doctor had prescribed after her hospital stay. If Teddy had to go on a trip, he portioned out the number of teaspoonfuls he figured she'd need while he was gone, and added them to a small bottle in her medicine cabinet. Then he took this bottle and locked it up in the cellar.

There were six months of doses in this bottle and she'd drunk it dry.

He saw her stumble up the gazebo stairs, fall to her knees, and get back up again.

How had she managed to get to the bottle? That wasn't any ordinary lock on the cellar cabinet. A strong man with bolt cutters couldn't get that lock off. She couldn't have picked it, and Teddy had the only key.

He watched her sit in the porch swing in the center of the gazebo and he looked at the bottle. He remembered standing right here the night he left, adding the teaspoons to the medicine cabinet bottle, having a belt or two of rye for himself, looking out at the lake, putting the smaller bottle in the medicine cabinet, going upstairs to say good-bye to the kids, coming back down as the phone rang, and he'd taken the call from the field office, grabbed his coat and his overnight bag and kissed Dolores at the door and headed to his car . . .

. . . and left the bigger bottle behind on the kitchen counter.

He went out through the screen door and crossed the lawn to the gazebo and walked up the steps and she watched him come, soaking wet, one leg dangling as she pushed the swing back and forth in a lazy tilt.

He said, "Honey, when did you drink all this?"

"This morning." She stuck her tongue out at him and then gave him a dreamy smile and looked up at the curved ceiling. "Not enough, though. Can't sleep. Just want to sleep. Too tired."

He saw the logs floating in the lake behind her and he knew they weren't logs, but he looked away, looked back at his wife.

"Why are you tired?"

She shrugged, flopping her hands out by her side. "Tired of all this. So tired. Just want to go home."

"You are home."

She pointed at the ceiling. "Home-home," she said.

Teddy looked out at those logs again, turning gently in the water.

"Where's Rachel?"

"School."

"She's too young for school, honey."

"Not my school," his wife said and showed him her teeth.

And Teddy screamed. He screamed so loudly that Dolores fell out of the swing and he jumped over her and jumped over the railing at the back of the gazebo and ran screaming, screaming no, screaming God, screaming please, screaming not my babies, screaming Jesus, screaming oh oh oh.

And he plunged into the water. He stumbled and fell forward on his face and went under and the water covered him like oil and he swam forward and forward and came up in the center of them. The three logs. His babies.

Edward and Daniel were facedown, but Rachel was on her back, her eyes open and looking up at the sky, her mother's desolation imprinted in her pupils, her gaze searching the clouds.

He carried them out one by one and lay them on the shore. He was careful with them. He held them firmly but gently. He could feel their bones. He caressed their cheeks. He caressed their shoulders and their rib cages and their legs and their feet. He kissed them many times.

He dropped to his knees and vomited until his chest burned and his stomach was stripped.

He went back and crossed their arms over their chests, and he noticed that Daniel and Rachel had rope burns on their wrists, and he knew that Edward had been the first to die. The other two had waited, hearing it, knowing she'd be coming back for them.

He kissed each of his children again on both cheeks and their foreheads and he closed Rachel's eyes.

Had they kicked in her arms as she carried them to the water? Had they screamed? Or had they gone soft and moaning, resigned to it?

He saw his wife in her violet dress the night he'd met her and saw the look in her face that first moment of seeing her, that look he'd fallen in love with. He'd thought it had just been the dress, her insecurity about wearing such a fine dress in a fine club. But that wasn't it. It was terror, barely suppressed, and it was always there. It was terror of the outside—of trains, of bombs, of rattling streetcars and jackhammers and dark avenues and Russians and submarines and taverns filled with angry men, oceans filled with sharks, Asians carrying red books in one hand and rifles in the other.

She was afraid of all that and so much more, but what terrified her most was inside of her, an insect of unnatural intelligence who'd been living in her brain her entire life, playing with it, clicking across it, wrenching loose its cables on a whim.

Teddy left his children and sat on the gazebo floor for a long time, watching her sway, and the worst of it all was how much he loved her. If he could sacrifice his own mind to restore hers, he would. Sell his limbs? Fine. She had been all the love he'd ever known for so long. She had been what carried him through the war, through this awful world. He loved her more than his life, more than his soul.

But he'd failed her. Failed his children. Failed the lives they'd all built together because he'd refused to see Dolores, really *see* her, see that her insanity was not her fault, not something she could control, not some proof of moral weakness or lack of fortitude.

He'd refused to see it because if she actually were his true love, his immortal other self, then what did that say about his brain, his sanity, his moral weakness?

And so, he'd hidden from it, hidden from her. He'd left her alone, his one love, and let her mind consume itself.

He watched her sway. Oh, Christ, how he loved her.

Loved her (and it shamed him deeply), more than his sons.

But more than Rachel?

Maybe not. Maybe not.

He saw Rachel in her mother's arms as her mother carried her to the water. Saw his daughter's eyes go wide as she descended into the lake.

He looked at his wife, still seeing his daughter, and thought: *You cruel, cruel, insane bitch.*

Teddy sat on the floor of the gazebo and wept. He wasn't sure for how long. He wept and he saw Dolores on the stoop as he brought her flowers and Dolores looking back over her shoulder at him on their honeymoon and Dolores in her violet dress and pregnant with Edward and removing one of her eyelashes from his cheek as she pulled away from his kiss and curled in his arms as she gave his hand a peck and laughing and smiling her Sunday-morning smiles and staring at him as the rest of her face broke around those big eyes and she looked so scared and so alone, always, always, some part of her, so alone . . .

He stood and his knees shook.

He took a seat beside his wife and she said, "You're my good man."

"No," he said. "I'm not."

"You are." She took his hand. "You love me. I know that. I know you're not perfect."

What had they thought—Daniel and Rachel—when they woke to their mother tying rope around their wrists? As they looked into her eyes?

"Oh, *Christ*."

"I do. But you're mine. And you try."

"Oh, baby," he said, "please don't say any more."

And Edward. Edward would have run. She would have had to chase him through the house.

She was bright now, happy. She said, "Let's put them in the kitchen."

"What?"

She climbed atop him, straddled him, and hugged him to her damp body. "Let's sit them at the table, Andrew." She kissed his eyelids.

He held her to him, crushing her body against his, and he wept into her shoulder.

She said, "They'll be our living dolls. We'll dry them off."

"What?" His voice muffled in his shoulder.

"We'll change their clothes." She whispered it in his ear.

He couldn't see her in a box, a white rubber box with a small viewing window in the door.

"We'll let them sleep in our bed tonight."

"Please stop talking."

"Just the one night."

"Please."

"And then tomorrow we can take them on a picnic."

"If you ever loved me . . ." Teddy could see them lying on the shore.

"I always loved you, baby."

"If you ever loved me, please stop talking," Teddy said.

He wanted to go to his children, to bring them alive, to take them away from here, away from her.

Dolores placed her hand on his gun.

He clamped his hand over hers.

"I need you to love me," she said. "I need you to free me."

She pulled at his gun, but he removed her hand. He looked in her eyes. They were so bright they hurt. They were not the eyes of a human. A dog maybe. A wolf, possibly.

After the war, after Dachau, he'd swore he would never kill again unless he had no choice. Unless the other man's gun was already pointed at him. Only then.

He couldn't take one more death. He couldn't.

She tugged at his gun, her eyes growing even brighter, and he removed her hand again.

He looked out at the shore and saw them neatly lined up, shoulder to shoulder.

He pulled his gun free of its holster. He showed it to her.

She bit her lip, weeping, and nodded. She looked up at the roof of the gazebo. She said, "We'll pretend they're with us. We'll give them baths, Andrew."

And he placed the gun to her belly and his hand trembled and his lips trembled and he said, "I love you, Dolores."

And even then, with his gun to her body, he was sure he couldn't do it.

She looked down as if surprised that she was still there, that he was still below her. "I love you, too. I love you so much. I love you like—"

And he pulled the trigger. The sound of it came out of her eyes and air popped from her mouth, and she placed her hand over the hole and looked at him, her other hand gripping his hair.

And as it spilled out of her, he pulled her to him and she went soft against his body and he held her and held her and wept his terrible love into her faded dress.

HE SAT UP in the dark and smelled the cigarette smoke before he saw the coal and the coal flared as Sheehan took a drag on the cigarette and watched him.

He sat on the bed and wept. He couldn't stop weeping. He said her name. He said:

"Rachel, Rachel, Rachel."

And he saw her eyes watching the clouds and her hair floating out around her.

When the convulsions stopped, when the tears dried, Sheehan said, "Rachel who?"

"Rachel Laeddis," he said.

"And you are?"

"Andrew," he said. "My name is Andrew Laeddis."

Sheehan turned on a small light and revealed Cawley and a guard on the other side of the bars. The guard had his back to them, but Cawley stared in, his hands on the bars.

"Why are you here?"

He took the handkerchief Sheehan offered and wiped his face.

"Why are you here?" Cawley repeated.

"Because I murdered my wife."

"And why did you do that?"

"Because she murdered our children and she needed peace."

"Are you a U.S. marshal?" Sheehan said.

"No. I was once. Not anymore."

"How long have you been here?"

"Since May third, 1952."

"Who was Rachel Laeddis?"

"My daughter. She was four."

"Who is Rachel Solando?"

"She doesn't exist. I made her up."

"Why?" Cawley said.

Teddy shook his head.

"Why?" Cawley repeated.

"I don't know, I don't know . . ."

"Yes, you do, Andrew. Tell me why."

"I can't."

"You can."

Teddy grabbed his head and rocked in place. "Don't make me say it. Please? Please, Doctor?"

Cawley gripped the bars. "I need to hear it, Andrew."

He looked through the bars at him, and he wanted to lunge forward and bite his nose.

"Because," he said and stopped. He cleared his throat, spit on the floor. "Because I can't take knowing that I let my wife kill my babies. I ignored all the signs. I tried to wish it away. I killed them because I didn't get her some help."

"And?"

"And knowing that is too much. I can't live with it."

"But you have to. You realize that."

He nodded. He pulled his knees to his chest.

Sheehan looked back over his shoulder at Cawley. Cawley stared in through the bars. He lit a cigarette. He watched Teddy steadily.

"Here's my fear, Andrew. We've been here before. We had this exact same break nine months ago. And then you regressed. Rapidly."

"I'm sorry."

"I appreciate that," Cawley said, "but I can't use an apology right now. I need to know that you've accepted reality. None of us can afford another regression."

Teddy looked at Cawley, this too-thin man with great pools of shadow under his eyes. This man who'd come to save him. This man who might be the only true friend he'd ever had.

He saw the sound of his gun in her eyes and he felt his sons' wet wrists as he'd placed them on their chests and he saw his daughter's hair as he stroked it off her face with his index finger.

"I won't regress," he said. "My name is Andrew Laeddis. I murdered my wife, Dolores, in the spring of 'fifty-two . . ."

25

THE SUN WAS in the room when he woke.

He sat up and looked toward the bars, but the bars weren't there. Just a window, lower than it should have been until he realized he was up high, on the top bunk in the room he'd shared with Trey and Bibby.

It was empty. He hopped off the bunk and opened the closet and saw his clothes there, fresh from the laundry, and he put them on. He walked to the window and placed a foot up on the ledge to tie his shoe and looked out at the compound and saw patients and orderlies and guards in equal number, some milling in front of the hospital, others continuing the cleanup, some tending to what remained of the rose-bushes along the foundation.

He considered his hands as he tied the second shoe. Rock steady. His vision was as clear as it had been when he was a child and his head as well.

He left the room and walked down the stairs and out into the compound and he passed Nurse Marino in the breezeway and she gave him a smile and said, "Morning."

"Beautiful one," he said.

"Gorgeous. I think that storm blew summer out for good."

He leaned on the rail and looked at a sky the color of baby blue eyes and he could smell a freshness in the air that had been missing since June.

"Enjoy the day," Nurse Marino said, and he watched her as she walked down the breezeway, felt it was maybe a sign of health that he enjoyed the sway of her hips.

He walked into the compound and passed some orderlies on their day off tossing a ball back and forth and they waved and said, "Good morning," and he waved and said "Good morning" back.

He heard the sound of the ferry horn as it neared the dock, and he saw Cawley and the warden talking in the center of the lawn in front of the hospital and they nodded in acknowledgment and he nodded back.

He sat down on the corner of the hospital steps and looked out at all of it and felt as good as he'd felt in a long time.

"Here."

He took the cigarette and put it in his mouth, leaned in toward the flame and smelled that gasoline stench of the Zippo before it was snapped closed.

"How we doing this morning?"

"Good. You?" He sucked the smoke back into his lungs.

"Can't complain."

He noticed Cawley and the warden watching them.

"We ever figure out what that book of the warden's is?"

"Nope. Might go to the grave without knowing."

"That's a helluva shame."

"Maybe there are some things we were put on this earth *not* to know. Look at it that way."

"Interesting perspective."

"Well, I try."

He took another pull on the cigarette, noticed how sweet the tobacco tasted. It was richer, and it clung to the back of his throat.

"So what's our next move?" he said.

"You tell me, boss."

He smiled at Chuck. The two of them sitting in the morning sunlight, taking their ease, acting as if all was just fine with the world.

"Gotta find a way off this rock," Teddy said. "Get our asses home."

Chuck nodded. "I figured you'd say something like that."

"Any ideas?"

Chuck said, "Give me a minute."

Teddy nodded and leaned back against the stairs. He had a minute. Maybe even a few minutes. He watched Chuck raise his hand and shake his head at the same time and he saw Cawley nod in acknowledgment and then Cawley said something to the warden and they crossed the lawn toward Teddy with four orderlies falling into step behind them, one of the orderlies holding a white bundle, some sort of fabric, Teddy thinking he might have spied some metal on it as the orderly unrolled it and it caught the sun.

Teddy said, "I don't know, Chuck. You think they're onto us?"

"Nah." Chuck tilted his head back, squinting a bit in the sun, and he smiled at Teddy. "We're too smart for that."

"Yeah," Teddy said. "We are, aren't we?"